A code blue killing. . .

"There wasn't much in the way of jobs–laying down track for the 35th transcontinetal, when the town of Barstow was merely a sign nailed to a post; working the borax mines and the opalite mines. From a distance the desert flashed a bluish silver beckoning you closer —"

A laundry list of items has been illegaly taken from the evidence locker including 1,300 kilos of cocaine; 1,000 psuedophedrine blister packs, a casement of red devil lye, iodine crystals and flamables and oxydizers; 400 packages of greenbacks wrapped in duct tape; and 25 throw away revolvers. A corruption case in San Bernardino's inner city takes Officer Isaiah Du Bois to a desolate desert outpost to watch the road on Highway 395 for criminal activity where he comes to lose his life.

Domino

by J. Lea Koretsky

REGENT PRESS

Library of Congress Control Number: 2004091844

ISBN 1-58790-068-8

Cover by Shawn C. Turner

Manufactured in the U.S.A.

REGENT PRESS
6020-A Adeline Street
Oakland, CA 94608
regentpress@mindspring.com

10 9   8 7 6 5 4 3 2 1

Wall of Darkness was a very ambitious story. It is extremely difficult to write a multi-character story. You do it exceptionally well. Your use of scene is crisp, clear and moves your story along. Well done!
–*James Frey*, author of *Night of the Wolves, mentor.*

J. Lea Koretsky brings her social worker's instinct and credibility to a chilling tale of the noir side of Hawaii that few tourists will ever encounter.
–*Jacqueline Girdner, writing as Claire Daniels.*

One of the most notable features of Judy Koretsky's stories is the vivid depiction of setting.
–*Ellery Queen Mystery Magazine.*

this novel is dedicated to truckers
without whose tireless perseverance
products would never reach
their destinations

about the author

LEA KORETSKY WAS BORN in San Francisco in 1949. She was educated in Berkeley schools, traveled widely in the United States and Israel, and received a master's degree and Magna Cum Laude status at California State University at Hayward. In 1983 she married a CPA who went on to produce film shorts. In 1986 she was awarded best short story by Northern California Mystery Writers of America and was published frequently under her pseudonym Lea Cash-Domingo in *Ellery Queen Mystery Magazine* and in *Third WomanSleuth Anthology*. In 1990 *Learning Publications* in Florida published *Leading the Recovery: A Guide for Adult Children of Alcoholics*, used as a textbook for her then private practice as a therapist specializing in substance treatment. She published a novella *Sitting in the Dark* in 2001 about a woman's depression over a divorce and the World Trade Center disaster. In 2002 Regent Press published *Wall of Darkness*, a novel about a journalist's coverage of a series of kidnappings in Hawaii with flashbacks to war-torn Cambodia and oil drenched del Oro plants in Ecuador. In 2003, *The Eternity Look* featuring U.S. Marshall Dalton Keys was released. Also in 2003 she was made a member of National Pen Association of Women Writers. Ms. Koretsky is known for her realism of the California High Desert and coastal ranch lands and for people who live off the land.

one

THE CLOCK ON THE DASHBOARD read fifteen minutes before four in the October afternoon. Although a mid morning rain had sent a flash flood pouring across the Landers wash at sixty miles an hour, the sand was drying out, segments of dark beige, trapped water shrinking beneath what was becoming a light powdery expanse. Marshal Dalton Keys found the high desert rivetting. He could sit reflective for long hours waiting for a case to break before he turned on the red lights and headed back to the Morongo Basin substation in Joshua Tree.

He was logging his summary to an out-call on a burglary-in-progress at a medical clinic onto a laptop computer. By the time he arrived to the scene the burglar had fled with a handful of codeine, barbiturate and I.V. morphine and several hundred dollars in cash. He dusted for prints, jotted the missing inventory and took photographs on a digicam.

"Drop what you're doing and come running!" Delora Montag yelled over the radio.

Dalton picked up the receiver. The urgency in her voice was unmistakable. He pictured her – a svelte golden haired glamour girl, her beehive hairdo and porcelain sculpted face a throwback to the Fifties when women were babes and men pulled up in Chevrolets and Malibus to admire their cool composure. "Keys here."

"It's an officer-down at Blue Water Casino at Crossroads."

He started up the engine. "Any idea who?"

"Tentative I.D. as Wally Simmonds. Coast Guard wants every available vehicle in the area."

"I'm on my way. Who else has been notifed?"

"My guess is they've called in everyone. Navy, DEA, ATF, State Bureau."

He wouldn't be surprised if officers flew in from Inyo or Imperial Counties. An officer-down was felt by every officer as an assault on law enforcement. Officers were dedicated and loyal a workforce as any military unit. In the high desert the bond was stronger because the desperate stretches of the desert placed every man at the mercy of solitude.

Simmonds was DEA. The tall, somewhat stocky red haired man with bushy owl-like eyes had trained in DuPage County Sheriff's Crime Lab in Wheaton, Illinois, some thirty-four miles west of Chicago, analyzing and identifying controlled substances and assisting sheriffs and marshals in San Bernardino County in clandestine methamphetamine laboratory seizures. He was more qualified than most, able to interpret inked fingerprints using the Henry system, able to adapt photographic equipment in extreme darkness without flash, and qualified to examine criminal evidence. This summer Simmonds had been called in to monitor a handful of Cessna and Beechcraft planes flying from Twenty-nine Palms to Red Mountain suspected of carrying cocaine. Using infrared scanning equipment Officer Simmonds was instructed to board and search the planes upon departure in an effort to track aircraft which were vanishing off radar scopes.

Within four months Simmonds had produced six hundred pounds of cocaine, seventeen thousand dollars in cash and fifteen arrests.

Now this. Dalton's chest was tourniquet-tight as he sped onto Highway 62 and turned on the siren and floored the accelerator. The day was a blustery eighty degrees, warm for mid October, a bit damp from the flash flood. A low cloud ceiling hung over the road. If the low visibility extended to the beach it could make a thorough search and rescue difficult, if not downright impossible. He passed the agricultural inspection station and Big River mini market. A string of pink stucco and yellow trim motel rooms advertised an overnight stay for twenty-two dollars. The desert spread out in riddled ravines. Saguro and spiny cacti stood along the roadside interspersed with purple wild flowers and olive green sagebrush. The cracked asphalt road rolled in huge dips. Metal towers with satellite dishes collected radio sounds from cars, trains, and incoming aircraft.

He swerved past the railroad beneath the bridge that led over the Colorado river to the town of Parker in Arizona. He sped along the frontage road toward Crossroads eyeing the beach for signs of activity. The river was a good eight to ten feet deep this time of year. It flowed at six miles an hour and could do its share of damage to anything it took in its current. At the sign to Blue Water Casino he pulled into the paved lot. He flashed his marshal badge at an officer who allowed him past markers of yellow caution tape marked *Crime Scene* which held back a gathering crowd. Parking behind a large navy blue mobile command unit of the Needles Police Department, Dalton called in his arrival to Delora. Then he logged the call onto his clipboard with date and time.

He squeezed past a barricade of five patrol vehicles with their red lights flashing at the water's edge. An ambulance stood at the ready. The drone of a helicopter caused him to glance up at the Desert Search and Rescue air patrol. A Coast Guard vessel in the river was searching the muddy waters. Coast Guard personnel gave a ping from a beacon on the upper deck of the boat to the Search and Rescue helicopter overhead. In response the black and white helicopter swept down, searchlight aimed at the greenish blue water, hovering at a distance of a hundred yards above the water near the vessel. Dalton surmised the search vessel was equipped with infrared, probably used to assist environmental police in cleaning toxic spills and DEA in detecting depth and identifying shapes below the surface.

He walked across the pavement and stepped inside the mobile command unit where a handful of men stood over a table to study a map of satellite imaging of known boats in the area.

"Did Simmonds go down in an aircraft?" He asked the group.

"Boat," replied Admiral Jacobs of the Navy, a short man in his late sixties with an egg-shaped face and balding greyish white hair who was in the area temporarily along with a meteorologist to monitor weather conditions. "He was positioned to intercept a suspected cocaine run coming up from Cibola. That's all we know,"

"Was he shot?" Dalton persisted, the urgent need to arrive on the scene replaced by an equally pressing need to understand what had occurred.

"Someone at *Shelly's Bait and Tackle* witnessed a man overboard."

"Did someone with him push him over?"

"The woman who made the report states that he fell and did not surface."

"How long ago did this occur?"

"A good hour."

"Who knew it was Simmonds?"

"The cashier at the bait shop." Admiral Jacobs thrust a wetsuit with mask into Dalton's hands. "Ever meet him?"

"I knew who he was, but I wish I had actually gotten to know him."

"Quite understandable. It's difficult even for seasoned men like yourself to face someone for the first time at death."

"You think he's dead?"

"We're fairly certain. Water temperature is twenty-eight degrees. Current is running at seven miles per hour."

"I gather I'm joining a search party."

Admiral Jacobs gave a nod. "You're joining a half dozen divers already searching to recover the body. There's no depth perception over the water is one problem," he said, as Dalton unstrapped the pistol he wore on his lower left leg and placed it on the table. "There's no real visibility below. My diver says the sea bottom is very murky – like swimming in a grey bowl."

Dalton donned a wetsuit over his uniform. "How many feet to bottom?"

"Ten, if that."

"Rocks?"

"And then some. Sounds insane but that's how it is. You'd do better in the ocean." The admiral accompanied him outside carrying a single oxygen tank. The temperature beneath the wetsuit was sweltering. Air visibility was good from shore to shore, approximately several hundred meters.

Dalton slipped the mask over his head adjusting it so that it fit snugley over his eyes and nose. Admiral Jacobs helped him with the tank. "No overconfidence, okay?" and looked with honest concern into Dalton's mask. "Simmonds should've alerted someone for backup if he was in trouble."

"I take it he was trained for the water?"

"His C.V. says he is accustomed to diving in mud-churning waters."

"Any idea how he was dressed?"

"Checkered blue and white shirt, navy pants."

"I'll do my best, Sir." He fastened the safety strap and tested it for tension. Satisfied, he inserted the mouthpiece. Grabbing the flippers he walked into the water. He gave a thumb's up. The admiral did the same.

The river bottom was indeed rocky. Irregular rocks placed at odd angles slowed his entrance into the water. At two feet of water he sank to put on the flippers then pushed off away from the bank. Through his mask he glimpsed several Alcohol, Tobacco and Firearms vehicles pull up behind his patrol jeep. If they were fortunate the media would not respond immediately to the call which would have been heard simultaneously over one of their receivers. All law enforcement needed was for local television and radio networks to clamour alongside some thirty deputies and officers.

He submerged. He flicked on the light above his mask. Dark filaments slid toward him. A large log blocked his view. He pushed it but it didn't move. Swimming around it he moved into murkiness. The water was a mix of darting silver-backed fish and dark greenish underwater weeds. He thought he caught sight of a man's arm but as he swam to it for a closer look-see, the current shifted him downstream into a quickly flowing stream. He fought to regain his former position but the water was stronger than he was. He swam toward the shore. When he thought he could see the bottom he attempted to stand. The sky emerged for an instant, loud with the sound of at least one helicopter, then he went under again. He floated over a density of silt and weeds. He checked the special regulator on his tank to be sure he had enough air. He did, enough for another five to seven minutes.

He moved to the place where he thought he had seen the man's arm. As he swam into the cold current he felt his way blindly. This time his headlight did little to diminish the obscurity. He swam face down looking for the discernible squares that made up a checkered blue and white design. He mentally marked off ten foot lengths focussing as he swam for the man, then he reversed and scanned the river in the opposite direction. Littered soda cans and a metal lunchbox glinted at him. He proceeded slowly but all he saw were plastic containers and reeds.

He sucked at air, and drew in a vacuum. He kicked to the surface, turned onto his back and removing both mask and tube, he kicked to shore. He removed his flippers and made his way to the mobile unit. A radio was on. Through it could be heard the musings of the Search and Rescue helicopter as it hovered above the surface.

Dalton spoke. "I need another tank. Got any double-tanks?"

"Not yet," answered a police officer from Needles. "As soon as Riverside arrives – they've got the heavy duty equipment."

Dalton outfitted himself in another single-tank and returned to the beach where a handful of boats and canoes had joined the effort and were dragging the water with nets. A wind had started up. No longer calm, the water was choppy, seemingly inhospitable. A U.S. Navy diver emerged and paused to chat.

"Not much out there, eh?" He said in an Australian accent.

"I thought I saw a man at two o'clock from the Coast Guard."

"Really? I'll join you in a sec, soon as I've replaced my tank."

Dalton donned the mask, mouth piece and flippers and swam to deep water and submerged. He waited for the filmy underwater shapes to reappear with real clarity. When he had adjusted to the dark, he pushed past the log into a burst of air bubbles and churning water.

A man's dark face rose to his. Simmonds! He grabbed him by the shoulder. The man rolled onto his side and fell away from him. Hope spiraled through him, although his internal voice warned him the man was dead by an hour or more. Dalton swam toward him and reached beneath his arm to draw the man toward him. Adrenalin pumped through his veins as he negotiated the man's size. He was a good six feet and heavier than Dalton expected and bumped at him causing Dalton to reposition his hold. Once he had him firmly in tow, the current wrestled with him for control. He scraped past a large boulder and the body wrapped itself around it. Dalton grabbed at the body and kicked hard to push away the rock. The body shot free and drifted over him knocking him backward. As he tumbled toward the current, then kicked frantically to avoid being swept downstream, he saw the Navy diver.

The Navy diver grabbed hold of the man's shoulder and motioned for Dalton to grab onto the left side, which he did. Together they hoisted the man to the rocky bank. Someone standing in the water reached for the man and drew him quickly from Dalton. Rising from the water he watched as the two men pulled the drowned man onto the beach. The man was African American, narrow at the waist and hips, shoeless. He was five foot eight, if that, with a lean body.

Not Walter Simmonds.

"I'm glad you got there when you did," Dalton said, and tossed his mask onto the sand. "I almost got carried away myself."

"I thought he'd drifted farther downstream," the six foot tall diver answered apologetically. "You know him?"

The other man, a sheriff deputy from Blythe with a dark tan and blond hair, had turned the victim onto his back. Dalton stared, stunned, at the raw, skinned body of a well known African American traffic patrol officer out of San Bernardino's Island Empire, as the inner city was called. Isaiah Du Bois had been transferred to Joshua Tree as a result of a corruption scandal in the police, highway patrol and San Bernardino city government. It was hard to look at him. His features were barely recognizable. His heart-shaped chin, broad upper face were scraped to the bone. So were his chest and limbs. His skin bled, bluish tendons showed through. Isaiah looked disposed of, his gangly arms and thin waist somehow out of kilter. On a taller man, one who approached six feet or more, the characteristic could be more easily understood, but in Isaiah it had often provoked a second look-see.

"Yes. He was sent to Morongo Basin CHP a year ago. Genuinely nice man, dedicated to the job, good friend," he replied, as the sheriff deputy out of Blythe knelt beside him and felt for a pulse in his carotid artery.

"Nothing," the deputy said.

He stood as a Coast Guard man – a sandy haired officer dressed in white uniform – hurried over to the body, inserted a stethescope into his ears and listened for a heart beat. Shaking his head, the Coast Guard turned Isaiah onto his stomach and pressed the stethescope to the victim's back. After a full minute of silence, he said softly, almost regretably, "I agree. He's beyond hope. He's been dead at least a half hour."

Isaiah Du Bois wasn't more than twenty-four, if that. Born in Mojave and raised in Barstow, he moved to San Bernardino when he was accepted into the California Highway Patrol as the first African American officer to serve the county. He had earned his merits twenty times over, serving on a city commission for neighborhood youth, hauling in drug dealers and petty thieves fleeing city and county jurisdictions and running interference for squad cops on stake-outs in the high desert. His older brother had seen already too much of death, having lost a son to Vietnam and their mother to death by heroin.

Dalton felt overcome with sudden grief. Isaiah's bony face, once alight with the passion of police work that comes with those not yet indentured to disappointment and burn-out, was scraped off, cut and bloodied. Dalton stood self-consciously feeling at once helpless and shocked as the Coast Guard's deft hands patted down Isaiah's body, reached into his pockets and removed the meager contents. A driver's license, wide-teeth comb, spare change, roll of film and a wad of bills. Absent were the card key and turquoise stone the officer usually wore around his neck.

As the fact of the drowning worked against his mind's instinct to shut out what he was seeing, Dalton realized the river had done more than a little damage to the facial skin. Tiny rock particles were grafted into the epidural. Dirt clung around the forehead and ears like a first layer of gauze. And the boulder around which the body had wrapped itself like whipcord had left a shadow of dark mangled tendons and tissue.

He pictured his first meeting with the officer when a container truck had turned onto its side on Highway 62 south of Twenty-nine Palms accidentally spilling a toxic chemical.

T HAT SUMMER THERE HAD been seven accidents involving trucks and spilled chemicals in the corner of southern California from Vidal to Winterhaven at the Mexican border.

"You the only officer on the job?" Dalton had asked upon arrival. He had been dispatched from Ontario where he was interviewing a handful of ranchers and sheriffs about poaching coyotes in the foothills.

Isaiah Du Bois strode across the road to shake his hand. "I don't take it personally. They do this to me all the time."

"Must be a small outfit."

"Same as yours. Morongo Basin."

"You're a block away."

"That's right. After Baseline Avenue, this leaves alot to be desired."

"I bet. What do you make of the spill? Besides the odorless part?"

"You don't smell anything?" Isaiah's attitude was half whimsical, half irony.

"Do you?"

"No," and he laughed a loud belly laugh. "What d'you say we break out the beers and shoot the breeze until your backup gets out here?"

"I don't get backup for this kind of assignment until I've conducted a prelim. If it's not Anthrax and this isn't, they call for a cleanup crew when time permits. Once I've eyeballed this affair, I'm expected back at Ontario. They'd prefer it be by nightfall."

"Must be an important conference."

"Poachers. Coyotes."

"Yeah, it's the food chain drying up in all directions. Real pyramid thinking."

IT WAS THE FIRST of a sporadic on-again, off-again friendship tapped out between winters and springs and cross-over investigations. After jointly tracking a computer hacker through the desert and comparing receipts for sleazy motel chains with sheriff investigators between Joshua Tree and the Salton Sea, Dalton looked forward to assignments that took him into proximity with the CHP officer. It wasn't until Dalton learned Isaiah was gay and his lover was dying of AIDS that he began to see another side to the southern California officer's life. This man spent long after hours in shanties and alleys seeking out the homeless dying of AIDS. He carried with him clean needles and syringes loaded with pain killers. He also carried food, sleeping bags, tents, small kerosene lamps. *The Press Enterprise* newspaper attempted to recalibrate the lives of homosexual professionals by countering public opinion but it failed to take the sting out of a community that regarded gay professionals, especially among the police and highway patrol, as little better than their derelict counterparts they were trying to help. There'd been nothing border town about Isaiah but the stigma of being gay followed him into the high desert where lack of discretion could censure a man permanently.

"WE DON'T TALK MUCH ABOUT the life at the office," Isaiah said one day out of the blue.

"You have to be careful."

"Yeah. I'm used to a good deal more openness, especially among associates." Isaiah was dejected. "I was married once."

"Couldn't take it?"

"Oh it was alright. She was pretty enough. White. My family felt I'd crossed the line."

"They didn't know?"

"About me being gay? I never told them."

"How come?"

"My grandmother raised me. It'd take the wind out of her sails if she knew."

DROWNING WAS A BAD way to die, Dalton thought. He couldn't imagine what caused his friend to fall overboard. Perhaps he went after a suspect in another boat or thought he saw the boat from Cibola carrying the suspected contraband. Dalton unwrapped a stick of gum and popped it into his mouth to steady his nerves. He walked slowly along the beach to sort through his feelings. Isaiah was so young, his life barely realized. He'd been a good officer. Dalton hoped he hadn't gone down in the line of duty.

"**Y**OU EVER WONDER about some of the marshals you work with?" Isaiah had asked at their last meeting two weeks ago at the Diary Queen in Yucca Valley.

"Wonder what?"

"About corruption."

"Not ever."

"You're a bunch of glory boys."

Dalton sipped his coffee. "I take it you have."

"You don't sound like you want to hear this."

"You can't afford to become a whistle blower."

Isaiah stared at his iced tea and toyed with cubes of sugar, stacking them side by side. With sudden impatience he flicked one across the table. "There's a DEA guy working with us on an interstate trucking case who plays Army three times a month. His whole apartment's a cache for computers, high tech equipment, forensics stuff."

"You think he's going to put out his own shingle?"

"The stuff rotates through his place weekly."

"Who's the fence?"

"I'll tell you who it isn't. He isn't selling this to the Girl Scouts. Jesus. The guy's not stupid."

"Neither are you. Leave it alone. If it's going onto the street then chances are database programs are going with it. Where's the guy playing Army?"

"At MCAGCC."

That was for Marine Corps Air-Ground Combat Center. "Really," he said.

"That's right."

"Leave it alone. If there is an investigation, lay low. Say you noticed some stuff but the guy's a hundred percent. Good record. Above board."

D ID THE CORRUPTION CASE OF a year ago in the city of San Bernardino have anything to do with Isaiah's death? Dalton hoped now that he hadn't been wrong to tell Isaiah to lay off. Then again Isaiah wasn't one to keep quiet. He would've asked questions, scoped out the picture, taken his hunches up the ladder. If he'd stepped on a few toes, gone after the wrong man, or if he'd interested too many people in his concern, he could've been fingered for death.

Dalton glanced at the beach. The ambulance had driven onto the sand. A dozen people – officers, deputies and Navy people – had gathered around the body. Because Isaiah was dead, his body would be driven to the county morgue for a tentative appraisal and autopsy before being sent to UCLA for a second opinion by a forensic DNA-trained Medical Examiner.

The Marshal Office would be assigned the investigation. They routinely investigated suspicious deaths of sheriffs and other civilian officers. Chances were his lieutenant wouldn't want to assign the case to Dalton because of his friendship with the officer, although Dalton was next up on rotation to receive a new referral for investigation.

Worse kind of case, having to investigate a death of law enforcement. Second only to family. You felt oddly exposed, as if you were being stalked by the taint of death yourself. And there was the shock of it all, no matter what your years were in the field. You could travel up and down the state twenty-eight days a month, eleven months a year, count the number of rain splotches that collected on the windshield and still not comprehend why anyone would kill an officer. Cop murderers were either stupid or arrogant as hell to think they could eliminate a man of the Law and hope to live. For the investigating officer, another officer's death quickly became a vendetta. The assigned investigator would cross any hurdle and move any obstacle to get to the truth.

Dalton joined the team of officers. Isaiah had been strapped onto a stretcher and placed inside the ambulance. The admiral eyed him. "You planning to meet the ambulance at the morgue?"

"The driver taking him to the county morgue?"

"Yes."

"If you don't mind."

"Coroner Teale wanted to know whether you'd be coming in with the body."

"You can let him know I will be."

Force of habit made him consider looking for Isaiah's patrol car before he left the scene, but he canned the idea for the moment feeling a need to put distance between memory and emotion. That, and he had to be available to be collected by the ambulance driver. He walked to the casino into the lounge and ordered a Miller beer and a bowl of chili. The Australian waved him over to a booth next to a window.

"Rough stuff," the diver said, nursing a cup of black coffee.

"I knew him."

"That's what you said. I'm Jonlin, by the way."

Dalton shook his hand. "Marshal Dalton Keys. My associates

call me Dal." He slid into the opposite seat. From the window he could see the boats on the river. The Coast Guard vessel was ushering boaters out of the area.

"Any idea where the suspected victim disappeared to?" Jonlin asked.

"None. I wonder why the witness didn't report a black man overboard."

"Maybe they couldn't see clearly. Could be from the angle of the sun, the man overboard appeared tan."

"But they didn't get a close-up."

"Apparently not."

"Did anyone look for his patrol car?" Dalton inquired.

"Doubt it. I came by heli as soon as the cashier at the tackle shop called it in. The mobile unit was sent from Needles. I'm surprised no one from Department of Public Safety in Parker showed up."

"Me too." He took time to eat his bowl of chili. "You know Simmonds well?" He asked between spoonfuls.

"Yeah. Nice bloke."

"Caucasian?"

Jonlin nodded, saying, "British, I think. From Los Angeles a while back, or so I was told. Was a conductor for the *Super Liner*, then was assigned to baggage on board southern Cal trains."

Dalton finished his chili and washed the taste down with a sip of beer. "You think the mobile unit is going to continue to look for Simmonds?"

"Only if they can't find him somewhere else," he said.

The ambulance driver approached their table. He was a small man in his twenties with a red face, dark wavy hair, and black tennis shoes that did not fit with the neat image his uniform and shoulder pads conveyed. "We're taking off, Sir."

"I'll follow behind."

"Very good, Sir."

"Nice meeting you," Dalton said to Jonlin.

"Likewise."

Dalton left the remaining beer untouched.

He called Dispatch as the ambulance driver pulled onto the pavement in front of his patrol jeep.

"You finished out there yet? The lieutenant's been asking for you." Delora Montag said in her usual run-on sentence chatter.

"I'm fine. We pulled in Deputy Isaiah Du Bois."

"Injured?"

"Dead."

"Oh lordy no. Oh gawd, his poor brother. This will be the third death in two years. Oh lord, what on earth happened?"

"It looks like a drowning."

"You going to the morgue?"

"Right this very minute."

"Call when you arrive."

"I will."

"You want me to notify Lt. Walker?"

"If you would."

"No problem. What time you think you'll put in?"

He consulted his wristwatch. It was one-twenty. "Ten or eleven, if the return traffic is moving."

"Will we see you in the morning?"

"I'll be in."

He followed the ambulance through a sheet of white sand which had drifted across the road in near-zero visibility causing vehicles to disappear and reappear as phantoms in a near dark fog. Dalton kept his speed to ten miles an hour. Seen through the smoke tint of the upper third of his windshield, the waning sunlight and blizzard conditions resembled snow. The dozen or so houses dotting the highway had windows boarded up with wood to prevent cracking from the wind and sand.

At Vidal the ambulance kept a beeline for Highway 62. The road unravelled like a ribbon, the white line on the edge peeling away centrifugally. A *Grubb & Ellis* sign whipped by. Here and there remains of markets stood like bleached bones awaiting the next descent of UFOs. Nothing seemed hammered down for too long. A mile or so down the road Joshua trees looking like medically injured hobos cropped up on the landscape. In the distance grey mountains reached toward the sky.

The sandstorm abated as they climbed elevation. The afternoon sky became a vast panorama of ethereal blue. A splash of yellow preceded hints of purple and infrequently red wildflowers. Isaiah's ghost resurrected itself in the rear view mirror as an elusive presence. It seemed to call out to him to pull off the road and return to the death scene. As the shadows of the mountain pass swallowed the ambulance in front of him, he felt as though death were reaching for him too, threatening his sense of safety and security as he approached the motels that made up the far reaches of the Eagle Mountains. The feeling that death was ever-present was irrational, but at least once it caused him to stare hard into his rear view mirror.

It was hard to imagine Isaiah's work taking him this far into the desert on a regular basis. Dalton's own work kept him in and around Twenty-nine Palms, Landers, Lucerne and Adelanto. He had been part of a special contingency that investigated drug trafficking, runaways jumping the probation system, and missing persons through unincorporated geography. Dalton understood the lure the high desert possessed for the hard-at-work. It was easy to become sucked into an investigation to such an obsessive extent that caution was forgotten. With the obsession followed depression. Every year there were a handful of rumored suicides found in their cars and among them, an occasional cop who appeared to have taken the easy way out, preferring to drink himself to death with a quart of Bourbon and a bottle of *Quaaludes*. The real story was usually different. The officer had turned his back on a lead suspect without considering the danger and was caught off guard.

Booze and pills were props placed in the officer's hand after the murderer forced him – and they were always men despite the fact that half the sheriff deputies and marshals in the high desert were women – at gunpoint to swallow enough pills to cause death within hours.

Ahead of him the ambulance careened down the incline of the end of the highway. Granite mountains sat in abundance. The sharp glare of the sun made the desert floor where Highway 62 met Freeway 10 appear caught in snowblind. Dalton slowed instinctively. A flat of windmills replaced the sea of Joshua trees. From here it was a straight shot to Highway 215 and San Bernardino.

He thought about the witness description. Nothing about it made sense. Isaiah would never have jumped off a boat without waiting for backup to arrive. He was not one to go after a drug runner alone. These people had teams lying in wait to divert a bevvy of officers. Isaiah had to have been jumped, snagged in a trap he had not anticipated. Perhaps he had been set up. Dalton wanted to get his hands on every last scribbled note Isaiah had left behind. That meant going through his home and his office.

As he backed to the unloading dock of the Emergency entrance, he was aware that the heat of the day had faded. With it had gone the limbo time – that certain detachment cops have after they survey death that allows them to absorb facts without feeling danger. He felt newly alert, ready to accept whatever truth came from the chief pathologist's head to toe examination.

R AND TEALE, CORONER FOR MORONGO Basin, eyed DuBois' body as an orderly wheeled the stretcher into the morgue. Dr. Teale was in his late sixties, slender, medium height, his face cast in a faintly golden tinge, wavy blond hair cut close to the scalp and intense blue eyes. Morongo Canyon was fortunate to have him – he had served on the marine corp base as coordinator for Search and Rescue missions while also doing weekend rotations performing autopsies for San Bernardino's inner city morgue.

"Jesus, Dal, where did you find him?" he said, as he reached into the abdominal cavity of a young male with his face shot off who lay beneath the examination lights and scooped out his intestines and dropped them into a pyrex bowl.

"We fished him out of the river at Blue Water," Dal said, and helped himself to a badly needed cup of hot coffee. "I got there too late. By the time I got him out of the water he was dead."

"Any eye witness accounts as to what happened?"

"A woman at *Shelley's Tackle and Bait* allegedly saw Isaiah jump overboard."

"Not a chance. Du Bois would've called Navy and they would've flown out an entire contingency."

"I agree."

Dr. Teale rinsed his hands and arms to the elbows, dried them, then powdered his hands lightly in talc to absorb perspiration and snapped on a pair of sterile surgeon's gloves. He surveyed Isaiah's face. "He really took a beating underwater." He examined each side, his neck and chest. He lifted Isaiah's hands one at a time and studied the palm and fingers for abrasions. "My guess is someone held him under until he aspirated water. Any idea how long before you hauled him to land?"

"A few hours. Way too long."

"Don't take it personally, sometimes these things happen." Rand paged the orderly who came seconds later through the double doors into the operating room. "Help me turn him."

The young man, a hispanic with nondescript looks and competent manner, helped to turn the body. Dr. Teale nodded his appreciation. Then he lightly touched Isaiah's back. Skin peeled off in his hand. Dalton backed away in revulsion.

"Someone's lying. Officer Du Bois was in the water longer than a few hours. The way the skin rubs off indicates time of death." He felt for fractured bones. The shoulder blades collapsed. The right hip appeared broken. "I think he was brought to the site unconscious and thrown over."

"Could the current have played a role in these wounds?"

"Yes. Seven miles an hour can do some mean things to a man. But I'm with you. I have a hard time understanding this idea he jumped in willingly."

"If someone did batter him and then threw him in, why not cart the body to the coast and dispose of him in the ocean where his body wouldn't be recovered?"

"It's probably essential to the case that his body was recovered in the vicinity. Any possibility Downtown reassigned him to Amboy or Needles?"

"He told me Morongo Basin. That's where his desk is."

"Because I think if you check on it he was spit out with the scandal case a year ago."

"He was incapable of corruption."

"Well, it may have been the excuse to get the manpower to the desert the county needed. The question I was getting to was, any possibility CHP storehoused him at Needles or Inyokern to watch the road?"

"I have no idea what he was assigned to," Dalton said.

"I'll tell you what I know," he said, and began palpating the torso and lower extremities. "Six months ago Search and Rescue was sent into the desert on report of a drug cavern up near Ludlow. Team of fifteen deputies were sent in. The whole thing shotgunned when a deputy lost his footing and fell off a ledge."

"I remember. He was injured dropping a rope over the edge —"

"In the dark, no less. I believe DEA went out, Du Bois among them, surveyed the situation and discovered the drugs had been slotted into the face of rock at the entrance. They brought in a man from back East."

"Simmonds. The officer-down call was presumably for him."

"My guess is Simmonds was the backup."

"Mine too."

Dr. Teale nodded, felt each kidney and grunted. "Good deal of swelling. Was he a drinker?"

"Lately, yes."

"Pills? Coke?"

"Doubtful."

"I'll check stomach sack for last meal. What kind of man was he in his personal life, or didn't you know him well?"

"No, I did. Homosexual. A San B. boy. Grew up on Baseline."

"Who in hell grows up on Baseline?"

"Well, you asked. He was an excellent investigator."

"Something happened. Someone somehow caused him to enter the water when he shouldn't have been in it. Could be he was too damned confident and didn't realize what he was up against until he went down," he said, with sudden anger. "He shouldn't have gone down like an inexperienced officer floating downwind clutching at air."

"How soon before you can give me a probable cause of death?"

"Tomorrow morning."

"That'd be terrific." He set his cup of coffee on the counter. "Thanks."

"Sure. I'll take good care of your boy."

DALTON GRABBED A SANDWICH AND coffee in Joshua Tree and headed home. He left a message on his supervisor's voice mail saying first thing in the morning he would return to the crime scene to look for Isaiah's vehicle.

He left at dawn. The drive to Crossroads found a patrol vehicle parked in the thicket of several cottonwood trees. The car was a two door, black and white, a San Bernardino Highway Patrol decal, standard outfit regulation. Inside, a clipboard showed a daily log. At eight that morning Deputy Du Bois had taken a vandalism call at *Fischer Storage* in Needles; at eleven forty he had been dispatched to *Just In Time Manufacturing* for a small fire. At three-ten he had been requested to check out a refrigerator which appeared in the parking lot of *Crossroads Bait and Tackle*. That was the call that had brought him here. Aside from the log there appeared to be no other clues. The black upholstered seats offered no stains or fibers. The black carpet looked as if it had been recently vacuumed and the glove compartment contained a handful of digicameras. He bagged and labeled these. He'd get the forensics team out to dust the upholstery down and Mylar steam the windows for prints, then to the auto lab for a complete workover. He wasn't hopeful, but you never knew. A spot of blood under the hood or a smudge on the door jam with even a corner of the ridges showing clearly was all one ever needed.

He returned with his Minolta to take photographs of the entire scene. Later these would become crucial in the process of evidence recovery to determine how the crime might have occurred. He snapped shots of the body, closeups of the damp tire tracks, the cottonwood trees and the location of the jeep. This done, he snapped on plastic gloves and cautiously extracted soil samples into paper bags. He took his time, concentrating on collection technique. He labeled each specimen and dated it. October 20th. In a notepad he referenced the specimens by letter and gave a brief description of his observations. When a suspect was brought in and the case went to trial, he could be certain his forensic and data collection met the code. Important if the case was going to survive the normal length of a trial with continuations, discoveries, lost witnesses or other obstacles which over time could jeopardize proceedings. Once during this process of data collection, upon realizing his ungloved hand had chalk or powder caked on it, he washed his hands from his canteen and dried them and snapped on a new pair of gloves and resumed his work.

His back ached. He stood to review his notes and count the

number of small bags. He accounted for all. The sun beat down on him. His shirt soaked sweat. He returned twice to his pickup, once for his Stetson, a second time to place his equipment in a carrying case inside his vehicle. Then he went back for the body.

two

DALTON'S FATHER USED TO tell him that you knew by the fields and tracts you'd hit the valley – bushels of money growing on corn and wheat as far as the horizon. He'd say the truckers had it the worst, two-timing a day's pay to make overtime. You thought you'd hit paradise when you shelled out a few hundred for the first mortgage until they pulled out the contract and told you it was a nickel on the dollar went toward the principal the first seven years. Life was created in the shadows of the sun's journey across the sky, his father told him about high desert living. Money was slow in the high desert. In the middle of tractors and plows and more water than in a nurse tank you had Morongo Basin, a California Water Service Company bulb lighting up the main highway like a tin can on the back of a newly wed fender.

Short of houses there wasn't much to recommend the chalk patch that made up the San Bernardino. No annual dog sleds or aerial tramway or ghost towns or mine shafts. If signs on the road advertised a room with a view, the only view was an eyesore of granite mountains and Joshua trees, ocotillos and yellow candles. A hundred years ago when gold was discovered, a man could pan a living independent of mine shafts. The only wealth to replace the mines was a storage shed of underground water, mesquite with roots reaching down some fifty feet and cacti, bleeders for a thirsty hobo run out of railroad steel.

Dalton's grandfather Clem Keys worked for fifty dollars a week in the then thriving town of Calico when it produced more than eighty-five million bucks of borax. There wasn't much in the way of jobs – Clem's brother Chaim Keys laid down track for the thirty-fifth transcontinetal, when the town of Barstow was merely a sign nailed to a post; and two great uncles worked the opalite mines detonating the ceilings and dropping as many rocks as could fill the wooden box containers that made for a rough and ready rail-road. Towns in the desert were slow to yield – Yucca Valley, Twenty-Nine Palms, Wonder Valley, Vidal, Needles. Ecking out a meal was pretty much the same from Johannesburg down Interstate 395 to the apex of the San B. through arid and riddled fingers of cracked sand some hundred and fifty miles to the Colorado River. Every so often the county talked about flooding part of the Mojave to bring water to new developments.

He would always remember how he felt the day he brought Nell home to meet his father and they found him barrelled into the big easy chair, exhausted. At sixty-eight he'd put up with all kinds of economic transitions around him, holding out against time and hardship never seeing what lay at the edge of misfortune. He remembered standing there, half a mind to turn around and leave and never return. What rooted him was his fear his father was dead and he was now the only survivor to a long line of Keys. But Sandy Keys awakened and Dalton was relieved and grateful.

Now as Dalton entered Isaiah Du Bois's two bedroom stucco house overlooking the College of the Desert he had that same feeling of abandonment. A rush of emotion flooded him causing him to feel immense sadness. Whatever it was Isaiah had grappled with he had done it alone. Dalton felt despairing aloneness inside this neatly kept and sparsely accommodated living room, with a light blue carpet over a hardwood floor, a jet black fold-out sofa facing a wall sized television, two lamps made from flowered china vases on cherry wood end tables, and a floor to ceiling aerial photograph of Joshua Tree National Monument. He caught sight unexpectedly of his reflection in front of a gilded oval mirror – his somewhat flat sculpted face, tanned complexion, receding wavy sandy colored hair, bluish green eyes and acquiline nose gave him an air at age forty-four, or so he was often told, of an engineer or surveyor rather than of a marshal. His eye moved from the mirror to a compartment full of blues and jazz ensemble CDs to a CD player in the dining room. Dalton removed a *Billie Holiday* CD and put it to play on the CD player. Billie Holiday's melancholy voice bleated out into the austere room.

Dalton moved through the kitchen to the study. Located in the first bedroom, bookshelves and wooden filing cabinets lined every inch of wall space. It wasn't true that road patrol cops didn't take home their work as much as homicide or materials management cops. Isaiah had kept meticulous files on everything from drug busts to internal department investigations. Dalton paused when he came to drawer of thick Internal Affairs folders.

The corruption scandal had altered the way every inner city officer perceived of himself. Internal Affairs Division concluded that top San Bernardino County brass including Police and Highway Patrol had taken bribes from drug distributors. When this became known men and women in the rank and file became resentful of working long hours for little pay. They wanted higher pay to augment the danger they encountered in the field. Also IAD found gross errors in documents for reimbursements and in log sheets for the evidence locker. Rumor alleged that in at least two trials documentation on mob-bought enforcement never made it into the computer database which were monitored by numerous agencies assigned to spot graft. Information was discovered to have been illegally deleted from written narratives, log sheets were changed, mileage accounts were altered, and evidence in the locker cages lost. Were it not for the ease that these changes were made, the third and fourth generation sons of immigrant Italians and Indians who were educated to become lawyers and who were themselves police officers, sheriff deputies and district attorneys would have found themselves in an unenviable position of prosecuting grandfathers and uncles. The ease however, accounted for by a bevvy of lieutenants on the take to enhance meager salaries and even less adequate pensions and benefits.

Isaiah Du Bois had been one of the names the audit spit out. In the wake of forced leaves of absences and time-off without pay, an African American officer whose counts against him were that he was gay and a periodic alcoholic had few options except to accept the desert Highway Patrol outpost the DEA assigned him to at Twenty-Nine Palms. A job with no advancement opportunities, the post called for routine surveillance of tourist activities between the city of Morongo Valley and Amboy. It was hoped that the small fry drug distributors and dealers could be swept into the net and put behind bars. A beat officer assigned this duty however found he could live and die in the heat and never find out who called in his marker and shipped him out to a gravelly hell of cacti and spiders and tin roof adobes and plexiglass enclosed brick patios. A road cop who normally patrolled a chunk of change the size of his fist on any state map was in for a rude awakening to learn he was newly placed in what might wind up an adobe shoebox.

Dalton removed the file. A typed sheet fluttered to the floor. As he bent to pick it up, he had a feeling of deja vu, that he was reaching for something intimately familiar. He sank onto the quilted bed as he read. *I felt I could no longer keep tabs with the investigation* once Eric became ill. His illness left him emaciated. I was certain the physicians had misdiagnosed him. Although he had a hacking cough he lacked the bruises and sores most AIDS patients have in the advanced stages. Sergeant Hague suggested I approach Hemal Ebenales about a cure. It wasn't long after we moved into Hemal's home Eric showed real signs of improvement. He was able to keep weight on. His spiritedness returned. The cough disappeared. When Hemal advised Eric to travel to the lake I did not object.

Eric was gone two months when I began to lose touch with reality. The normal associations one has, the normal socialization one has, to think of certain things in a certain fashion, I no longer thought of in that fashion. I believed at first it was because of Eric's departure that I began to contemplate too much. Desperation had not been a characteristic of my relationship with Eric but the longer we were separated the worse my preoccupations became. I don't know when I realized Eric was having an affair – whether I sensed this or discovered him with Hemal's partner – but at the point it hit me I was assigned a new DEA intern. I split the surveillance with Simms sixty-forty. Simms took on far too much. I see that now. As I began to rely upon him to a greater extent I found myself relegated front-end assignments, conducting surveillance of suspects without being given the opportunity to adequately track them. In retrospect I see I should not have dragged Simms into this mess. It wasn't fair to him to shadow suspects through several counties from Imperial to Inyo. But I was fearful of losing a four year long investigation. As it turned out I lost Eric.

I don't know what happened. Did I snap? Lose perspective altogether? It was like running happily along a path feeling my life was restored and then suddenly my will or my spirit went on a different track and I was lost. Everything suddenly seemed disordered. Nothing seemed to mesh and it had meshed in the past so well.

I hadn't known the evil people are capable of. The hatred, and their not holding back their hatred. Chief Cobb's man Dimes came at me. Hemal kept showing up to places where Eric promised to meet me but *did not show. Then Eric died. I felt I was introduced to a breaking point and I let myself be broken. I must have been crazy to trust Hemal. I knew long ago what he is capable of.*

Dalton sucked on his cigarette, then squashed it out in the ashtray. He hadn't known about Isaiah's depression although he imagined at the time he knew. Loss of a lover to AIDS must have been frightening – the emaciating and wasting away, the hope that a cure might be found, the terror of facing eventual death, the fear of saying too much in mixed company – and the DEA cops' world was indeed mixed company.

Dalton spread the two articles written by Sergeant Bowman about the IAD investigation on the floor. The photo shots of Chief Cobb with Sergeants MacIntyre and Hague sent a shiver down his spine. A second photograph to hit the front page of the *Gazette* spelled the end of an era of diehard cops and brutal, hands-on show of force as the preferred way to correct crime. A night photo, mysteriously taken through a one-way mirror with a camera checked into the evidence room two days earlier, showed Sergeants MacIntyre and Hague bludgeoning a witness for a confession in an interrogation room. As a result of the photographs Bob Hague retired before the investigation was well underway, Chuck MacIntyre admitted himself for a coronary and did not return and a handful of cops went the way all censured cops go – onto the streets of San Bernardino and Riverside Counties as private dicks. The witness was sent to a private hospital in the mountains and was attached to a feeding pump. It was expected that once the guilty parties retired the problems – whatever they were – would go away. But that hadn't happened and a handful of other men, decent men, were implicated, Du Bois among them.

The Department buried the results of the investigation along with six officers it farmed out to the outskirts of the desert. If these men discussed their censure in the open, they did so with their wives and with each other. More likely they didn't discuss it and the memories and considerations festered in open emotional wounds. Isaiah probably sat on his anger and disappointment waiting for the day the DEA would again become tolerant, liberal enough to revisit some discussion of his return to inner city work.

Dalton folded the articles and returned the file to the drawer and shut it. He entered the second bedroom. Powder blue carpet matched light blue walls. White ceiling, white window trim and white comforter on the bed gave the room an airy, spacious feel. CD speakers sat on ledges above the bed. A tall mirror stood in front of a Thomasville dresser. A small antique writing desk sat in an alcove of an arched window that looked onto a deck with a glass patio table and rattan wicker chairs.

A lost life, Dalton thought as he opened the closet and examined five uniforms and black and grey dress slacks, Arrow wrinkle-free dress shirts, David Taylor blazers and khakis, and four pairs of Barrington wing tip and Moc-toe Oxford shoes stuffed onto a shoe rack. Organized drawers contained pressed handkerchefs, a small velvet lined drawer with silver and gold cufflinks each stamped with cursive letters *IdB*, and neckties hung from cloth hangers. Isaiah Du Bois had lived well in his materialistic possessions. He had served his community fairly in good conscious. Still it was not enough. Something – or someone – had sent him into the desert, to an eastern-most corner, for insanity or death, and he had found both.

three

THE MARSHAL OFFICE SITS ON White Feather Road off the main highway in Joshua Tree. Its offices take up the rear half of the building which is also habited by the Morongo Basin Sheriff Department. The building sits on a southwest corner – a tan stucco and red brick building with a security checkpoint in the lobby and a deputy seated by the door. Together the Sheriff and Marshal Offices are the law enforcement for civilian crime in a handful of communities dotting the highways along 62 and 247. Morongo Basin takes in Twenty-nine Palms, Wonder Valley, Yucca Valley, Flamingo Heights, Johnson Valley, Landers, Morongo Valley, Pioneertown and Yucca Valley. Whereas the Sheriff Department's jurisdiction is local to these towns, the Marshal Office covers investigations into teen runaways and related homicides, intracounty contraband and laboratory seizures, aircraft crashes, warehouse arsons and drug related kidnappings. They work with Alcohol, Tobacco and Firearms; with the Drug Enforcement

Agency; National Transportation Safety Board; and Federal and State Bureaus of Investigation.

O N MONDAY MORNING DALTON strode to his cubicle pausing to nod hello to Marshal George Maciel, a lanky man in his mid thirties. He was an amiable man whose training in aerial reconnaissance frequently placed him on military cases often involving friendly fire. In his own cubicle, a sixty square foot space which he shared with Marshal Lina Crandall, Dalton removed his navy jacket with yellow letters stamped across the back and hung it on a hanger in a closet behind his work station.

"My phone ring?" He asked Lina who was entering a report into her computer, a pencil between her clenched teeth as she typed a narrative.

At eight in the morning, Lina Crandall should have been at her best, her dark blond hair parted in the middle and curled under. She had been accepted into the ranks of U.S. Marshal because in addition to her usually freshly groomed appearance, she gave the brass what they wanted. Neatly typed notes, punctuality and in every other respect a team player.

What he liked about her though when she wasn't being argumentative, which she did when she was harried or tired, was her tough, shrewd ability to nail the correct suspect and an unflappable, seasoned manner. Excellent backup in the field. Nothing hurt her feelings, but then she allowed nothing to become an obstacle between the evidence and her investigation.

Not his type of romance by any stretch of the imagination. He liked a windblown look, casual manner and something of the rugged individualist, a woman who could stand on her own two feet if she had to.

"Haven't been paying attention," she replied without glancing at him. "Heard about Officer Du Bois. I'm sorry, Dal. It's a hard thing to get over."

"I'm sorry too. He was a good man."

"Looks like Marty may have put Ian on the case," she said of the African American marshal who was frequently assigned boat death cases.

"I wasn't aware he had."

"He's already assigned witness interviews to him."

Dalton left his computer without typing in his password. He passed Ian Spender's office and indicated with a nod he was going to talk to their boss. He pushed open the door to Lt. Walker's office. Marty Walker was on the phone, his shirt sleeves rolled up, a notepad on his desk with notes scribbled diagonally across the page. From where Dalton stood he could tell his supervisor was talking to Admiral Jacobs about the sequence of events.

Lt. Walker was tall with a severe crewcut that caused him to seem strict when in fact he was friendly and approachable. A law enforcement man from a line of sheriff deputies, he had been accepted into the Marshal Office in his mid forties. After ten years in the field he was promoted to the position of lieutenant. He oversaw a staff of seventeen marshals assigned to three outposts – Joshua Tree or Morongo Basin, Amboy and Needles – for a salary of one hundred thousand dollars a year. He offered his men solid support backing them up in the field with whatever reinforcements he could find. Salt and pepper crewcut, a long face with large hollows, long neck, he sat comfortably, a fan situated on a bookshelf behind him blowing cool air on him. Through an arched window the rugged desert stretched, the chalky white landscape dotted with adobe one-story homes and here and there Joshua trees and saguro cacti.

Dalton took a seat and waited for his boss to get off the phone. Ian joined him in the chair beside him. Ian was a good ten years older than Dalton. He was strident in manner, silver haired, narrow shouldered, thin all the way down no matter what he ate, which was frequently donuts and coffee. When Lt. Walker got off the phone, he said, hands held in mock protest, "I haven't yet assigned this case, Dal. The file is still on my desk," he said, indicating with a nod to a stack of folders on top of a two-drawer filing cabinet.

"I can handle it. I already know more about it than Ian can. I'm not going to overlook anything precisely because it is personal with me. I know how Officer Du Bois thought; I know what his life was about. Ian isn't going to go into a gay bar if the case calls for it."

"Not so fast. The problem with Officer Du Bois is that he was assigned to CHP because the corruption scandal involved the disappearance of cargo on several desert routes. I can't afford to have Chief Lenny Salvo breathing down my neck when you turn the case into a vendetta as you undoubtably will."

"It's bound to be a vendetta for all of us," Ian interjected. "It's fine by me for you to handle the case."

Lt. Walker sat silent for a moment. Then, "okay, we can do this. When you finish writing up your notes," he said to Ian, "turn them over with a copy to Dal. Be sure you have compiled a chronology of interviews and leads you have followed up on."

"Not a problem," Ian said, and stood to leave.

"Okay, that'll do it." Marty Walker said. "Where are you with all of this?"

"I found Isaiah's vehicle," Dalton said. "I did a complete workover. I sent the vehicle to the forensics lab. I took several rolls of photos which I am having developed as we speak. I submitted soil and fiber samples to the lab."

"Has Teale completed a prelim?"

"Not yet. He thinks the water action may have forced water into the lungs, but he won't know until he opens him up."

"I see." Marty Walker was reflective. "Admiral Jacobs thinks a log rolled onto him."

"It's a possibility. The question for me is who was Isaiah pursuing?"

"Ian interviewed Nick Casille. I'd like you to also question him."

"Already done. Nicholas Casille is under the impression the man who went after Isaiah was someone by the name of Carmichael."

"Did Casille say where this man works?"

"I don't think he knows."

"We have anything on Isaiah's last six months?"

"Just that he brought his partner to Hemal Ebenales for some kind of treatment for early onset of AIDS."

"How do you know this?"

"I went through Isaiah's home. I came across his notes. The situation with his partner may in fact be tied to the Cobb/Hague scandal of a year ago."

"Be discreet. What's your next step?"

"Do a look-see through his office, obtain a list of cases, put my hands on any paperwork which might suggest where he went and what he was after."

"I want you in contact with me around the clock on this one," Marty said. "No independent moves, okay?"

"I understand. What else did Admiral Jacobs say?"

"Simms isn't where he's supposed to be."

"And where's that?"

"At Red Mountain airport waiting for Piper N16374."

"Whose plane is it?"

"Man named Kyle Scott owns it. He was supposed to have flown in from Costa Mesa."

"He's what? Drugs?"

"There's nothing that says he is. He was allegedly bringing in electronics."

"And what happened?"

"Radar picked the flight up somewhere over the Cady Mountains."

Dalton said, "Pretty far east from Newport Beach area. What does Jacobs think?"

"He's concerned that when Du Bois went down so did Simms. So I don't want any heroics."

"You won't get any."

Lt. Walker gave him a glance that said he knew better. "Call my pager each leg of your investigation."

Dalton left. In the hall he dropped a few quarters into the *Coca Cola* machine and snapped open a *Diet Coke* and walked to his cubicle.

"You okay?" Lina asked him when he entered.

"Fine. I convinced Marty to give me the case."

"It was either that or have you watching over Ian's shoulder every step of the way."

"I wouldn't have done that. How's your day going?"

"I spent all morning from four to seven-thirty sprinkling sand on 395."

"Another spill?"

She nodded. "Oil."

"Tanker?"

"Yes. Messy —"

"Real douche bag."

"You do so have a way with words. I wound up drenched in the stuff. It was all I could do to show up here."

He turned on his computer and punched in his password.

"You're the better detective to handle Du Bois' drowning," she said. "Spender doesn't have your years tracking suspects."

"He's the best with boaters. I don't think there's a single cuff he's failed to bring in. So, Lina," he said trying to lighten the atmosphere between them, "when are you going to say yes?"

"When are you going to ask?"

"You want to go steady? Wear my ring? Kiss my dog?"

"The dog sounds interesting. What breed?"

"Big, slobbery."

She grimaced. "Yuck," and returned to her data entry.

He put in a call to Dr. Teale who answered on the second ring. "Any update on the autopsy?"

"Your man had a heart attack."

"Cause?"

"He drowned first. His lungs filled with water. I'll FAX my report to you by tomorrow."

"Did you cut open the stomach sack?"

"Practically empty. Du Bois ate breakfast around six. He didn't eat lunch."

"You have a time of death?"

"I'd say noonish."

Dalton nodded into the phone. "What are you listing as official cause of death?"

"Homicide. It's always homicide when an officer is dead for unknown causes."

"Thanks." Dalton put down the receiver.

"You get what you need?" Lina asked.

"I had hoped for more. An autograph would've been nice."

THE MORONGO BASIN HIGHWAY PATROL was located in a stucco building a block away from the Marshal Office. Obtaining a security clearance from the Public Safety Officer as he had done many times in the past proved no problem, and he wound his way down a hall to Isaiah's office. Dalton pushed open the door and switched on the overhead light. His gaze fixed on a red jade vase with fake wildflowers. A remembrance came at him as if out of nowhere, with a jolt.

"What the hell're you doing out here?" Isaiah asked, as Dalton crossed the threshhold of his kitchen and stared out at the oblivion of the desert and then at the roof tops of the Copper Mountain Campus of the College of the Desert.

"I was told you're on my case as an assist." Dalton said.

"Jesus. Am I really? What the heck time is it?"

"They'll shoot you in the balls, Isaiah, if your hangovers take over your life."

"No hangover. I'm putting in back-to-back shifts for the Highway Patrol in Riverside and Inyo."

"Is this for the DEA? Or are you moonlighting?"

"Moonlighting. The CHP came to me."

"I thought you told me you'd learned your lesson, that you were going to stay home and watch television."

"Can't handle it. Not since they packed Eric on ice."

Dalton didn't say much as Isaiah stumbled out of bed and jogged into the bathroom and vomited. Isaiah looked bad, his body too thin, his ribs showing through like some crack head or dildo boy. It was a good cover if he was gathering information for the DEA, but Dalton worried about his friend's health.

Dalton went into the kitchen. He fixed coffee and toast as Isaiah dressed.

"You want to tell me why Riverside when you could punch in after-hours for San B?"

"I can't, Dal. It's an emotional thing. There's too much of Eric in the desert. Everywhere I travel at night I come across something to remind me of him. It just fucks with my brain."

"Why did you move out here?"

"CHP felt I'd work better."

"They probably thought your commute from downtown San Bernardino would be too great."

When Isaiah responded with an expression that said a man had to make a living any damn place he could, Dalton turned to the matter at hand saying, "You could at least tell me what case we're running out on to Joshua Tree College."

"Bunch of blasters found on campus."

"What composition?"

"Standard revue, amonium nitrate."

"Was a threat made?"

"Yeah, from the Desert Liberation Army. They want to stick our aircraft in a marble display on Twenty-nine Palms Highway."

"Why you? The feds couldn't bother with one of their Emergency Recovery Technician experts?"

"Oh fuck off," said Isaiah, suddenly coming to life. "Some fuck-face has been doing all the small airports near the colleges and universities in the Southwest. Began with UCLA. It's a nuisance. I mean, why the hell doesn't this butt-head just melt his finger in the cigarette lighter and get it over with?"

On the way to the college, Dalton handed Isaiah the map. "Anything else out here besides an extension campus?" Isaiah copied the route onto his small notepad, took a sip of coffee from his thermos cup and considered. "Maybe the military's hoping to set up posts that can more effectively respond to drug traffic."

"That's as likely as anything else," said Dalton.

"Don't knock it. The campuses have become the sites of surveillance."

"How about of experimental contaminants? Beats housing some of this stuff on military bases."

"Stupid to create that kind of threat on a campus."

"That may be but sooner or later it's all wrapped into one sushi. Some places suggest a certain type of crime. Riverside and Los Angeles are up the butt with computer hackers; San Diego with airline crashes. We've got the last will and testament on highway crimes. Whatever goes on the roads affects a good percentage of our industries."

"I see you've given this some thought worth a bit of salt."

"Whole Southwest from southern California to New Mexico is a chili pepper waiting for its ass to get lit."

IT WAS THE LAST TIME he had seen Isaiah alive, he thought as he sat at Isaiah's desk. Isaiah had been right about crime and industry. There wasn't much to grow in the desert except suburbs and storefronts.

A road map of the San B. had been thumbtacked onto the wall over the desk. Dalton looked through the lower half of a metal filing cabinet where the files were kept. He withdrew a file containing mileage logs and unpaid receipts. He leafed through them. Some were several years old. As far as he could tell the receipts were for meals and hotels in the lower southern California area. He jotted down the dates, places and amounts. As he copied the information he wondered why the receipts showed that Isaiah had travelled numerous times from Big Bear Lake to Inyokern. Big Bear was a wilderness resort and the stops along 215 and 395 were remote desert gasoline stops. Apart from a smattering of fast food stands and mini markets, there was nothing else out there except sand and wind.

Next he opened the drawer for Cases and removed a file marked, *Cases in progress*. It contained reports. They appeared to be original reports, not yet submitted on the forms that a supervising CHP would sign off on. Isaiah had headed each report with the last name of the suspect or in those situations where the criminal's identity was known, the last name of the doer. *Gardino, McDougal, Carey, Azul, Bahe*. The only name he recognized was the last one. Bahe was known for bringing hate mail to ranchers and farmers in the forms of sewage water pumped into private vineyards, fruit flies to destroy orchards and truckloads of dirt delivered to one's driveway to prevent automobile access to the garage. While no one caught him in the act, he was known for his willingness to do just about any mean nasty thing to rid a community of self-styled entrepreneurs who intended to sell goods sold by small mom-and-pop shops.

Next Dalton unlocked a file drawer on the right side of the desk. In it were a handful of digital cameras, an Ricoh RDC-5300 worth a good seven hundred dollars, a Mavica MVC-FD88, also worth a cool eight hundred, a Nikon Coolpix 950, and a Fuji SLR-style digicam that featured a zing camera that could plug into a USB port on a computer. The collection was the best in state-of-the-art, high tech cameras that had optical and digital zoom lenses for closeups and photo quality posters. One camera was able to provide high speed continuous shooting, another provided eight million pixels for better imaging and scanned 35 milimeter negatives and slides onto a computer. Isaiah also had the Quickstitch 360 software that placed the photographic image in an eliptical grid for use on Windows 2004. Together the cameras made for unusually viable surveillance. He bagged them.

Isaiah's computer featured a *Nokia 800Pro* monitor with a smaller CRT and good color. The keyboard was an *Acer Airkey* and operated without a mouse. Beside it, unplugged and still wrapped in plastic, lay a *Key Tronic Secure Scanner Keyboard*, a state-of-the-art item that relied upon fingerprint-identification software. If it were installed, the program would reject Dalton's fingerprints.

But it wasn't installed and Dalton accessed a handful of cases using the password he found taped to the side of the monitor. *Jon Carmichael, Jason Carey and Carlos Azul.* If this was *the* Carmichael Nick Castilles had spoken of, it was an easy find. Dalton jotted down the information, then as the sound of footsteps approached and passed the office he flicked off the computer and let himself out.

four

THE VOICES FILTERED INTO the hall. Dalton was surprised anyone was still in the building on a Tuesday at four in
the afternoon. He strained to hear who was talking.

"Good excuse to watch for faces," George Maciel's voice became clear after Dalton passed the room with the copier in it.

"Or to study who is doing what to whom," Lina replied. "Not
much out on 95 to warrant continuous oil spills."

Dalton found Marshal Maciel at his desk, feet propped up on
the ink blotter. Maciel swung his feet off the desk as Dalton placed
a stack of Sheriff reports on the desk.

"Recognize any of these names?" Dalton handed Maciel a copy
of the list he had compiled from Isaiah's case files.

"Sure. Vail Bahe. He's a little stink bomb living in a nice sized
tin roofed ranch house in Vidal. His mother's Margaret Bahe. She's
a produce trucker who resides at Mahogany Flat."

"Know anything about her?"

"Her husband was a drunk Spaniard whose bones were so shot to hell he couldn't stand up."

"Remember his name?"

"Gardino."

"He any relation to Gardino trucking?"

"Could be. Check with National Transportation Board."

Dalton sat at his desk.

Maciel hesitated at the door. "Mrs. Bahe used to volunteer for the Catholic Social Services going out on the street and getting young men on the AFDC dole to train as pipe fitters, electricians and construction workers. I can't be certain but I think she was an electrician for half a dozen construction companies piecing a living together between her husband's periods of insobriety and winter rains."

Dalton handed the list to Lina. "What do you make of Isaiah's list?" He asked her.

She gave the list a once-over. "Looks like a drug case."

"Officer Du Bois' death definitely smacks of drugs."

"Azul is a trucking company."

"What does it ship?"

"Produce primarily. You remember when the county expanded Inland Empire funding? It did so with the idea that small businesses would enhance the number of customers they shipped to. A number of small shipping companies signed up to train drivers so these fellows could eventually get hired by larger companies. The funds were a shot in the arm for smaller businesses in places like Barstow, Hinkley, Kramer Junction up 395 to Inyokern and Olancha."

"Interesting."

"Well, that was part of the scandel Chief Cobb created. There's very little on the road to begin with apart from *Cal Trans, PG&E* and a half dozen fly-by-night resorts. Chief Cobb created all these businesses and expanded the shipping routes."

Dalton asked, "Any idea whether Gardino received county funds?"

"I'm pretty sure they did, but I can check."

"If you can obtain an entire listing of every company that received funds that would be terrific," he said.

"I'll try."

He looked up Margaret Bahe's name in the telephone directory. She was one of ten people listed. He dialed the number.

Margaret Bahe's voice struck him as intensely familiar even though he was certain he had never spoken to her. She suggested he drive up to Mahogany Flat. He told her it would take him a good four hours.

He stopped at his house for an overnight bag and a change of clothes and several plastic bottles of Crystal Geyser spring water, packages of beef jerky, string cheese and a package of Almond Roca. He filled his jeep with gas at the mini market at Twenty-Nine Palms and purchased an extra set of maps for Inyokern County and Death Valley National Park. It was ten after five before he made Pioneertown and Landers.

I don't know why I love you but I do bleated from the jeep stereo. Except for the fact he would be working through the weekend, he admitted to himself that he felt most productive when he was working a new case. Back-to-back shifts were frowned upon although widely practised and relied upon. Without double shifts the county jails would face understaffing and a third of the workforce – divorced or underemployed with mortgages and child support burning a hole in the back pocket – would go broke. For himself the after-hours work was more challenging than the seven to four routine.

He gunned his jeep at sixty miles down the rust colored gravel landscape that extended into infinity off Highway 247. Joshua trees flashed by, their angular disjointed shapes like giant spurs against a solid blue sky. Dalton switched radio stations. For a moment the music wailed at him, unrecognized. Then sense and familiarity broke through and he drummed a beat as he sang along with Randy Sparks' song, Sinner Man. *Who you gonna run to, who you gonna run, oh sinner man, who you gonna run to, all on that day.*

The uphill climb past Apple Valley and up 395 to Adelanto where Federal Express had brought in a bevvy of airplanes to its expansive airport was wearisome in the hot sticky heat. Wind blew drifts of sand across the road to a church that stood at the outskirts of civilization. Distant bluish mountains formed a bowl in an ethereal stone landscape. The journey to Kramer Junction was a straight shot down an asphalt road to a shimmering horizon that promised water but delivered thirst and emptiness and disappointment. He stopped for gasoline and a cup of iced coffee. Sweat soaked his undershirt. Hot wind provided no relief to the exhaustion he began to feel. For an instant he thought he should have insisted upon a telephone interview, but instinct had told him to take a look-see at the terrain, and at her. No matter how many times a month he travelled this stretch of road, every case was different and conjured up its own woes and despair. It was the passing through the landscape, the opening up to the road and the cataloguing emotions a case stirred up that he trusted.

The badlands stood like an inhospitable barrier to travel. They were parched rolling mountains consisting of yellow and chocolate swirls. The road sliced through them and through a lithic wilderness of salt flats and riddled veins of sand. The sharp piercing sound of a jet cracked the solitude and faded somewhere in the distance. Whatever solace this jumbled stretch of color was intended to offer, it aggrevated rather than reassurred. Dalton snacked on beef jerky and string cheese and took sips of water to alleviate anxiety more than to satisfy hunger.

All around the air smelled of sulfer. Occasional sand dunes cropped up between the chocolate and yellow mountains. An overlook for the passing tourist allowed for the marking of time and for photographs. Dalton took a break from driving and got out of the jeep to stretch his legs. The searing heat of the day was replaced by a more temperate, almost sultry evening candescence. He considered the trips Isaiah had made to visit Mrs. Bahe. This area was irritatingly desolate. To a man who feared going over the edge, this was a fool's errand. Better to have stayed at the computer and whiled away the hours manning the tip hotline or playing Solitaire or Free Cell.

Mahagony Flat stood at the mouth to Death Valley. It was a trailer park with a scattering of tin roofed one-story houses where desert rats holed up to escape the blasphemous sunlight. Drunks lived here; so did dry drunks and drying out addicts hell bent on salvation. Dalton half expected a scrunched up, tight lipped woman with more than one person's share of complaining. He didn't expect the sleek beauty of a woman with ash blond shoulder length, fly away hair in an open necked, white blouse, matching pedal pushers and red sneakers. The shock of her gave him quite an impression of surrender.

"The road people come out twice a year now," she said, and led him through the two room trailer out back to the stoop. She had planted a small vegetable garden of zucchini, lettuce and pumpkins that reshaped the usually cracked ground into something hospitable.

"If you refuse there's not much else they can do." He responded.

"That's what this friend of mine says when he comes up."

"I'm here about Isaiah."

"So you said. Is he alright?"

"He's dead. He drowned in the Colorado."

She was speechless. She sat for a long time before she spoke. When she did, her voice was searching as though shock absorbed her ability to think. "He'd just met someone, gotten newly involved."

"Do you know who with?"

"He didn't tell me the man's name."

"Did you ever meet Eric?"

"Once. Nice man, very introspective."

"Did Isaiah tell you anything about him?"

"Just that Eric was a computer programmer. He was building

an interface for a camera to download photographs onto a database."

"Do you know whether Eric joined Isaiah in his work?"

"I wouldn't know."

"Were you ever to their home?"

"No." She poured two cups of sun drenched tea.

He sipped his tea slowly and savored the sweet berry taste. "How did you meet Isaiah?"

"He rode with me a few times when I used to drive a load into Coachella. I asked him for advice about how to handle the real estate agent who was up here trying to buy land properties. This man was going to offer me sixty grand for this patch of dirt." She laughed. "Isaiah suggested I take the offer and relocate closer to my son. If I could've imagined going anywhere else, I would've jumped at the offer."

"Tell me about your son."

"He works for a man named Cater."

"Do you know what he does for him?"

"He hauls equipment from Arizona to Tahoe."

"Did Isaiah ever ask about your son's hauls?"

"No. He wanted to ride with me."

"Where did Isaiah ride with you?"

"Twice to Coachella and back."

"Back where? To the Flat here?"

"The return trip is through Lone Pine and Independence to Big Pine."

"Not much there."

"Depends when you drive. About forty percent of the State's hauled traffic takes 395."

"What was Isaiah interested in?"

"He asked everything I was capable of telling him about trucking." She looked into his face, her expression searching for something akin to approval. He gave it. "Department of Transportation, Federal Highway Administration, Office of Motor Carriers. He said he planned to spend several months as a highway inspector. He wanted to know about our records, codes we are subjected to —"

"Like what?" He interrupted.

"All truckers have to carry insurance. Some fleets have drug testing programs. All lines have to pass safety audits. Drivers have to carry fire extinguishers, spare fuses, reflective triangles and red electric lanterns. They also have to turn in a checklist on their rig after each day's work."

"What sort of checklist?"

"Condition of the brakes, the parking hand brake, steering, reflectors, tires, horn, windshield wipers, rear vision mirrors, emergency equipment."

He scribbled notes as she spoke.

"Also the cargo can't shift. The driver has to make sure it's tied down tightly and that it won't block the driver's view of the road."

"Do you know what kind of case he might have been on?"

"He was following some kind of foul weather case he called it."

"What did you understand him to mean?"

"That the situation was dangerous."

"Did Officer Du Bois say anything to you about the assignment he was on?"

"Well, the first time he came with me there was ice all over the road. Plowing through it was like driving through slush. A truck had jackknifed. There was garbage strewn across the road. He wanted to know about times and places of road accidents I'd seen."

"Were you in an accident?"

"Never. But he'd seen a bad one. He said the truck had landed on its side."

"Where was this?"

"On 395 up near Little Lake."

"Could you say what caused it?"

"Speeding. Accidents on the state's backroads, especially on the steeper grades, occur all the time. Sometimes it's because the road is too slippery to drive on, due to ice or oil, or the driver had pulled out of the dock late and was hoping to gain time on the delivery schedule. With produce a driver has a refrigeration time clock to beat. With high value commodities the driver has to keep the wheels to the tar, otherwise he is a sitting duck waiting for a highjacker to come down an empty stretch of road.

She said, "My guess is he was investigating a hijack, maybe a string of them."

"What are high value commodities?"

"Surveillance equipment, computer upgrades, automobile parts, that sort of thing."

"You'd need a fence to sell the stuff, wouldn't you?"

"For most of it unless you were part of a hijack team that planned to use the surveillance equipment to pull robberies."

He was thoughtful as he dropped an irregularly shaped brown sugar cube into his half drunk tea and stirred it with his finger. "Does hijacking usually occur on the Staircase?" he asked, after a long silence.

"Well, generally it's not on 395. Cargo apart from cocaine or heroin comes into Long Beach and Costa Mesa and winds up in trucks on Interstate 5 or on small planes headed for Vegas."

"Any idea of the return ticket for a hijacker on 395?"

"I always thought the trucks that were headed toward Bishop got hit somewhere around Independence. The fence is probably sitting up there at Bishop or Bridgeport."

"Can you recall anything Isaiah actually said to you?"

"He said something like, the way to hell for a Mexicali Rose was up the interstate chasing after the prison drug trade. If the Asians didn't slice you at Mecca, the whites would make a grab at Red Mountain. If you got as far as Olancha or Owenyo, you had the real crazies to deal with."

"What was a real crazy?"

"He didn't say and I didn't ask."

"You have any idea whether Isaiah had a specific hijacker in mind?"

"He wanted me to take him to Big Pine on a number of occasions. I said no, so you know, your guess is as good as mine. Maybe if I had said yes, he'd be alive today." She smiled sadly and sensing his inqueries were drawing to a close, she said, "I'll miss him. He was the only DEA I knew who I liked."

The hair on the back of his neck prickled. "Have you known many DEA?"

"They used to check the produce as it was unloaded onto the dock. At any given time there might be two or three agents."

"Ever heard of Gardino?"

"John Gardino? He's a small time trucking company that brings produce to fifteen or so markets in and around the city of San Bernardino. Has a daughter Dani, early twenties."

He stood. "Thanks for your time. And for tea."

She took the cup. "Any time you're out this way, feel free to stop by."

"I will," even though he knew he'd never see her again. "Keep the faith."

He returned the way he'd come trying to decide upon the most likely race of bandits patrolling the after midnight corridors. He thought they were probably Caucasian. The road through Inyo to Mono County was a lonesome road through uncharted mountains. Notwithstanding tumbleweed and cacti and long heat and high pressure thirst, there was nothing to think about, nothing to see. You could dance a gig with old wily coyote and no one would be present to see you do it or care that you had gone a little nuts. And between Lone Pine and Big Pine and Bishop and Mono, discounting the angry ticked off bears that had ripped off a door or two at Yosemite and had been tranked and flown to the wilds of Bishop, the only real castigating eye was an occasional plane airport-hopping up the Owens River. Besides recovering alcoholics who were putting in double shifts carting tomatoes and corn up the state, the highway was a trail for burnt-out scriptwriters and producers, a place in the trees to contemplate a hundred ways to split a navel orange.

"YOU GOT A PERMIT FOR THAT THING?" Nell asked as he stepped between her legs and inched her across the floor of her one bedroom apartment.

"What, this?" he asked, and unclasped his holster and gun and tossed them on her sofa. "What I've got I don't need a permit for."

"Oh, Dal-face," and she smothered his face with kisses.

She knew how to humor him through the dismal hours of a crime scene discovery. For all the overtime he clocked he couldn't tolerate a relationship that took his mind off the work and gave him an inferiority complex. A half foot shorter than he was, she was a dark moody type who wept over late-night movies and bit into a dozen chocolates before she decided on one she liked. The conversation was deep when he needed it to be and the love took him into the depths of passion. Nell was practised at tenderness and in her arms he felt they moved as one. The breath was one, the rocking slow and easy and temperate, and the joining was comfortable.

"You want to go out tonight?" he asked.

"Do you?"

"I'm wiped." He admitted.

"Poor Dal."

She led him through the bedroom to the sunken bath tub and undressed him and walked him into it. He closed his eyes and leaned his head against her arm. The hot waters took his tension and damn near everything else he had held onto in the past few days. If he was going to break he'd break in the circle of her embrace but when she embraced him from behind as was her style he shook himself loose and without explanation sat beside her, holding her hand, mute.

"Want to tell me about it?" she asked him.

He searched for a way to call forth his grief but it had frozen inside him like permanent disinterest, a sullen reality.

"Max called." Max was his cubicle partner's mate. In ten years Dalton had spoken to him maybe four times. Conversations with him tended to be short, an exchange of information about a planned absence or the need for duty coverage.

"About Lina?"

"He wouldn't say. He was pretty obtuse."

"Did he sound urgent?"

"No, just if you could call him when you had a chance."

"I'll call him," and he lapsed into silence, letting the water do its restorative work. He wished he could fall asleep sitting up as he had done when he was part of an experiment at UCLA sitting in a floating isolation tank in warm fluid darkness. Too long trained in danger to his own vulnerabilities, he got out, towel-dried himself and Nell, and made his way into her bedroom.

Her room was shaped with rounded walls like a dark cave. Made of adobe the walls in day light were chalk white. Small opaque glass windows studded one wall against which was a bed with a head board in the room's center. A rattan sofa, a host of knicknacks among them a flannel blanket, stress squeeze toys and tiny glass candles; solar panels and framed watercolor paintings of the ocean made the desert residence seem modern and enduring at the same time.

Dalton let sleep take him. He dreamed dreamlessly, startling awake, nearly jolted into consciousness. Moonlight filtered in through one of the overhead solar panels and dark clouds cast obscure shadows over the walls and carpeted floor. Then recognizing his surroundings he drifted back into slumber. Once or twice he cried out in sleep, the only acknowledgement was Nell hugging him to her and shushing him and like a small child he responded by curling up beneath her mothering hands. In fleeting visions he remembered he had forgotten to call Max and that Lina was sent alone too early in the morning to clean an oil spill. His mind, freed of the ties to routine and service, unlatched other doors. The oil spills were grease on a predawn wheel of misfortune responsible for truck skids and overturned automobiles, sometimes for wrecks that left a handful of vehicles on their sides or burning carnages of some unnamed war.

He awoke at four thirty. Knowing his habitual crisis behaviors, Nell had awakened and put a fresh pot of coffee to brew and then returned to bed. He closed her bedroom door softly and took a cup of hot coffee on the deck overlooking the distant desert mountains. This was a sight he craved – when the night lost its flush of stars and pink light crept into gradual visibility. He sipped coffee and allowed the new day to possess him. He thought of the landscape sprawled out along Freeway 15, of the brownish beige soil and dense shrubbery, a hodge podge of dark and light greens, of olive leafed, low lying trees and purple and yellow wildflowers interspersed with a barely visible dash of crimson for a high desert beauty. Sorrow welled up inside him passing itself off as anguish. He readied himself for tears but they were dormant now.

T HE AUTOPSY REPORT sat on Dalton's desk.

CITY AND COUNTY OF SAN BERNARDINO
Chief Medical Examiner
Necropsy Department
Name: **ISAIAH ALEXANDER DU BOIS** Date & Time of Necropsy: **16 OCTOBER 2003 0845** Age: **24** Height: **5'10"** Weight: **190**

PRELIMINARY EXAMINATION:
The body is received enshrouded in a white sheet and identified by an appropriately labeled Medical Examiner's tag. The body is cold,

rigor is present and lividity is fixed posteriorly.

Dalton glanced at the section marked **EXTERNAL EXAMI-NATION**. He let his gaze take in the physical description of the body along with the description of trauma. **INTERNAL EXAMI-NATION:** for the section marked **LUNGS:** described the abnormal collection of freshwater and the presence of algae confirming that the scene of death was the Colorado River. He scanned for the diagnoses. *Focal trauma was due to pulmonary edema, cardiomegaly and left ventricular hypertrophy.*

He took the report and went to the conference room where Lt. Walker was conducting a weekly staff meeting.

"**W**HAT'VE WE GOT?**" Lt. Martin Walker began the weekly briefing. Crewcut, long face with hollows, no nonsense mien and wiseacre expression, he stood at the white board, a black marker in hand.

Present in the room was the investigative team comprised of Ian Spender, Lina Crandall, Margo Sam, George Maciel. Their supervisor Lt. Walker filled Dalton in on the week's take. Ian and Lina had seizured a clandestine laboratory, and Margo and the lieutendant had served warrants on a handful of single wide mobile homes and radiator shops where methamphetamine was manufactured. Lt. Walker was looking to replace Margo Sam – a petite Korean Chinese woman, five foot five, clean sparse look, who had settled in Yucca Valley with her husband and three children from San Francisco where she had formerly worked for the Medical Examiner's Office of the Sheriff Department – in court hearings where the judge would begin to hear testimony on these cases. Margo was being called north at the end of the week to Folsom, a suburb near Sacramento, to review findings with the Family Services section of the District Attorney's Office on one of her high profile Hmong cases. Because she was usually assigned as a duo with Ian for gang activity and had a sixth sense for spotting violence before it went down, whoever replaced her had to be able to point out to the attornies appearing on the cases what potential problems might arise. Lina offered but Lt. Walker needed her to investigate a vandalism at the Willie Boy Grave Site and to look into a second oil spill on Highway 95. That left Marshal Maciel who agreed he was the best marshal for the job anyway. His all-American good boy appearance, blond hair, blue eyes, firm physique wooed even the more resistant attornies to see matters his way.

Lt. Walker scribbled the assignments on the board. To Dalton he said, "How're you doing on Du Bois?"

"So so," Dalton answered. "I went through papers in files both at his home and office and found a list of names in a in-progress file. Also I sent in a dozen or more rolls of film from various state-of-the-art cameras and have photos for a look-see. I interviewed a woman trucker with whom he rode and received feedback from her about a situation he was investigating. Isaiah apparently spent time as a fleet investigator but I have yet to confirm it with Department of Transportation."

"What's your impression?"

"I think he was on a hijacking case."

"How soon before you know definitely?"

"I plan to conduct surveillance of the names I found in Isaiah's cases in progress."

"These Officer Du Bois' photographs?" He pointed to a pack of photographs.

"I recovered this off one of his cameras," Dalton put in. "More than half of the exposures are too dark." He spread the photographs on the table.

Lina reached for a photograph of a Ving card key. "Great clip."

The five marshals in the room rifled through the pictures. One was of nightfall and street lights taken from a motel through wooden slats.

"This location shouldn't be hard to pin down," Maciel remarked. "How many motels have slats for window coverings?" He pushed aside several failed exposures including one of too much light and picked up a photograph of a lobby. "That's the *Schoolmast Inn* on Waterman Avenue. I know because I've stayed there."

The lieutenant said, "Check DMV registrations against Du Bois' unresolved cases. You need assistance?"

"Wouldn't hurt." Dalton said.

"Margo, you will ride as a second until you need to leave for Folsom. Maciel, you and Crandall take the vandalism at Landers and Ian, ask CHP to give you a hand with the overturned rig at Del Rosa. Cut and dry narratives on all out-calls."

Marty Walker said, "Officer Du Bois went down in the line of duty," he began. "He was engaged in tracking routes between 95, 62, 15 and 395 all the way up the Staircase. There's some belief DEA relocated him out here to the Highway Patrol. If you hear of anything that you feel might be connected, call it in. There's some likelihood of a switch hitter on the road, so be extra careful."

"We looking at a dirty cop?" Ian queried.

"Very, very doubtful. My guess is we have a businessman who is bringing in contraband. Or possibly a dirty Department of Transportation. Keep your ears alert to the street. That's a go."

Dalton waited until the others filed out of the room. "I received the necropsy report."

Lt. Walker took a seat at the long table. He poured himself a glass of ice water, put on thick wood framed eye glasses and turned to a fresh sheet of paper in his yellow lined legal pad.

"Cause of death?" he asked.

Dalton read from the report. "Lungs took in freshwater, the heart ruptured and so did the spleen."

"The freshwater says scene of death was the Colorado. He either drowned accidentally or was killed in the river. He wasn't dumped from a saltwater pond or lake. You were at the scene. What does cause of death suggest occurred?"

"He couldn't get out because the water was flowing too fast. Given the river – its width and depth – six miles an hour is fast enough to prevent a man from climbing out to safety."

"Or he had help staying in the water. Any idea where he went in? At the site where he was rescued, or closer to the dam?"

"His patrol vehicle was parked a quarter of a mile from the casino."

"How deep is the river there?"

"Same. Fifteen feet."

"Depending upon where he went overboard, if this were closer to the dam, the turbulence of the water would have been sufficient to kill him. Once under water, the wake of boats could have prevented him from surfacing. What do you think occurred after he parked his vehicle?"

"I think he was following a suspect who took his boat out on the water and Isaiah took a boat to follow."

"Do we know in whose boat he was?"

"No."

"Have you learned whose fingerprints have been identified on his vehicle?"

"No."

"Call the auto yard, see what they've come up with." Lt. Walker made notes on half of the pad, then considered questions raised by what he had written. On every case Lt. Walker carefully interviewed the investigating marshal's findings once the cause of death was known. This was done early in the case and then periodically every three to four days until the facts of the case were well established.

"You think Officer Du Bois had learned his quarry's routine?" The lieutenant asked him.

"He must have, because he had chronicled various truck stops by motel and restaurant receipts."

"What do the receipts show about activity in this area?"

"They walk the line from Inyokern through Red Mountain and Boron to Barstow, Daggett and Needles. One of the names on Isaiah's database - Vail Bahe - lives at Vidal."

"So presumably this man's territory for whatever it is he does is marked by his residence. Did you attempt to research the other names on Du Bois' list?"

"I only had last names. I learned from this man's mother that Gardino may be Danielle Gardino."

Lt. Walker gave a nod. "A trucking firm."

"Carrying produce. Same with *Azul*. They are also a trucking company for San Bernardino city."

"Why do you think Du Bois did not make an arrest?"

"I wondered about that. It seems Simms made the arrests. Perhaps he lacked documentation to make an arrest that would stick."

"Du Bois covered roads and boats. Simms covered railroads and airplanes. Do I have that correct?"

"Yes. Isaiah recently checked on air traffic at Red Mountain."

"What exactly did Du Bois do that tells you this?"

"He followed someone there and took a plane home."

"Maybe he took a plane to avoid getting his cover blown. Do you know how many times he did this?"

"Isaiah's documentation doesn't say."

"Or more precisely who he was following?"

"No. That's what I hope to find out."

"You plan to investigate activity for places which Du Bois compiled a string of receipts?"

"Yes." He waited for his supervisor to think through his concerns for accuracy. Whereas Dalton worked by intuition, years in management had made Lt. Walker a precise man who required clear details which could later be used to build a court case to sustain a conviction.

"How will you ascertain who on Du Bois' list is committing the crimes Du Bois investigated?"

"I plan to photograph all the activity I observe."

"Which is what Du Bois did."

"He did not directly link the photos he took with any of the names nor with any crimes."

Lt. Walker sat thoughtfully for a long time. Whatever impatience Dalton felt in this question/answer process receded. He usually came away from these discussions with greater clarity.

"It's possible these names Du Bois compiled are known to CHP under aliases," Lt. Walker said.

"I considered that. It could explain the reason Isaiah was assigned to the CHP out here."

"Any idea why the activity Du Bois photographed is still occurring in the same places?"

"I haven't ruled out that it is. It could be the activity of the ring is dependent on other things these drug dealers have no control of. Such as when other rigs arrive and depart?"

"I'm not convinced that what brought Officer Du Bois to Blue Water was drugs. We have no way at this point in time to know whether the call he responded to was in any way related to drug traffic."

"You're right. It's too early to tell."

"Until we know the crimes, I want you to submit a careful chronology of every place you go to. Put it on your laptop and back it up to me. We'll stay in contact by air touch pager. Perhaps if Du Bois had been relentlessly cautious he'd be alive today.

"Okay, Dal, that's all for now. Keep up the good work."

"Thanks for your time."

Dalton went to find Margo Sam. By nightfall he wanted to learn the establishments that utilized Isaiah's card key.

five

BY THE TIME THEY reached the town of Yucaipa it was a breezy eleven o'clock in the morning. Dalton headed for a motel he thought used Ving card keys. The key turned out not to be theirs. The butterfly appearance made by the strings of small punched-out dots on the plastic card belonged to the *Alhambra Lodge* in Redlands.

The manager for the Spanish style, red roofed two story adobe motel recognized the photograph of the motel key with five numbers printed below the design. He selected an identical card key and inserted it into a scanning device. Data appeared on his computer which told him a man by the name of Isaiah Du Bois checked in at 4:13pm on September 20th and was given room 206 on the second floor above the mezzanine. Prior to that night Mr. Du Bois stayed one night in June and one in July, also in the same room. He was not observed to be travelling in a party nor with another individual.

They drove to the *Night's Inn* on Waterman Avenue in San Bernardino. The manager, a small petite brunette who looked as if life had passed her over, told them that there were a handful of motels that used the Ving card key. They were Night's Inns in Victorville, Barstow, Red Mountain and Lone Pine. Margo inquired whether it was possible to say which nights Mr. Du Bois had stayed at other motels. The brunette inserted the card key into her computer and told them that on September 21 Mr. Du Bois spent a night in her motel in room 219. The petite brunette checked for other Night's Inn locations. On September 22nd Mr. Du Bois spent a night in Victorville in room 204 but left in the middle of the night after claiming that large cockroaches had crawled under the door from the parking lot. He drove to Barstow where he booked into a double occupancy at a Night's Inn in Room 109.

Room 219 on Waterman Avenue faced the street at the angle taken of the street lights in the photograph. Dalton could think of no reason Isaiah wished to have a photograph of the street, but he took note of the place on the street that the photograph represented and determined it was of a truck stop because of an all-night hamburger joint across the road. He and Margo sipped coffee and packed in several glazed donuts watching for rigs along that stretch of road. Within an hour four, eighteen wheeler, fifty-three-foot long trucks pulled up for approximately half hour breaks. Margo said she would check which rigs had stopped here the night Isaiah paid for the room.

At Margo's insistence they drove to Victorville to see the motel there. It was an L-shaped two story building consisting of forty rooms. Room 204 faced the road. Directly across from motel was a corner on which sat several gasoline stations, a Burger King, a Taco Bell and a mini market. The bright lights made it impossible not to see people and cars with absolute clarity.

They drove to Barstow. The Night's Inn was a block from the airport and faced both a local coffee shop and the train tracks.

Dalton and Margo walked through a four-block radius. Rigs, some without their cabs, lined the main road. One was parked a block west of the coffee shop in front of a church which advertised Alcoholics Anonymous groups every Thursday evenings at six o'clock.

Another time Dalton would attempt to hammer down other stops Isaiah may have made that third week of September. He and Margo rode back down Highway 15 most of the way in comfortable silence. He thought about drivers who made a career out of driving rigs. He decided the way they managed the silence and the monotony was by talking often to other drivers on their route. He wondered how it was one driver of a company could be heisted without anyone else in the company hearing it and decided the heists were done late at night, perhaps into the wee hours of the morning when the company's dispatch was poorly staffed.

In the next twelve hours they would discover that on September 23, Isaiah stayed at Inyokern at the only lodge in town, a *Best Western*. The night clerk, a short elderly woman with frizzy blond hair who smoked incessantly, saw him arrive. The hidden camera eye recorded the transaction with minimum fanfare – Du Bois wore dark grey pants and a light grey turtleneck cotton top and matching woolen scarf and gloves. He arrived, the manager said, shortly after a businessman known to them as Mr. K. Scott arrived. Officer Du Bois was put in the room adjacent to Mr. Scott. Coffee and scones were served the next morning but the tape did not record the presence of either the officer nor of Mr. Scott. Officer Du Bois had dropped off his vehicle at Hertz at the airport and hopped a flight aboard a six seater bound for Ontario. He travelled into San Bernardino by a rented automobile and drove to the desert to his home.

"WHAT DO YOU THINK?" Dalton asked Margo. They wolfed down hamburgers and milkshakes at the truck stop in Red Mountain. Temporal shades of hunger diminished as they sipped cups of coffee and considered the dead man's journey represented by a four day excursion of withheld receipts in the life of an officer. Dalton had spread out a map of San Bernardino County on his dashboard and pencilled in the route Isaiah had taken. It charted a fairly desolate stretch along Freeways 15 and 395 from Redlands to Inyokern.

"What do *you* think?" Margo asked him, in her clipped accent.

"Well, I think he took the routes taken by the people he was tracking."

"Judging by the information we uncovered he tracked them a handful of times."

"It's questionable whether this is a drug route or something else," he said.

"I agree. The operation was fairly straightforward."

He gave a nod. "Someone gave the card key for the motel room to a dealer to conduct the sale of drugs for a night."

Margo removed a notepad and turned to a fresh page and began taking notes as he continued.

"The operation may have been set up in this manner because the head honcho – Hemal Ebenales or Cater – wanted there to be no obvious way to track these transactions. The upside was he could bring in a lot of customers from the road without arousing suspicion of them or his operation. The downside may have been that in a sting his dealers were picked up."

"How would he get the key back?"

"From the motel manager. It's probably a simple matter, especially if he owns the chain that utilizes this type of key."

"Any possibility we have prostitutes at these motels?" She asked.

"A good likelihood," he answered. "I counted four strip joints in Victorville alone. Why not call girls?"

She spoke, thinking aloud: "So a driver pulls into town, gets a little jazzed, turns over his truckload to the hooker and —"

"No. My guess is there's no exchange of goods. Whatever's in the rooms arrives there prior to the driver's arrival. The trucks are allegedly not getting heisted at motels. That's happening on the dark backroads late at night under a cloudy sky."

"If the heists do not require exchanges conducted at motels, why the stopover to a motel at all?"

He thought about it. "What do Isaiah's receipts say?"

"Where the route is."

"For what type of crime?"

"We may not know that yet."

"My informant said he was interested in a series of hijacks."

"Maybe the use of the room was not for drugs," Margo said. "Perhaps it was for Isaiah's friend. Eric."

"And being assigned CHP duty was a caviat his boss threw in? Doubtful."

"Isaiah's friend became ill prior to Isaiah being transferred to Morongo Basin?"

"Yes."

"Maybe Hemal put Eric up in different motels because he was too sickly to be seen or because he wanted Isaiah to be able to see his friend."

"Also unlikely. This route was a crime scene."

"You think Hemal Ebenales kept Eric in motels along this route in order to distract Isaiah?" she inquired, and lit a menthol cigarette.

"That would make sense. You realize Isaiah moved in with Hemal?"

Her face paled. "I didn't know." Margo considered this information. "Do you think he did this because of the situation with Eric?"

"I'm not sure. It's hard to know based on the scant information Isaiah left behind whether he moved in with Hemal to satisfy concerns over this investigation or because Hemal was the one who had a possible cure."

"I thought Eric had AIDS," she said.

"He did."

"I think Isaiah moved in with Hemal to keep tabs on his lover's treatment."

"For that he could have moved closer to Eric."

"I see." She brushed her jet black hair behind her right ear. "It was an opportunity that presented itself. You think Hemal ever caught on?"

"I don't think it mattered. Isaiah was one of the investigating team tracking his operations. If the DEA thought he'd be an unknown in the desert, they sadly underestimated the situation. My belief is Hemal made the lives of all investigating officers absolute hell. I think he engineered the situation so that Isaiah never knew where Eric was at any given time."

"That would've worn him down, easily played on his anxiety."

"Over time I think he caused Isaiah not to like himself or to trust himself."

"Do we know when Simms was brought on?"

"Less than a year ago."

"If Simms began by obstructing Hemal's drug trade and subsequently by arresting motel managers and dealers for permitting the sale of drugs," Margo speculated, "then Hemal probably wanted everything done to move Simms and Isaiah out of the way."

"I agree." He said. "Chief Cobb went into early retirement because of the scandal. Officer MacIntyre became a private investigator in San Bernardino and Officer Bowman, a Pinkerton man in San B., Riverside and Imperial conducting surveillance of warehouses. They fanned out to where the bees went once they broke up the hive."

"I keep coming back to the reason Hemal uses a card key. He must have a reason for choosing this type of security."

"It may provide entry to several warehouses or to a computer system or even to a home, in addition to motel rooms. Depends upon how extensive the trade on the road is."

She said, "Some idiot could break the code and walk off with a fortune by committing a robbery, assuming they knew all the locations of this man's operations."

"I think that's what Isaiah did."

"Then he was either stupid or a fool, and it got him killed."

He waited out her sudden anger. He too felt anger at Isaiah for not backing off or simply moving out of Hemal's home.

"This man was very clever, Dal. He changed Isaiah's focus somehow."

"He did that. Isaiah's journal describes his perceptions that everyone looked like people he knew, his feeling that he couldn't match up what was on the page —"

"Hemal probably hired people to follow him around, determine to whom Isaiah reported, where he went, who was paid per diem, who was a fulltime regular deputy or officer, and the hours they worked."

"And then, what? Assigned criminals who resembled snitches?"

She eyed him. "Hemal must have given Isaiah the illusion of roping in many crooks so that after six months or a year, CHP assigned him solo duty. It's possible Hemal changed the routes depending upon which officers were available for backup."

"That's a lot of effort to dupe one officer."

"I think it's done more than we realize. I think it's the reason there are so many adult gang members on the streets. We put officers into the field to respond to the types of criminals we encounter and the criminals in turn staff their operations in outlying areas with people who resemble us."

"I think Hemal fooled Isaiah into thinking the situation was less dangerous than it was."

"Or to confuse the police and make identification of suspects more difficult."

"Also to prevent arrests. Could be with so many similar looking people on the road the person the police were after disappeared into thin air."

They smiled at each other. Dalton went to the outdoor hamburger stand and ordered two additional coffee drinks.

"Isaiah must have penetrated a good deal of Hemal's road action," he said, sitting on the bench.

"I just can't figure why he actually moved into this man's house."

"I think it was a risk. I wouldn't have done it."

"I wouldn't have either." She took a sip of coffee. "This is a big operation."

"Huge. Involving many trades, not merely drugs."

"Perhaps the key was used with one of these groups of people who look alike. It might appear as though the same individual was in four or five different places in the same motel chain. Perhaps when a manager signed a person in, the code automatically appeared at a second motel. When the person showed there the next day, registration triggered another reservation at another motel."

"I think you might be correct."

"And by taking the key," she added, saying, "Isaiah may have eliminated a convenience for registering people to designated rooms where certain equipment was stashed."

Dalton laughed. "That key certainly meant something to someone. I can't imagine anyone going to so much trouble to set up an operation that has hijackers bringing in equipment to warehouses and then having an officer steal their key."

They were thoughtful. After a long moment, she said, "Isaiah's theft of the key hasn't stopped the crimes from occurring."

"Maybe not, but I'm sure it's been a real pain in the butt to establish a new trustworthy system."

"Do you remember the strangulation case sheriff deputies had about four years ago? The body a train conductor discovered at Red Mountain?"

"What about it?"

"A refrigerator had been thrown off a container train?"

"And?"

"The scandal began with that case. There was a trial. Chief Cobb testified. MacIntyre and Bowman testified. I think Officer Du Bois was called in."

"It centered on a series of refrigerator discards, one with the body of a child."

"Yes, that's it. Internal Affairs talked to Lina about it. She had a companion case."

He smiled. "All our cases are companion cases."

"In a sense that's true. But Isaiah misplaced evidence. On the stand he couldn't recollect the names of informants. He improperly tagged one of the refrigerators. He effectively stalled the hearing."

"That's *why* he was shipped out to the desert."

"I think he had his life served up to him on a platter and there was no other way out."

L INA STRETCHED OUT on the flowered sofa, her head in the lap of the man she had lived with for eleven years, her dark blond hair neatly parted in the middle. Although fifteen years older than she was, Max was the more energetic. He ran every morning for four miles, clocking himself and taking his pulse at intervals. He had prepared English Breakfast tea, made blueberry scones from scratch and created the comfortable easy-going atmosphere by which Dalton, shoeless and sockless, let himself be accommodated.

"You talk to her?" Max asked. "The truck lady? Bahe?"

"Yes," Dalton replied. "Interesting lady. She thought Isaiah was tracking a truck hijack ring. He apparently travelled with her twice."

"What do you think he learned?" Lina asked, rising.

"I was hoping you'd help me sort through this puzzle."

"He must have seen a hijack," Max put in.

"Good," Lina said. To Dalton, "you have the route. It starts where? In Colton?"

"The receipts say Yucaipa but I'd say Crossroads is tied in somehow —"

"I agree," Max said. "Otherwise how do you explain Isaiah's entry into the Colorado."

"That's easy," Dalton responded. "An eyewitness saw him in a boat go after a woman who had rented an outboard."

"My point is, if the call were simply a traffic problem he probably wouldn't have gone into the water unless of course the suspect were drowning."

"I believe someone did go overboard and Isaiah went in."

"Any idea what products these hijackers are after?" Lina asked, and poured herself a cup of tea. Sipping it, she winced at the strength and dropped in two cubes of sugar and added a touch of cream.

Dalton considered. "I don't think it's produce, although one of the names on Isaiah's database was *Azul Carriers*. My guess is it's computer or electronics equipment coming over the border from Mexico corporations."

"And these hijackers work for a competitive company?" Lina queried.

"Who knows. If the product is computer enhancements, the ring probably resells the goods at a lower cost."

"Or conducts Saturday markets at local high schools."

"Isaiah had digicamera gadgets all over his office and in his patrol vehicle."

Lina reflected. "Digitals might bring in some spare change assuming the market is not going to churn out an upgrade overnight. You thought about where these products are delivered to?"

"Haven't even got there."

"That's where I'd start. I'd get a list of products, their carriers, schedules. If there's drug involvement, DEA might be able to tell you who is on the road and what the carrier is bringing in. If it's routine theft —"

Max shook his head. "These victimized truckers haven't turned in incident reports. I doubt companies with drivers getting injured bother much with reports."

"You don't even know who is getting heisted?"

"No."

Lina sipped her tea. "I'd try to obtain information on time schedules from the Department of Transportation."

"Good idea."

"Jesus, you don't even know what you're up against."

"Isaiah did not spell it out in black and white."

They lapsed into silence.

"You miss him?" Lina asked, about Isaiah.

He nodded. "Feelings come and go. I don't know what happened with the new lover except the man must've hurt him."

"I think Isaiah believed people are basically good at heart. I doubt he would've put up many defenses if he needed them."

"He should've remained single after Eric's death and taken a leave of absence from the job."

"Not everyone grieves that way, Dal."

"I feel badly for him. What can you tell me about a case Isaiah was on that Internal Affairs questioned you?"

"The Becker case. Three teen victims, one child in a refrigerator and one adult deposited in train compartments of various trains also carrying scrap metal and car parts. A child death at a boathouse on the river. Gruesome."

"I wasn't aware Isaiah had been an investigator on a mass murder." He took a sip of tea. It was still too hot to drink quickly, although weariness would predispose him to several refills before he was satiated.

"Apparently so. It was the worst case of Lt. Cobb's career but Isaiah apparently wasn't fazed. He found the first body. He took photographs – unbelievable quality of photographs. Sharp closeups, you could see the spinal dislocation, the odd placement of the head, as though the killer arranged the body when he dropped it. Isaiah reviewed the collection of tapes after the murders stopped. He pointed out to me the patterns that demonstrated Becker was the killer."

Dalton asked her: "Why were you asked about Isaiah?"

"He refused to disclose his notes when the case went to trial. He apparently eliminated information off his database; it was presumed he misplaced or stole records from closed files. Internal Affairs wanted other law enforcement who could testify as to his ethics."

"You think this case led to the IAD investigation?"

"The timing is right, although nothing else is. The Becker trial was what, honey? Three years ago?"

"Two." Max thought it over. "Two and a half."

She turned to Dalton. "IAD didn't feel Isaiah's actions resulted from protective camouflage. Internal Affairs seemed to believe he had deliberately concealed crucial contacts."

"Who? Did they say?"

"A man named Cater, for one."

"I think Hemal Ebenales works for him. Hemal's the one who provided a temporary cure for Eric."

"I met Hemal," she replied. "It wouldn't surprise me to learn somewhere down the road he broke Isaiah. I think he got in the way of Isaiah's relationship with Eric and I think he did it so Isaiah would be taken off whatever he was investigating."

"Did Hemal testify on Becker?"

"I don't think so." She let Max pour her another cup of tea. He made excuses about returning to his decoupage hobby. When he left, Lina said, "It makes him nervous to hear these kinds of cases discussed."

"Nell's the same way." Like Lina he tried hard to keep talk about serious murders in the office so she wasn't likely to come into contact with the evil that ran tandem with these cases.

"Did Eric die during the Becker trial?" He asked.

"No, he got AIDS during this time. I'm sure it was very difficult on Isaiah."

"I'm sure it was."

"I told IAD what I knew. Becker used a boathouse at Needles for one murder. I think Isaiah's life was threatened."

"He wouldn't tamper with evidence otherwise. He was a solid cop. He cared about his reputation."

"Any possibility Eric's death was a murder aimed at Isaiah?"

"Could be," he said. "Eric after all was the man who kept Isaiah going."

"You plan to speak to Hemal?"

"I'd like to. You have an address for him?"

"He has a warehouse in Ontario out near the airport, one at Needles as you pull into town from 40 and one at Inyokern."

"The man is well-situated."

"He's in the drug racketeering business. He needs the stations."

"I'm sure he does. What name is on the warehouses?"

"*San Bernardino Manufacturing, Co.*"

"Is he the manager or owner?"

"I'm not sure. Owner, I believe. Doesn't it strike you as odd especially in light of the way IAD came down so heavily on Isaiah that they shipped him out to Morongo Basin?"

"Not if he were actually DEA sent in specifically to watch Hemal's operation. The IAD investigation probably rubber-stamped his relocation."

"You think Isaiah had arrangements with Chief Cobb to transport contraband?"

"Yes, specifically to lure Hemal to him."

"You think Blue Water owner Nicky Casille was pressured by this man Hemal to store cocaine in his freezers?"

"Doubtful. He wasn't given a permit he wanted to expand his deck service to the waterfront."

"I know Casille attended the hearings for the Fort Irwin Road project to make improvements to the road to reduce accidents on Highway 62 between Vidal and Crossroads."

"My impression of the Fort Irwin hearings was they were a public vehicle to obtain additional funds to post Cal Trans workers on the road who could observe drivers passing through the terrain," he said.

"I think you're right," she responded. "One of the matters discussed during the Fort Irwin Road hearings was why so many small planes came down in Owlshead Mountains. The pilots weren't asleep or inebriated and the FAA towers recorded no unusual activities other than high winds."

"All the airports were on 395?"

"That's right. From Apple Valley to Big Pine. Documentation cited that planes got tangled in power line wires or plunged into tree tops or hit the airstrip too soon or burrowed into a snow peak. Passengers said immediately following announcement of estimated arrival time the plane veered off course."

He considered this. It sounded as if the planes lost altitude or hit icy wind. "Know whether Isaiah may have talked to anyone at Fort Irwin Road?"

"I have no idea."

They sat quietly. Her place was small with the comfort luxuries of mixed furniture that didn't belong together, stained glass table lamps, modern wall lights and round throw rugs on top of square oriental and Turkish rugs. The desert pressed in at the windows as a vast inland sea of a multitude of silence and tumbleweed. He thought he understood the way she collected solitude, for he collected it in a similar fashion - with an ethereal eye toward a chalky wilderness, desolate beneath an indomitable sky, a home that stood witness to raging winds and summer thunderstorms and silent shadowless hours. He was comforted to know they were two of a kind, that they had been fortunate in purchasing adobe homes that overlooked a placid rugged shawl of the desert mantel. It comforted him now as he allowed his strong emotions about Isaiah's death to wander toward him and make him its accommodation.

He gazed at his tea and met his reflection. "I wish I had saved him."

She nodded. When a comfortable silence had lapsed, she said, "I think when Eric died Isaiah wished he had died too."

"They were together a long time." Dalton acknowledged.

"You didn't know? Isaiah had an affair and passed on AIDS to Eric as a result."

Dalton was stunned. "I had no idea."

"I think he tried to kill himself in half a dozen ways."

"I love you, Lina."

"Oh Dal —"

"I don't mean *that* way. It's just that if anything happens I want you to know what you've meant to me."

"I love you too, Dal."

"It's late," he said.

"For me too."

He stood, wondering as he helped her clear the cups about women and how they managed to squeeze the rarest confidence from men while men shared comraderie often without tenderness. If it wasn't the stigma of being perceived of as homosexual he didn't know what it was. He honestly missed Isaiah. The emotion was powerful and irrational for it went against all the values he was taught to maintain his authority. He could say *I love you* a dozen times to Lina in the certainty she would understand him and know that in this moment, this hour it was permissible to say words like those. But hours from now, or in a day, he'd return to his world where words meant something other than the sounds they suggested and feelings were detached and objective.

She walked him to the door.

"I thought I'd go to the funeral," she said as they stepped outside, as though she had thought about it during his entire visit and decided only now to confide it in him.

"I'll go with you."

"Good. I was hoping you would say that."

H E FOLLOWED THE backroads home. He hated funerals. He didn't want to accept Isaiah's death but his mind was crying out for consolation and for ending. He considered the newly learned reality of Isaiah's life. Realizing he was an AIDS carrier, watching the disease gradually kill his lover of fourteen years – How had he lived with this knowledge? Dalton unlocked the door to his house. He crossed the patio and lawn that made up the courtyard and unlocked the second door, stepping inside the dark coolness of his living room. He felt sickened. Had Isaiah latched onto Hemal out of guilt? Dalton felt overwhelming sadness for his friend. He groped in the dark for the stairs and finding them leaned against the rail as he descended the three stairs into the sitting and dining rooms. The house whispered back. The lingo of the evening came as a promise on a distant shadow and he knew the promise would never become fulfilled.

He dialed his father's telephone number in Needles.

"Dad?"

"Son?"

Sorrow swept over him. Struggling to keep emotion out of his voice, he said: "It's good to hear you. How are you?"

"Can't complain. You coming home this winter?"

"In a few weeks if Mom's up for it."

"You sound worried."

"I'm okay." Even as he uttered the words he could palpate a rising swell of emotion. "I wanted to ask you who I could talk to in Transportation. I need to know who sends high tech cameras, surveillance equipment, radio transmitters, computers —"

His father cut him off, saying, "*Radio Shack.* Call Joe Eisler," and looked up his friend's number in his address book.

"Thanks. Say hello to Mom."

"I will. Work going okay otherwise?"

"I'm keeping busy."

"I'll tell your mother you called."

"Nice talking with you, Dad."

"Take care of yourself, Son."

Dalton sucked in his breath as he lowered the phone into the receiver. Tears crowded in the corners of his eyes. His face quivered and his jaw redefined its contours.

I N THE MORNING HE called the number his father had given him for his contact at the Department of Transportation.

"How is your father?" Eisler sounded as though he were at least his father's age. "I hired him at eighteen, you know. Did he tell you?"

"No, Sir. I'm calling because I'm on a case. I work for Lt. Walker."

"Marty Walker? Good man, Marty. You one of his?"

"Yes, Sir. We're Morongo Basin."

"When I knew Marty he hadn't made lieutenant yet. He was new to San Bern's Marshall Office. So? What can I do for you?"

Dalton told him.

"Your rigs are probably losing their balance as a result of carrying too heavy a load. Either that, or a *Mountain Cascade* machine. It's a small standup equipment, smaller than a small tractor. Another rig will carry it on a flatbed to the construction site. Positioned at a slope the machine can cause quite a disturbance. Main purpose is to scramble airwaves or ding your odometer. Also good to disable a truck and not allow it to have radio contact with anyone."

"Any idea who uses the machines for the not so nice projects?"

"Anyone who can get away with it. My advice if you think

victimized rigs lose contact with their foreman is to sit on that portion of road where trucks are tipping for several weeks and try to catch the thugs in action."

"This Cascade machine. Does it work on small aircraft?"

"Stalls the engine; at best scrambles the compass. You see the *Saladino* truck coming at you and you might as well pull over and abandon ship."

"Why do you call it a Saladino truck?"

"Because it looks like something the mob created. It's a twin cab in one. Seats four, two in front, two in the twin. This allows for hijackers to surprise the trucker because in the dark the driver can't see much."

"Any idea how they take him?"

"None. Probably they sneak up on the right. Most drivers have one eye on the left, one on the road."

"You know anyone who's been heisted whom I could speak to?"

"I have my hunches. But none of the men talk about it. They say they stopped for a bite to eat and when they returned their load was gone."

"One last question. What types of loads are stolen?"

"Well, our single line recorder *Radio Shack 43-236B* is popular; listening posts, mobile receivers and recorders with voice activation are sought after, and *Doppler* and *Watson-Watt* antennas for voice monitoring."

"All surveillance equipment?"

"Right. These are professional jewel thiefs. They want to know who's at the target site, who the security is, whether FBI is involved, that sort of thing."

"Did an officer by the name of Isaiah Du Bois ever talk to you?"

"This the guy they're saying walked into the Colorado at Topock?"

"At Crossroads. He was an African American male in his thirties?"

"No. He didn't contact me."

"What about a Lt. White? That would've been his supervisor?"

"It doesn't ring a bell."

"Thanks. You've been enormously helpful."

"Don't mention it. Say hi to your father."

He promised he would.

six

"TAKE A GOOD LOOK AT the photographs," said Lt. Walker from behind his desk.

Dalton did so. The color prints showed a Caucasian male, approximately thirty years old with light brown wavy hair dressed in a checkered black and white shirt and black cotton trousers, squeezed between the gravel and rusted steel railroad tracks, his body tightly wrapped with the plastic coil that attached a truck cab to its load.

"This is Maciel's and Spender's overturned rig found out on 15 past 127 headed toward Tecopa and Shoshone," Marty said. "Man was stabbed in the left arm. Cause of death was heat from a torch. His face was charred."

"How do we know this death is connected to the hijacks?"

"We received an anonymous tip."

"Jesus. I bet that person vanished into the woodwork."

Lt. Walker gave a decisive nod. "Now here's the way we're

going to treat all investigations related to road crime. I want daily debriefings. If you're going to be out in the field for a day or several days, you carry a cellphone. You call in twice a day regardless of activity. If I don't hear from you I'll send someone to find you.

"We have reason to believe," Marty Walker continued, "this death may be related to Du Bois'. When you spoke to Teale did he say whether there were internal signs of trauma?"

"There were none."

"Go to the morgue anyway and eyeball this driver. I want you as informed as possible when you get on the road again."

"Anything other advice?"

"I want you to enter your narrative summaries at the end of every contact onto your laptop. I've already asked the Department of Transportation to issue a warning to truck carriers travelling 15, 40 and 395 and alternate routes. If the driver is subject to a holdup, he is to comply to the letter. No heroics."

"Do we have any identification of any single hijacker?"

"Nothing." He continued, saying, "You tell me in advance who you intend to interview to allow me time to check out the subject. If there's any question as to safety I will tell you. If need be, we'll squash that aspect of your investigation until it's safe to send investigators into the field. Any questions?"

"I was planning to sit on 395 to watch for hijackers Isaiah may have been tracking."

"Drive in to see Dr. Teale first. Whatever is going on out there, we need to be prepared."

Dalton drove to the Hall of Justice, parked in the lot, entered the building and walked through two clearance checkpoints to the rear where the morgue and forensic laboratory were situated. There he found the chief medical examiner eating lunch in the morgue.

Rand Teale seemed to appreciate his caution. "Can't be too careful," he said, as he slopped Italian style eggplant and pork into his mouth from a carton. Despite the cleanliness of the linoleum and of the stainless steel sinks, the room reeked of death – it hovered like the overwhelming smell of urine or of cancer. One autopsy was completed and lay on a gurney ready to be taken to the freezer. The flap of breast skin hung uselessly from the exposed ribcage. With the right shoulder crushed, the body looked as if it had never been human, a robot created for a movie set.

Dr. Rand Teale said, "My guess is the victim was cornered by several rigs."

"You think he let down his guard?"

"Or was working a double shift and was tired and wasn't paying attention."

"Any indication of struggle?"

"None. My guess is several men jumped him from the sides and steered him off the road to the place he was found. One thing you might care to know: the victim had an ear infection and was taking medication for it."

"What about that fact interests you?"

"I'm not suggesting anything. I am merely pointing out a known medical condition this victim had. Du Bois was a drinker, seen frequently at bars. Victim selection of rig drivers may be operating here." He tossed the empty carton in the garbage can. He donned a surgeon's coat, snapped on plastic gloves, and sat down to examine a small breasted Indian woman. In death she looked mute. "The killer or killers probably operate with considerable secrecy, late at night, perhaps under cloudcover. If they believe it is safer to kill people who come across their operation rather than to scare them off, you have a sizable problem, Dal."

"Couldn't these two deaths be retaliation for DEA seizures of drugs?"

"Very possibly. I do think you have more than one killer. I think they wanted this driver off the road. Possibly they choose times when the only driver on the stretch of road was the intended victim. Who knows. Du Bois, I suspect, faced a similar proposition.

My belief is he was held head down under water until he was dead. If you can prove it without risk to yourself, terrific, but don't go looking for the impossible. You may be one of the best fugitive hunters in California, but if you fail to estimate the cunning of your quarry, you're as good as dead."

"Lt. Walker read me the same notice. I'll be careful. I'm not going to gamble with my life."

"Your trouble is you have no sense of fear in a potentially violent situation, Dal. With this type of crime you have to trust your inner sense of worry, not ignore it. If I were Walker, I'd stick you on something less exotic."

"I'm not going after a killer. That's Maciel's and Spender's turf."

"You don't know what you're after. If this hijacker sees you sniffing around his haul and thinks you're getting too close, even if you're only watching the road, if you're on his domain he may figure the best thing is to ditch you."

"Any advice?"

"Don't let anyone catch you watching them. Tone yourself down if you can."

"Thanks." Dalton rode the elevator up to the first floor and walked past the gift shop and desk of the advice nurse. The modern hall with scenic desert oil paintings restored his sense of himself. But the taint of dried blood and mortality followed him like a penetrating illness which after he recouperated would remain in his memory.

INTEGRATE YOURSELF INTO the environment, his stepmother used to tell Dalton. Picture yourself emerging from the bowl of mountains that encircle the San Bernardino into the chalk bone of the desert. He hadn't felt close to her and had resented his own parents' breakup and going to live with his father and his new wife. For a year Sonora watched him out of the corner of her eye. Pinning wet clothing to a clothes rope to dry or standing on the beige soil as the school bus deposited him in front of their home, he felt her presence strongly. He resisted her. He convinced himself the desert always reclaimed the soil like a desperate mother setting eyes upon a lost child.

You could stand on your head or stand on your feet but it was the same damn elevator. Same picture going down the grade or rising out of it. You hopped on the tail of Freeway 215 and took the tail past the college and past San B Steel, past the big DQ sign that stood for Dairy Queen. Her voice echoed inside his mind.

He passed Little Gateway cemetery and revival stuff at the gold club. Behind him in the rear view mirror were scalloped mountains, in front of him a seascape of scattered sagebrush through which he could see hardened sand and beyond, buttes, plateaus and ridges crested with basalt. Their webbed flanks were predominantly brown with shadows. A sign read: closed to commercial traffic. There was a campground at Hole in the Wall and at Mitchell Caverns. He was aware only of himself, of small silvery brush, of the bumpy road and a chalky frontage road. Up close the buttes and table tops and mountains were bluish. Sadness kicked in; it came and went sort of like it does when the isolation of the desert wilderness begins to make a man restless.

The soil turned rich coffee brown. Rows of orange groves and strawberries lay as far as the foothills. Fields narrowed at the pass. He passed ranches. It was a very private rule of living where agriculture dominated the land. Just as he moved up the incline he saw the mountains rising in their infinity and merging with the Sierras. You had the reality of small towns dotting the highway and all the mesmerizing that went with it on a late Indian summer day. You could still see the older ruling world market with pipelines going over the mountain shoulder and oil being pumped out in smaller quantities than in the flat desert where iron horses moved slowly up and down as the shaft rose from the well. Oil lay barely fifty feet below the mantle where a milenium of dinosaurs made beds of fossil fuels. Gravel pits and sawdust mills, orange and citrus in plentitude, the tops of the trees trimmed to form hedges so they appeared from the air like diamond-shaped sections that you could walk across from one end of the field to the other. Here and there infiltrated into the desert perched quietly like adobe homes the color of chalk, officers sat awaiting a truck run that could come at any time between midnight and four in the morning. The hope for an arrest – for cuffing the greaser in a pair of rain shoes so he could spend the remainder of his life on an iron bench – was all the prison reform desert badges banked on.

seven

THE ROAD FROM VICTORVILLE ON 18 ambled along verdant greenery, with craggy peaks forming a bowl around the last of the world before he entered the ravine road between two sharply rising peaks. Orange trees gave way to tomato fields. Opposite these fields were metal water tanks and a hundred or so wooden crates and new vineyards cris-crossing the hills. As he drove through the windy pass rows of shiny stakes flickered past, the color contrast between the soil and stakes made more beige than brown by the fading daylight.

When Dalton was sixteen, his father Sandy Keys taught him to label land title documents and other papers he kept in his safe. A rigorous process, it conditioned in Dalton an understanding for identifying normal as well as unusual aspects of plots so that after many years of tracking criminals this process converted into a perception of jurisdiction according to county land. Definable units of geography were described under many listings – plots on a map, boundries, dwellings, fences and water wells, and government authorities such as city, county or state or military. In addition categories were further broken down according to day, month and year, season, chronology, historical event, and schedule. Over time all this carved out in him attention to detail as well as to significance.

Based upon what Dalton had seen of Isaiah's files, he didn't think Isaiah composed his thinking in a structured fashion. Since he lacked a point of comparison, he was unable to determine whether the scandal adversely affected Isaiah. If his note taking came under scrutiny and censure and he was penalized for specific references, it was conceivable that he made a new practice of not taking notes. If he had been threatened because of what came to light during the trial as a result of his documentation, this too could have affected him. Dalton found it irritating that Isaiah's notes seemed incomplete. He appeared to document the importance of investigative events through photographs he took. Whereas Dalton collected his thoughts in scribbles on notepad paper which at the end of the week he lined across his desk – as a way of making the sometimes imperceptible concrete and of putting a seemingly intangible or poorly perceived reality in front of him so that thoughts were not simply thoughts in his mind but he could see them and begin to separate from them – Isaiah collected photographs by types of events. The events suggested a highway crime. Because Dalton relied upon written narratives for information, the value of the photographs struck him as incomplete. He wondered why for example Isaiah had not more overtly tied the names to the crimes and why he had not labeled the significance of each photo in its relation to the task of the crime it represented. It could be Isaiah had not decided who was doing what to whom. It could be that without specific identifications Isaiah left a window of investigative opportunity open for as long a time as possible. Or it could be that in residing with Hemal Ebenales he simply could not write anything definitive down. It was possible Isaiah thought his database was being tampered with or at least spied upon. It was possible also that information from the office was leaked into the community and that Isaiah had proof of this.

The photos were primarily of truck stops and motel rooms. Dalton did think Isaiah knew the purposes the motel rooms were used; he also thought Isaiah knew who the hijack ringleaders were and what their connections were to the drug industry. Isaiah in his function as CHP of being able to remain hidden without being sensed in advance of being seen by the suspect was able to keep the possibility of danger at bay. That ability made for him to observe frightening circumstances relatively unscathed.

Or at least up to a point. Dalton thought it was Simms who endangered Isaiah. Once Simms was taking forfeiture, all agents and officers actions were suspect. In closing in on Isaiah, who it seemed thought in linear components waiting for events to suggest links in response or in proportion to preceding events, Hemal would have made use of any weakness in belief system or mental process. Isaiah's weakness was that he believed there was an underclass that was continually exploited. He believed law enforcement primarily protected the rights of those who amassed property over the rights of those who could not or did not, and he believed there was a need for political pressure to be applied to all levels of authority that kept the power of property holders in check. Because Isaiah made psychological room for underclass citizens, Dalton believed he could have permitted people who were unworthy of trust too close to him who then deviously or maliciously weighed him down. Dalton believed Hemal Ebenales was such a person. Isaiah's written statements in his journal indicated Hemal had changed him – had altered the manner in which Isaiah set about an investigation and had induced him to relax his standards for criminals who Hemal knew. Dalton was hard and fast on zero tolerance and would not have ventured so close to Hemal, no matter what the objectives of the DEA were.

That weakness uncovered, Hemal could easily have utilized Eric's disease to place Isaiah in such spiritual pain that Isaiah could not see how Hemal was dragging him along the bottom undercurrent.

Dalton revised his thoughts. Isaiah had after all written his worries down. He had maintained a careful journal in which he had tried to make sense of and take apart what was happening to him. This suggested to Dalton that Isaiah had become aware that something was not quite right but he could not pull back far enough to get the objectivity he needed. Isaiah had been ambushed. He had been duped somehow. In spite of his extensive knowledge about the southern California drug industry, the knowledge was not enough to protect him.

The countryside was lonely and the road to Littlerock cut through a dark forest as it wended up an upcline. Had Isaiah made this drive? It was more direct, less steep, not as demanding on the brakes. There was no summit to Adelanto nor icy mountain passes to gamble one's life on. As Dalton whisked by a rig that had pulled over, he wondered how many times Isaiah had stopped to talk to big rig drivers. He wondered also whether Isaiah had signed on as an inspector at the scales.

Halfway up the incline the road ran out of forest. The land stood vacant and stubbly, a rude sight for people long used to seeing fields of trees. Dalton thought of the foolishness of running out of forest. It was an expensive proposition – retirement of a logging community had taken the form of K-Marts and McDonalds and golfing greens and tin-roofed double wide manufactured homes. Each stretch of clearcut revealed itself to resemble a type of home-steading on someone else's creekbed claim until you ran out of water or claims and you just couldn't continue to sustain a mining or manufacturing industry. The game of getting the product to market long before you had to pay a salary on the man's labor who moved it was now on the state and national chessboards.

Dalton again considered the Night's Inn motel key. In his mind's eye he saw a handful of card keys that went with a string of motels and another string of warehouses located closeby small airstrips. Although they seemed predominantly situated along the spine of 395 there was some question in Dalton's mind as to the width of territory the hijacking business covered. Vail Bahe lived at Vidal off highway 95; the Azul trucking line was situated in San Bernardino city and Bishop; and Ebenales owned a handful of warehouses throughout the desert. The death ride occurred along 395, a fact borne out by Isaiah's photographs. It went as far south as the state border at the Colorado River and as far north as the railroad at Red Mountain and lonely motels in Lone Pine and Big Pine. The crime scenes suggested a language of danger - railroad tracks brought in a methamphetamine train; Crossroads and Earp were symbols of stark lawlessness and the dam, a continuous overflow of water for electricity. If those symbols were not enough to suggest mobile home stoves and tin shacks utilized for methamphetamine manufacture, the fact that refrigerators were abandoned in railroad yards and parking lots certainly gave the investigating sheriff a picture of what he or she was dealing with. Desert officers had an expression: the nearer in sleep to the drug send off, the sooner your ride at the other end could pick you up.

At Rosamond the weather was a cool forty-three degrees. Clouds passed over the suburban redefined desert landscape and you could see all of the emotion of the sky. There were a few buttes the colors of salmon and vermillion and a sea of sagebrush and olive shrubs. In either direction as uneventful as the orange groves were growing up any tillable hillside, were quarter acre plots of squash, potatoes and corn. Everything you saw, all the shadows and the breath of the land, was enhanced by the light reflected in the clouds and in the storm that pushed the clouds north.

Two big piles of dirt left in front of a gravel quarry could have been hate mail left by the mob in retaliation for the air force flying their planes too low and shrieking across air space over Palm Springs and Laughlin at early hours of the morning. It was a not-so-amusing joke in the U.S. Marshal that the Air Force sent its new fliers out to test their abilities of sound to shatter glass over the paths where the Arab-infiltrated Italian communities had built their ten million dollar homes. The Air Force retaliated for oil burning trucks on the road. Destroyed cargo on the road was part of the game of stacking up retaliations – thugs for the underworld burned huge piles of wood positioned at angles to an airstrip. The burning firelight interfered with a pilot's ability to accurately see a landing strip.

At smaller airports along 95 and 395 alike, bonfires were lit to keep planes out of the air during those times contraband was transported by aircraft so that there were no eye witnesses – at three in the morning, before test flight pilots would normally begin their day.

Dalton turned at Mojave. Sand blew across the road. A train outfitted with black containers of asphalt or oil stood motionless, and cableless. He passed a row of temporarily abandoned rig loads and a row of cheap motels. At Kramer Junction he stopped for a soda and a tuna sandwich. He filled his jeep with gasoline. The desert here was flat. The soil was sandy chalk, the shrubbery comprised of tumbleweed, few Joshua Trees, sagebrush, and cacti with vivid pink, red and yellow colors. By the time he arrived at Independence where the road on 395 was most desolate, it would be dark.

He headed up 395. The maze of tan tinted solar panels sat on the road like rows of irrigation, mirrors turned toward the flight of the sun. They extended a quarter of a mile, beautiful mirrored glass to provide electricity without the toxic effects of a power plant. The desert in its back stretches where it was once uninhabited, and would probably to this day never be inhabited, always made Dalton feel lonely. It wasn't just the demoralization of being alone for long periods of time; it was a necessary depression, a way of getting in touch with the sadness he felt about himself and about the world – the fast pace of living, of being made to conform to an ever increasing series of rules, and made to consume products one had

little need for; of seeing one's function as being essentially a con-
sumer rather than an artist, scientist or other self-directed wage
earner - and sadness for people he knew. It was a way to grieve the
inevitable or what would surely become the inevitable. You grieved
the unknowable pieces of your life because these pieces were gone
too soon or because they came upon you too quickly and you were
a loner, unable to appreciate who they were in the moments you
knew them until they were gone. Dalton felt this way about himself, about Nell and about his work. He was a loner charting paths
into the wildernesses of other people's lives. The work drew him
away from his comforts, and his personality and his need for isolation did the rest. He told himself he didn't mind the desolation but
in deepest night when he awoke and, barely conscious, reached for
Nell and startled into wakefulness at finding her absent, it was
despair that shook him, despair that made him uncomfortably aware
of himself and of his need to be dependent upon someone or something other than just himself.

He shook himself free of the thoughts thinking, you couldn't
survive out here for long if you let the desert landscape absorb you.
You had to resist. You had to take back that piece of yourself you
called your soul and make yourself small. You had to tell yourself
you were complete as you were, capable of rational thought and
shirk self-doubt and envy. If your emotions didn't rob you of calm
or confidence, the road, if you gave yourself over to it, eventually
would. You had to know the road was capable of robbing you in
order not to be robbed.

At Red Mountain rows of delapidated tin shacks had been set
up against beds of gravelly ore. You knew right away these were
once mining towns and they brought the silver dollar down the
road. This was a different kind of reality, a different kind of world:
homes were boarded up and cars disintegrated on lawns that were
no longer lawns but were tired, worn out straw mantles. The
backroads lay beneath extensive wildernesses of mountain clouds.

The distant mountain peaks had nothing sitting on them, not even rays of light. No act of living – small casinos, postage stamp-sized farms, roadstop coffee houses - made a dent in any of this. Dust would settle the final score, no matter how many re-inventions time and man discovered. Nothing was forever – not the rich beds of gold ore nor of iron or silver, not the railroad lines laid down chink-a-chink, nor the mining camps and their apartheid one and a half room houses, nor fossil fuels - drying up or dried up. In the end it was just the land. Awareness of it caused you to know that you were alone, apart, separate, isolated, growing old and possibly not having enough possessions to steer by nightfall up that spiritual lonesome road.

He passed through Randsberg. At six thousand feet altitude the air was chilly and windy. He passed small, one-room houses and mobile homes parked at the edge of the highway and *Moon Dreaming Thunder*, a tribal arts shop. These were low-to-the-ground living - worm farms, knife sharpening, hide tanning, a mining museum and rising in the distance were the lords of time, *duenos del tiempo*, incredible blue mountains, snow on their peaks, fog settling halfway down the grade, silver sheets of rain and flutters of snow blasting his windshield. Shadows cast palm prints on the mountains and here and there he glimpsed a school bus winding up the incline disappearing into the hills. A man could lose his soul out here and never know he was a ghost and not a man. He could play at the edges of his life and wonder why the more he chased the less he obtained and then come out here and understand that it wasn't the having of things that counted, it was being in the environment that counted. If he wasn't conscious enough of being in the environment, his whole life could pass him by and not until he reached his sixties or his seventies would he know he had lived too fast.

Dalton travelled this way half a dozen times a year, when he was tired and nerve-wracked with all the responsibilities of living.

He'd come here in order to still his thoughts and be emptied-out by silence and wind and moonlight washing over the parched desert changing the landscape into resemblances of bone. After he was made quiet he'd know what it meant to become humbled – made small as a small creature on an expansive landscape.

Up ahead against the prairie hills stood the links of the grain trains and silver-rusted container box cars for borax. The soil swept across the road by perpetual gusts of wind and was made to re-shape itself into new deposits of grey and yellow, sometimes swirled together, to form ravine-riddled land. Tin-roofed, white chalk houses with corrals which you didn't see until you came right up on them stood on gradual inclines visible off the land. You had a very mean impression of gold rush territory, that miners flooded the land in all directions slaying Indians and villagers and poor people, taking advantage of the weaker or the uninterested; and all that remained between Johannesburg and Inyokern were single dwell-ings spaced miles apart, a tenuous quiet living without livestock, hid by swellings and mounds, oblivious to any modern-day gold rush. Ridgecrest was an empty place and Inyokern was a cigarette stop for truckers before they hit Little Lake or Olancha. These outposts were just postage stamps, barely villages inhabiting the road for a spell and then they too might move on if the elements became too inhospitable or the snow dropped down this far, which it rarely did, and took out the road for any length of time.

At Olancha a stream of snow had come down the mountain and looked like slush gushing in rivulets over the low elevation. There were no trees here for a small plane to lose speed and snag a tree top but it could be that if you were planning to pick up a passenger out here that the clouds might come in too fast and knock out a lot of sunlight or worse obscure the pick-up point from view. You'd be flying above the clouds and come down into grey and black cloudcover. Landmark coordinates or not, no visibility with high winds and snowfall spelled getting bufetted about, thrown clear of the landing or crashing, especially if there were any interference with equipment.

AT LONE PINE DALTON pulled off the road. It was after nine at night. A block away bright lights from a gasoline station removed the black ink silence of the country town. He wandered across the street to a small coffee shop where he purchased a newspaper along with a cup of coffee and steak and salad.

"You passing through?" the redheaded waitress asked him.

"Going up the road to Bishop. Vacation."

"First time there?"

"Oh no, I drive up a few times a year. You new?"

"Started this summer."

"You must have a few truckers come in."

"Every day. It's how we earn our living."

"Milly!" The chef shouted from the kitchen.

She looked forlorn. "Sam hates it for me to talk to customers. Says it's bad for business."

He reached for her hand and let it slip from his grasp. "You have garlic toast?"

"Sure."

"I'll have that with my salad."

He ate, with an ear to the conversations around him. Old men talked about snowfall, two women asked directions to June Lake. The chef scolded Milly for dawdling and suggested she make herself useful and clean out the sugar jars. At length Dalton slapped a ten on the table to cover the tab and tip, and left.

The gasoline station manager couldn't tell him anything about rigs on the road. He was young, in his twenties, and he said he usually slept through the night. Dalton asked a handful of motel owners what they knew or saw but no one was willing to say, if they knew anything to say.

Dalton drove toward Independence. In the rear view mirror a strip of light lit up the ribbon of asphalt that was the road. With only intuition to serve him he stopped at Manzanar and made camp for the night. He parked his jeep off the road behind a stone monument which marked the wartime memorial to the Japanese detention camp. The shoulder on either side of the road was a quarter of a mile, if that, to the flanks of the cement riddled mountains. The road was a straight shot in either direction, an empty corridor where he could wait like a new docent for dead night and peace of mind. Dalton set up a grill with charcoal and warmed a a cup of coffee. He thought about time and space and about men and wars. What a bleak world this must have seemed to Japanese interned here, after being shipped by train to bunker-style longhouses and surrounded by barbed wire in a landscape as tenacious as any prison camp and left to inhabit desolate hallways and even more desolate imaginations. Whatever occurred here had occurred beneath star scattered skies that kept all the secrets of the human condition and let its inhabitants know they were far from help, too far to be seen or heard in their tremoring pleas for help.

Dalton settled against the tire of his jeep and read a book of Robert Bly poetry by lantern light. A lizard emerged out of a crack in the parched soil and languidly crawled over the page, his tan and beige lines causing him to fade and reappear. When the chill night arrived Dalton bundled up in a lamb's wool jacket, thick gloves and heavy socks and boots. He ate cheese strips and salami and crackers from a plastic package and washed the meal down with cherry flavored gatorade. Then he put out the lantern and killed the grill coals, mashing them into a pit he dug in the ground and stuffed the grill in the back of his jeep.

Deep night came in its vastness, an all-encompassing void of stardust and the faintest motion of wind. The air smelled of some intangible herb and he rested inside his jeep in his seat, a pair of binoculars hanging from his neck.

eight

HE CAME TO, STARTLED awake to the blaring sounds of yelling above a din of rock-n-roll music.

Ya-hee! Ya-hee! came an eerie voice of what sounded half-human, half-beast. *Oh boy I got you now! You bettah pull ovah, boy, or ah'll land you smack dab in the balls.* Dalton rivetted into the shock of awareness. The hair on his neck prickled. His mouth went dry. He thought he heard the roar of a truck careening upwind, its heavy weight cutting the wind. He lifted his binoculars and positioned the lens on the asphalt strip of road. An eighteen wheeler rounded the bend like a bat out of hell. Two tall cabs without loads chased the driver at fifty or sixty miles an hour onto the shoulder of the road. A rig the same size as the victimized one bore down on the driver like an animated Tyranosaurus out of *Jurassic Park*.

"Oh lordy, lordy," the driver yelled through a loudspeaker, "if we ain't got you now! You wanna pull ovah, turn off your radio and don' turn around!"

The driver pulled over offering no resistance, defeated in the agog of fear. Dalton couldn't imagine what the driver was thinking. No doubt his heart was pounding, fear exploding in every orifice, his hands shaking too severely to control the weight and turn of his rig.

Dalton's own hands shook as he positioned the binoculars over the drivers, their bright headlights too bright to see them, their cabs lit up like small blocks of yellow. Dalton pushed open his door and threw himself onto the ground and crawled on his belly to hide behind a two-foot high sagebrush.

The hijacker jumped down from his rig onto the soil, a rifle pointed at the other driver. The hijacker ordered him to the ground. The man obeyed. He climbed down from his cab and lowered himself face to the soil. The hijacker stood at the ready, antsy on his feet, while three or four others flung their doors open and transferred the load from one rig to the other. They worked quickly. It took forty to fifty minutes to get back on the road, going south in the direction they had come.

Dalton ran to his vehicle, charged inside it and started up his engine. He followed, his lights off. His heart throbbed. He was too scared to think. He rode with his window rolled down, the mountain chill throttling adrenalin through him. Ahead the cabs raced against time leading the way for the stolen cargo. The sound of their tires slapped a lingo on the asphalt.

At Owenyo they pulled off the road onto the narrow shoulder beside several smaller trucks. They worked quickly to unload the stolen cargo into these. Dalton left his jeep somewhere on the shoulder away from the road and crept as close as he could, a digital camera and night vision goggles in one hand, toward the operation. He found an area protected by low-lying trees. Lying flat on the ground he snapped photographs of the smaller trucks, the men and the two tall cabs. At this range, he could determine that the hijackers wore gloves, denim pants, light shirts and heavy boots. Although they wore masks over their heads and faces, Dalton presupposed they were Caucasian, in their late twenties or early thirties judging by their stockiness and agility. They wore night vision gear.

No one's radio was on. When he obtained the prints, perhaps one or two of the men would have distinguishing tatoos or marks, but he doubted it. They probably had been selected because they had no remarkable characteristics.

He thought one of the hijackers was female but wouldn't know until he saw the photos. He would try to take plaster of paris molds of their shoe prints, assuming the dry earth offered up any visible clues. A half hour flew by. When they departed they took all the cabs and rigs with them abandoning silence to the scene of the crime. He lost them as they entered the Panamint Mountains.

nine

IN THE DARK DALTON RETURNED TO the hijack scene at Manzanar. The driver and rig were gone. Since he hadn't passed him on the return, he decided the driver had headed north. He drove cautiously with night vision goggles with an eye to the flat surface where a rig may have parked off the road. The goggles cast the entire landscape in a greenish tinge making it possible for him to discern objects near and far. There was about an acre distance between the shoulder of the road and the distant mountains. The landscape was barren and empty.

The chill air raised goosebumps on his arms. Terror was an adrenalin pusher that jolted through his veins as though he'd drunk twenty cups of coffee. The moon floated above the fog and clouds in a silvery green light. In the glow of moonlight the landscape resembled a bleached surface. Felled tree trunks looked like driftwood or pale bones. He sped up the incline noting how the road narrowed. Rapidly descending clouds swallowed the horizon. Perhaps the driver would go as far as Bishop, or perhaps horrified by the ordeal he would drive all night. Dalton entered Big Pine where he drove city block by city block in search of any rig that resembled the hijacked cargo. When at last he had not discovered it he headed to Bishop. Large pine trees stood rooted nearby a cluster of motels. He passed along the main artery through town, then went street by street until he found a rig he thought might be the one he was looking for. He wrote down the company name. At length he pulled into a gas station and called dispatch.

Delora answered. "Good grief Dal. Where are you?"

He told her. "Can you track down a truck with a decal of a computer and antenna for me? It's *Coachella Valley Access*. I need to know destination and what she was carrying."

"That could take half the night. Why don't you ask Crandall to run it for you in the morning?"

"Can't wait."

"Sure, sure." She was irritated, probably more at being a single parent than at spending her graveyard shift chasing after a stolen load. "You want me to call when I've got it?"

"Yes, page me."

"Will do. Coming in tomorrow?"

"If I can. Depends on where I put down for the night."

His watch read 15:50. He was worried for his driver. After a hijack the driver's mind was dealing with the assault and not necessarily functioning rationally. If he were holed up in a nearby hotel, and Dalton felt certain he was, he might take off in two or three hours and head to the destination on the bill of lading as if nothing were wrong. Any ominous situation along the way could result in flight. A sheriff pulled over with his lights doused might be suspect. Dalton was fairly certain his man wouldn't go to the police for help. He was more likely to wait for the arrival of his mechanic or to ditch his rig altogether and hire a car rental home.

Dalton parked within sight of the rig. He waited out the

remainder of the night playing a game of chess on his laptop computer. No driver emerged and no mechanic or foreman arrived.

In the morning he called dispatch again. Delora came on the line, her usually throaty voice quietly contained. The warehouse destination was *Flynn Accoustics* at Mammoth. They sold home theatre. She rambled off a list: Yamaha two zone surround receivers, DVD players, Mitsubishi rear projection television, Sony VCR, Sony satellite receivers, Sony CD changers, Lexicon remote control audio systems and M&K subwoofers. He thanked her.

A call to the driver's shift manager confirmed his fears. The driver had abandoned his load and walked off the job. As soon as he could make it to Bishop he'd bring his own private investigator to look the rig over.

He grabbed a light breakfast of oatmeal and coffee. By 6:15am he headed south toward San Bernardino. Patches of pine trees studded the foothills. Grassland and leafy trees made for uneven grazing in an area that not many years ago had supplied half the state with lumber. He drove without thought, his mind not yet ready to chunk down to size the events of the previous night.

He organized his next several tasks. First he would drop off the film of the hijack at the postal instamatic across the street from the Chamber of Commerce, then he would return to the office to write up his narrative. When he was finished he would consult Isaiah's supervisor Lt. Taylor of the Highway Patrol for a printout of highway crimes in Inyo and San Bernardino Counties for the last half year to assess for a crime ring.

Video and audio cables and components were big business for semi illiterate young adults who had not graduated high school or passed the GED. He hoped at least one of the hijackers matched the names he had taken off Isaiah's computer. If he could tie a hijacker or a carrier to Ebenales or some other shady businessman, he could start building a surveillance strategy to make an arrest.

He didn't see the cab until it was almost upon him. It came up fast, horn blaring, rivetting his attention to his rear view mirror. The white cab took up the entire rear window and was too close to see anything except the grille plate. The grille had five large strips of metal across it with wire meshing behind the strips. On the second strip the name *Chase* appeared in dark cursive. Dalton downshifted and stomped on the accelerator. As he sped up to ninety miles an hour, the cab also sped up. It kept pace down the incline, its grille a few feet from the rear of his jeep. The gravelly desert flew by, creosote and sagebrush, low dry trees and tumbleweed sparse conclusions in a wilderness that called forth only wind. Fear shot through him. So did nausea, panic, claustrophobia, horror and impending doom. He'd be killed in an instant. Blood coursed through his head. The back of his neck prickled. His mouth went dry. *Help me, help me* – all the way to Independence where the cab miraculously swerved onto the shoulder just as a wide load bearing a mobile home whooshed past him in the opposite direction. He kept moving, his gaze fixed more on the retreating road, checking and rechecking to be certain he was no longer being followed. He didn't know whether to cry or to vomit. All he thought of was he had to take a piss and he didn't dare stop. He'd been threatened before, but not like this. He was badly unnerved. Vomit rose to his throat. He swallowed it and tried to convince himself he would be okay. His hands trembled badly making it difficult to grip the wheel. He should pull over but he didn't. He kept pushing on, oblivious of the sandy landscape, silently uttering his prayers, unable to well up emotion.

The road could own him in this mood and then he'd be washed up. That's all it would take. If the road took him today, now, he wouldn't be able to get through the night without needing Nell to remain awake, without a light on, or a glass of water on the nightstand. It'd be months on disability.

He pulled into a gas station at Lone Pine. He made his way into the bathroom. He couldn't urinate. The piss in him had frozen. He was having a God damned tension reaction. He winced as he relaxed and the urine leaked out painfully.

He picked up a sandwich and quart of milk and sat on a lonesome road west of town for a good hour. He thought about rodeos and branding irons and cowboys and good looking women. The food went down slowly. His stomach did not rebel. The windless air and the quiet had steadied him. Only once when he thought of Nell he became choked up with tears.

BY THE TIME HE GOT BACK on the road the weather was drizzling. He rode to the place he thought the final transaction of the night had occurred, somewhere near Cartago. He recollected the sparse landscape, the fact that it was pitch black with only the pollen scatter of stars visible at the horizon. He looked around for a warehouse or silo where the men might have taken the hijacked goods and found none. He got in his jeep and rode to the Panamint Mountains. There was nothing anywhere, not even a market, just a scattering of one story, delapidated adobes whose tan chalky color made them seem to fade into the ethereal air and beige soil. He stood off the road and surveyed the landscape. Here and there purple wildflowers gave some accent to mildly hilly surroundings. He thought about the hijack and the speed at which they departed; the timing and precision meant these men had pulled many similar heists in the past. A fierce wind trembled. But for the faint sound of an aircraft motor somewhere in the distance, the sweep of land was vast and silent. He strained for the motor sound but it could no longer be heard. He told himself that faroff desert sounds seemed closer than they usually were and that the aircraft had turned in a different direction causing the motor sound to be obscured.

A single propeller plane flew low over Dalton's jeep. Dalton raised a hand in a salute. This far out into the desert with no tower closeby nor landmarks to direct it, the pilot would fly by instrumentation. He applied climb power, then turned the plane to the left angling back in the direction he had come. A cloudcover had descended and the plane flew into it. Dalton waited a moment imagining that the turn coordinator indicator was oscillating and the pilot would have to fly an average position for the heading indicator to avoid a spiral.

He returned his thoughts again to the event of the night. The hijackers had a smooth routine. They had the hijack operation timed to an hour. It was conducted at a time when there were no other trucks on that stretch of road and the next truck to come along would do so much later. It was disconcerting to think that once they obtained the goods the truck had vanished in any number of directions or to take some of the goods to another destination, possibly to a fence in Las Vegas. For Isaiah to have observed the routine many times told Dalton something about his friend's ability to track a ring of several people. Tracking criminals on the ground was one thing; tracking each member, determining contacts, friends and families meant years of surveillance, weekends lost to followup.

All at once the small propeller plane moved out of the clouds. It's nose began dropping in a steep turn, increasing airspeed. It didn't have far to fall. A tight knot of anxiety gripped him in the stomach as he listened to the choking of the engine. The inside wing must have stalled. The plane rotated abruptly toward the low wing. He stopped again, his gaze fixated on the plane's light. From where he rested he could tell recovery was possible. The plane's nose came up and the pilot, his face now visible through the small window, gave him a thumb's up as he turned to the right and regained airspeed. Some vague idea about weather and destinations blipped across Dalton's mind. He steadied his pen to his pad and tried to grab onto the image, but it was gone. He drove to the Morongo Basin station.

H E KNEW LT. WALKER WOULD expect a thorough narrative before he would assign him or anyone else in the office to followup on the hijack. Marty pushed for step by step descriptions of who was at the scene and what each person was observed doing as well as what other observers, if there were any, observed each subject to do. Once the actions were well defined, Lt. Walker wanted photographs of the crime scene that showed or shed light on what had occurred. A pencil sketch of the scene showing distance of hijackers to the truck they were unloading and of the smaller trucks would provide additional clues. It was not unusual for Lt. Walker to send a man back into the field to the scene to reconstruct what may have been seen by unknown observers based upon the angle of houses or buildings and windows looking onto the scene.

In this event he would want to see what the scene looked like by day. He would ask Dalton to lay out with tape where the trucks and hijackers were, to the best of his recollection. Because daylight could appear to change a site in one's mind, the impressions of tires which he had photographed would show more precisely what had happened.

Dalton took care to lay down his foundation for telling the events. He recreated the narrative first. To do this he wrote his observations beginning first with the trucker who had been chased off the road by the two tall cabs. He described the size of the victimized cab, the approximate amount of space between it and iron bar that supported the load, the number of axles, length of load, then went on to describe the hijackers. The cab was standard size, a good furnace under the hood, able to carry a fifty-three foot load of one long container riding on five axles or eighteen wheels. This particular load was a metal container bolted at the back, similar to *Genstar* or *De Salvo* freights which had the capability to be transferred as box freight to a railroad train.

He reviewed what he had written. Satisfied he had produced what he saw or thought he saw, he went on to describe the hijackers. There were four men, three of them lanky, well muscled, careful. The fourth had appeared antsy as though under the influence; he was the one in charge, shouting commands, moving from man to man as if to oversee the complete function of each. The film prints would help hone in on whatever details he did not remember accurately. He sketched each hijacker, scribbled notes about each to the side of each drawing and then recalled what he could about the way each individual walked, sound of voice – rough, impatient, coersive – manner and degree of intimidation wielded. He was fairly certain that although the team had a woman, she was younger than the others, neither a backup nor a leader. He had the impression she was an occasional participant but as to the reason he thought it he was unclear. She had as much toughness as the men and she kept her activity to a well rehearsed routine.

The final piece of following the victimized driver to Bishop and of being chased down the incline on the return - took time to discuss. His brain tried to recall the details while terror held the experience at bay. He drafted what he felt was an incomplete set of descriptions, feeble in impact because he had become a participant in his own investigation. He had expected the stolen cargo to be a bevvy of listening posts and high speed/low light cameras and synch oscillators. A reasonable take for an outfit that planned to utilize the equipment for pulling burglaries. Instead the cargo was state of the art sound control, surrounds, video component switching electronics for home entertainment. He doubted the gang intended to resell; this loaded had been jacked to clear the way for a competing seller probably in the same area.

S OME FOUR HOURS LATER after Dalton had finished with the graphic artist and had two pencil sketches of the night scene, he and Marshal George Maciel took a coffee break to discuss the implications of their respective investigations. Marshal Maciel was under the impression that his killer operated alone, even if he worked with associates to pull off burglaries or heists or river piracies. He gave a list of businesses he thought his killer might operate with, among them boat detailing, autobody finishing, bringing in weapons or drugs in drywall on trucks, chemical production and transportation.

"My thought is this man has his own aircraft parked closeby his desert adobe wherever that may be."

"For diversion or courier?"

"Courier. Of course it's all guesswork at this stage."

Maciel who had spent much of his ten years in some sort of aerial reconnaisance to identify landmarks had worked with the National Transportation Safety Board to create maps for new roads. They weren't the only agency to handle theft booty by vanishings in small aircraft. Depending upon how large this case mushroomed to, they could have statewide DOT involvement along with area Cal Trans, and private operatives within days.

"Walker going to bring in Du Bois' supervisor Lt. Taylor?" Maciel asked.

"He wants no suggestion that we're going after Du Bois' death."

"That'll be difficult if not downright impossible to conceal once we all begin interviewing witnesses to hijacks. Word hits the street within hours." Maciel rendered him a look of frustration as though to say he could work faster, produce leads and get more accomplished if he didn't have to check in so often with the brass.

"Once you rule out other truckers and train conductors, what do you see as your next step?" Dalton asked him.

"Oh well," Maciel said with a laugh, "then we get down to real work." He fished out of his pocket a map of Class B airspace for Boron to Inyokern. Heavier lined circles determined the boundaries of altitude limits for incoming airplanes. The ten miles of veil around the airspace over Inyokern showed the radio beacon and frequency 350, below which there was no voice facility.

"You and Spender understand this stuff pretty well," Dalton said.

"This," he responded, rapping his knuckles on an outer boundary some seventy miles southeast, "is where my body wound up —"

"Right outside Baker."

"And here," he said, tapping the veil area, "is last known sighting of your hijack, right?"

"Here," Dalton corrected him. "At Olancha."

"I thought it was further down."

"No."

"So for all you know their deal was to get to an airstrip and hustle the stuff out of the state?"

"Right," Dalton answered. "Or deposit the take in the river."

"Not stuff for heists?"

"No. No Radio Shack, no Pac Bell. This was sound equipment. Stereophonics for the home theatre." He took a closer look at Maciel's map. It was clear small aircraft required no towered airport for clearance. "What are you looking for with this map?"

"Where these aircraft take off from in conditions of minimum visibility. Both areas – yours and mine – are subject to weather. Any idea what the weather was down at Crossroads when Du Bois drowned?"

"Low cloud ceiling, warm front," Dalton replied.

"What about last night?"

"Possible ice on the windshield."

"That, Dalton, spells certain death if you run into freezing rain without warning."

"If you're escaping into air."

"Well, *that's* my point. I haven't found anyone on the road who has any idea how my John Doe came to be on that stretch of road let alone who else was on it with him who killed him."

"You chart the weather for your John Doe?"

"For two consecutive nights – warm, moist air circulated into a cold front causing AIRMET SIERRA conditions of fog and drizzle."

"And no visibility."

"Almost none. So here's my thought: Du Bois hunkered down with one mean sourpus in order to lay his hands on vital information as to who was running off with drug forfeiture. He probably wanted to know whether there was sheriff involvement since that's who is out here."

Forfeiture involved capture of suitcases of cash and cocaine from drug transactions. "It's not sheriffs. They're too close to the bench."

"Meaning?"

"Every prisoner between here and the Pacific ocean can identify sheriffs. They're the last people to become involved with forfeiture. My guess is it's military or Highway Patrol, if there's any police involvement at all."

Maciel said, his mood expansive, "it looks to me as if DEA was setting traps to take the cash themselves and they lost sight of it."

"Not necessarily. They could've made a handful of arrests and taken cash into evidence."

"How much money do you think we're talking about here? Half a million? A mil?"

"At least."

"Think it was enough money to get several outside parties involved?"

They both knew they were talking about the scandal that removed a police chief from his duties. Along Baseline Street from the inner city clear into the outer reaches of Highlands amid palm- and lawn-lined haciendas lay a handful of drug dealers waiting in unidentified vehicles for the drug forfeiture to roll in from the desert.

"You think Chief Cobb is still running the show?" Dalton asked.

"No, he's washed up. My guess is we're looking at a brainchild who no one's ever gotten close enough to who reroutes the drugs and brings in the more serious terrorist action to make sure the drugs stay on the road."

"Good luck to us."

"Office rumor says you have Hemal Ebenales on your list of players to interview."

"Yeah. You want to come?"

ten

THE USUAL BRIEFING THAT Lt. Walker led at the noon hour every Monday had been cancelled. In its place he was meeting one-on-one with each marshal, going over the rigors of the next task of each investigation. He had elected to temporarily assign night duty only and to keep all units off the road during the day. His fear was that with the hijack, road talk over the radios would be at a justifiable high and he didn't want his staff getting mugged, chased or in any other way compromised.

"The issue," he told Dalton, "isn't how to ask the question but on the subject's manner. When you talk to Ebenales I want you to write his answers verbatim as well as tape him. We need to verify everything. If what you observe doesn't match with the answers, you'll need to interview again. In ninety-eight percent of what he says some things will match while others won't. Most people tell some truth most of the time."

Dalton flipped through his small hand-held spiral bound notepad to refresh the points they had discussed. "You want me to obtain a list of equipment he keeps at his Needles warehouse."

Lt. Walker nodded. "We had a sheriff deputy there a year ago. Ebenales had a man who was bringing in mobile receivers and recorders which we determined were used in a handful of burglaries throughout Redlands and Upland. We put the man in jail and the whole operation dried up."

"I'll verify what he's bringing in and then ask him why he invited Isaiah to move in with him."

"Chances are he didn't realize at the start that Isaiah was CHP."

"But you want some sense when he did arrive at that realization?"

"Yes. See if you can unsettle him. Ask him about the scope of his business, if he will say much of anything about it. Talk to him about where his men stop for maintenance repairs and who he has on the road to handle mechanical problems."

"What's your working premise?"

"I don't have one at the moment, but it's beginning to look as though he steers his trouble the way a rancher rides cattle - at flying dirt and thunder to the watering trough under forecasts of twelve and twenty-four hour Instrument Flying Reference."

It was pilot talk for ceilings of less than a thousand feet visibility. He, Maciel and Lt. Walker were on the same wavelength.

Ebenales was the devil, Dalton would decide later as he parked his vehicle beside the aging cement warehouse that sat at the V of the off ramp into town. For the moment however he was trying to grab onto his boss' idea as to what he should be looking for.

Lt. Walker said, "His distributors fly under dewpoint, temperature and sky highs and sky lows with last minute restrictions to cancel a truck run. We're busy studying weather charts and pressure systems, whereas he's looking for color presentations and intensities," the lieutenant added dryly, making no effort to conceal the dislike he felt for this man. Ebenales was a man with a long reputation whose dedicated dealers had recycled in and out of jail and prison and still the law had nothing on him to convict him with.

Dalton said, "Sounds as though he uses visibility readings to plan drug runs."

"It's simpler than that. Minimum visibility corresponds to elevation with each stop-off point being a numbered station. Crossroads is Station 1 with a low cloud ceiling of standard three statute miles. Twenty-Nine Palms is overcast at 1400 feet; it's Station 2. I tinkered around with his operations and conceptualized it as so: he has stations marked up the grade with stops at Yucaipa, Redlands, Del Rosa, Baseline, Adelanto, Barstow, Johannesburg, Inyokern and Lone Pine, all measured pretty much the same."

"So that when he's on a walkie-talkie, he's not using a foreign language that makes his delivery people stand out."

"Precisely. He's a sharp cookie. East of Eben is what the sheriff deputies next door call him."

"He's never been caught."

"Not in years since he was in his twenties. With age he's toughened. He enjoys his privileges, believe me, but don't underestimate him. His brain is going a hundred percent of the time, sizing up weight and balance envelopes expressing everything he's got on the road in pound-inches and pound-feet."

"What dialect is that exactly? Weight and balance?"

"Airplane-in-flight talk. His logbooks probably read like baggage loading and tie-down instructions."

Already Dalton could foresee a myriad of problems; one, to decipher a drug run from pilot or trucker chatter, another, to guess at definitions about weights for fuel, passengers and baggage. If the local airports didn't detect problems in advance, how the hell would he?

FIRST THINGS FIRST, Lt. Walker cautioned him. Write down all questions in advance of the interview. During the interview, record the number on the tape of where the answer was. Keep the discussion respectful and straightforward. He changed his mind though when he saw the large jeeps and vans parked in the unpaved lot in front of the warehouse at Needles. The feel of the environment was at once formal and professional and he opted for an interview style that would allow him to breathe some spontaneity into the questioning.

Hemal Ebenales was tall and dark complected with remarkable features. Wavy brown hair, an aquiline nose, intense brown eyes, a long neck, slender shoulders, thin, almost no waist, his looks were enviable by all standards among deputies and marshals whose long hours conducting surveillance or sitting behind a desk for twenty-hour stretches gave them misproportioned overweight in the stomach and thighs. He gave Dalton a mildly intolerant once-over that was probably meant to offend, although Dalton made every effort to maintain an emotional distance. Dalton showed him his badge.

"I am investigating the drowning death of one Officer Isaiah William Du Bois. Is there somewhere private we can talk?" asked Dalton. He took in the warehouse at a glance. The walls and pipes were newly painted white. To the right were stairs leading to a loft which overlooked the entire square footage. Equipment was stored in boxes stacked on twelve-foot high wooden shelving for which each item was labeled.

Hemal showed Dalton into an office with brick siding, a wood floor, a large desk which they sat facing each other for the interview, and a handful of placards on the wall over a cabinet. Not too shabby - although the price this came at Dalton surmised was all part of operational expenses. As he sat Dalton instinctively felt for his pistol, can of Mace and two way radio attached to the side of his belt. He expected his navy uniform with gold letters that said

U.S. Marshal across the back of his shirt carried more clout than did the uniforms of a sheriff deputy or highway patrol officer. Most people who faced an officer of the law shed any bullying or coersive manner and Hemal Ebenales, Dalton knew, was known by some as very intimidating.

He showed Ebenales the glossy black and white print of Du Bois. "You knew him." Dalton removed the microcassette tape recorder.

"Is that really necessary?"

"We tape all interviews in investigations of officers. We can go to Morongo Basin if you like."

Ebenales shook his head. "Yes, I knew him."

"For how long?"

"Approximately a year and a half."

"He was your roommate?"

"Yes. I asked him to move in shortly before his lover Eric died. Isaiah was in a bad way."

"What was his disposition exactly?"

"He was distrought. He had been with Eric for nearly ten years."

"Do you know how they met?"

"I introduced them. I knew Eric before he met Isaiah."

"How old was Eric?"

Hemal smiled deprecatingly. "He was ten years older than Isaiah."

"Which would've made him thirty-four."

"Yes. I'm forty," he said.

"Into which home did Isaiah move?"

"My home here. It's up the road near the creek."

"What is the address?"

Hemal gave it.

"Did you know Isaiah was an officer?"

"I thought he was DEA."

"When did you learn he worked for Highway Patrol?"

"He told me a week or so after he moved in."

"Do you recall the circumstances under which he told you?"

"I believe I was getting ready to move a shipment of deli goods. We ship some restaurant supplies regularly," he explained. "Isaiah told me what the code was."

"For interstate travel."

"It had changed."

"Were you surprised to learn of the change?"

"Not really."

If he guessed this was Isaiah's foot in the door to his operations, he didn't let on. "How many trucks do you have on the road at any one time?"

"Three hundred."

"And they transport goods to your various stations as well as pick up for deliveries?"

He shifted in his seat. "Yes."

"Has any of your drivers been hijacked?"

"Not yet," he answered, with obvious irritation.

"Then you know about the holdups?"

"Yes, everyone in the industry does."

"They appear to be predominantly for surveillance equipment."

"That's a good deal of what I catalog. I have wireless intercoms, *Cony* and *DECO* multikilowatt transmitters, listening posts, mobile recorders with voice activation including *Capri* and *Sherwood*, *CANTRAC 360s*, *Dopplers* and *Watson-Watt* antennas for voice monitoring utilizing bumper beepers."

Dalton nodded appreciatively. "High resolution cameras?"

"Those too."

"Why do you think they haven't held up your trucks?"

"Hopefully because they don't want the headache of dealing with me."

"Who handles mechanical breakdowns?"

"I hire a work crew to ride with my fleet. If a driver is experiencing difficulties, each mechanic is no more than twenty minutes behind. We have to do it that way or we're out of business."

"Hiring a mechanic – is that standard practice?"

"For every last fleet on the road."

"What about overnight runs? Your men sleep in their trucks?"

"Too dangerous. I book them into one of a handful of cozy corners I own."

"Like this?" Dalton showed him a copy of the Ving card.

"Yes." He acknowledged warily. "Where did you get that?"

"It was among Isaiah's possessions found in his vehicle," Dalton said, lying about the place of discovery. He didn't want to learn that in several hours the CHP office would get thrashed. "Why?"

"We are the only establishment in the desert who uses those kinds of electronic keys. I can't afford to have these things floating around."

The simplicity of the card key was it could be changed daily to be coded with a new set of numbers, not unlike tumblers in a high profile vault lock. Dalton probed, saying, "It shouldn't be too difficult to change the configuration of your cards, if you're concerned about that." He watched Hemal's face for secretiveness, or sign that there were other operatives observing his operation whom Hemal hadn't taken into account. "Would you have to rekey the locks as well?"

Hemal gave a deliberate nod. Dalton thought Hemal was about to say something but after a long silence, Dalton moved on. "Did you know anything about Isaiah's schedule the day of his death?"

"He started off here before he received his first call."

"Was that usual – for him to join you here?"

"Yes. I open at four-thirty and he'd come with me."

"Do you know whether he had anything on his mind?"

"Like what?"

"Well, had he discussed any concerns with you? Any cases, for example?"

"He didn't carry cases the way you federals do. He was patrol."

Shoot for the eyes, was U.S. Marshal George Maciel's posture for serving up a confrontation. Dalton said, "Don't you find it interesting that Officer Du Bois was transferred off one assignment after a scandal and placed in an area where all he had to do was to watch the road?"

Hemal sat quietly before answering. "Why would that interest me?"

"Well he wasn't a threat to you if all he was doing was watching the road."

"At no time did I consider him any threat to my operations."

"A few more questions. Please."

Hemal continued to sit quietly.

"Did you consider that Officer Du Bois had skillfully convinced you to invite him to move in?"

"No." He was adamant. "He was coming apart at the seams. I rescued him. Believe me, it was no other way. He alternated between uncontrollable tears and moods, he apologized every ten seconds for not being professional enough. He wasn't being coy or seductive. He was in pain. If I thought for ten seconds that my business was in any way at risk because of his presence I would've offered to put him up indefinitely at one of my other homes, but he needed to be around someone."

"You sound like you came through for him."

"I tried to."

"Why did you move Eric around from motel to motel?"

"I did that twice. He required privacy."

The back of Dalton's neck prickled. "Who were you afraid saw him?"

"You know I really don't appreciate the inuendo. Isaiah was a man I cared for – deeply." He stifled emotion. "I wanted to look after both him and Eric. I wanted Isaiah to know I was there for him."

Dalton studied his notes and eyed the slow wind of the tape recorder. He didn't believe this man. "You must've had your hands full, what with overseeing several warehouses and trying to keep Isaiah from sinking into depression. It would seem something had to give."

Hemal glanced at the floor. Sorrow rose and subsided. At length he reached for his computer monitor and turned the screen toward Dalton. "Everything on here belongs here. You can sit in your jeep outside and screen my website twenty-four hours a day and decide any damn thing you want."

"Who saw Eric at your home?" Dalton asked again.

"No one. You're making inferences which don't apply. Eric's health took a sudden decline. He required a good deal of machines, round-the-clock nursing staff, a lab tech who could run blood samples every five minutes. He was dying for Christ sake."

"I'm sorry."

"I am too."

"Thank you for your time." Dalton rose, closed his notepad, stopped the cassette tape recorder and deposited it. He got what he had come for, he thought on his way out.

eleven

D ALTON INSERTED THE COLOR slide prints into the projector. One at a time he switched them onto the wall. In the darkness the green night vision lens of the camera was like the developer for prints in the darkroom. The lens had frozen the hijackers movements with startling clarity allowing their visible features to become evident. Dalton could appreciate Isaiah's instinct to find a camera capable of revealing to him the various aspects of his four- or five-year long investigation. He must have settled on the few digicams with e-film and e-ports which Dalton had come across in his file. Isaiah must have experimented with zoom *PowerShots* and *Fuji FinePix* and higher resolution compression, shutter speeds, standout features, time videos with sound and black and white and sepia modes until he was able to capture the incriminating details of this ring. If the photographs or diskettes were not to be found among his possessions nor in his patrol vehicle, it meant they were somewhere – in Hemal's possessions or in a train or bus locker. Or destroyed.

Of the four hijackers one remained hidden by a black and white snafu over him. Dalton stared at the zigzag motion on the film, puzzled, wondering what his camera had captured. It wasn't lint on the lens because none of the other prints had it. At length it occurred to him he was seeing the hijacker's red or reddish overshirt. If they knew they had been photographed extensively then it stood to reason the gang utilized clothing which could obscure the ability of an observer to correctly assess his or her quarry.

Dalton clicked onto the next slide. A slender man or woman with armpit-long dark curly hair stood beside a stocky built man with a scalp cut. He honed in on their thighs and decided after a handful of seconds both were male. He clicked in reverse to the hijacker with the oddly printed black and white overshirt. He'd put this image on computer via a file format conversion and press the zoom key until the image pixellated into boxes to obtain a better idea of the dimensions the shirt was designed to deliver. For now it was clear to him that to the uninitiated the image would appear distorted, perhaps causing the observer to discard it as an over exposure. He magnified the image until a wavy color pattern took up the entire view. He wasn't quite certain but he thought the image was intended to obscure the hijacker's sex. He clicked through a handful of slides until he found another shot of the person. The individual had bent to check the hookup and in doing so was doubled over, hiding breasts or midriff. The legs were slender, from a side angle, the torso twisted somewhat. He should've brought along a mini DV video and shot a moving picture in addition to the slide prints for better comparison. Because he hadn't known what he was looking for he couldn't recall what he thought each hijacker was like.

At length he took a break. He'd return to the site for another few nights of surveillance, this time with a partner and a handful of cameras and camcorders. Chances were there were two or three teams of four hijackers who rotated jobs. He poured himself a cup of coffee and considered what it meant for this particular ring to operate from Ontario to Big Pine. He thought about Isaiah's DEA agent whom Isaiah had alleged was stealing equipment. Except for the fact that high tech surveillance equipment was getting raided and probably stored at Hemal Ebenales' various warehouses, little else made sense. If backcountry highways were used to bring in drugs then the hijacks were needed to create diversion. If the hijacks were to chase down a competitor then the hijacked good were probably sitting in storage until scarcity drove up the prices or bit into the competition's edge.

He methodically viewed each slide. He took notes on the transfer of trucks. He checked the individual's overshirt for design. In a store the image when viewed on a video might depart from being a blur movement and show as a grayscale-block image. He sipped his coffee. These folks assumed they were being watched. This was the allowance they had accomodated.

Dalton took the SmartMedia diskette that had originally contained the photographs and punched it into a computer. He isolated the headshots of all four hijackers and interfaced them into the Sheriff Department's database for CLETS for identification. It would take the rest of the day for a sheriff to download the photographs and run them through several databases to produce names and last known addresses.

He turned off the projector. When he returned to his desk at his workstation, a list of traffic calls for the past month lay on his desk.

A truck carrying lighting equipment had tipped, so had an unmarked truck containing United States Mail. A vehicle had been cited on a 27158 for operating in excess of thirty days without a smog certificate of compliance. Approximately one automobile a week was given a 27360 for failing to have a child under the age of four restrained properly with an approved safety belt. *ABC Trucking* was cited for a 27903 for carrying hazardous cargo; a tow hitch was not securely mounted; bailed hay was transported by a farmer in violation of California Highway Patrol regulations. A tire company was given a 31560 for failing to notify the California Integrated Waste Management Board forty-eight hours prior to departure. A child under age fourteen was cited 38505 for riding a motorcycle without a safety helmet. A man had been issued a ticket for 10751 for altering a VIN number on a automobile and for using it to commit a 10853 malicious mischief.

"IT'S ALOT OF ACTION BETWEEN Adelanto and Little Lake for what's out there," Dalton told the lieutenant an hour later over a late lunch of sodas and pizza. "It tells me something else is going down."

"You have any names yet?"

"One. Vail Bahe, a kid out near Vidal."

"Jesus, Vidal." Lt. Walker set down his soda.

"I know, there's nothing out there."

"Without links none of Du Bois' findings mean a thing."

"I know."

"Just because he felt he needed this high resolution camera stuff, it doesn't prove he actually came across the same hijackers you have."

"I know."

Lt. Walker considered. "We still have no connection to the call that took Du Bois to *Blue Water*."

"I don't know where that's going to come from. I don't have a hijacker who matches any description we were given."

"Well, what have you learned? One man is from this county. The foursome in all likelihood know they're at least periodically under surveillance. What else?"

"Nothing that can be hammered down yet."

Marty Walker picked the olives off his section of pizza. "You know how they succeed in getting a driver to pull over."

"Yes, and that they cut the radio wires so the driver is helpless. Maciel have any progress yet on his dead driver?"

"He's been identified as Wallace Simms."

"The DEA man?"

"Yes. They matched him to his dentals. He was actually headed to Amargosa Valley to a small resort there."

"It's shocking that anyone would murder DEA. Was he carrying contraband?"

"It hasn't been reported as such."

"Does DEA or Transportation have any theories about his murder?"

"Retaliation for the cocaine shipments he yanked. There's some speculation he may have witnessed police involvement."

"I thought the rumored police involvement was simply rumor, that it was the headliner that enabled DEA to expand its investigation into the high desert."

"I hear what you're saying. I think this one was very real. All that money sitting in the evidence locker was too big a temptation."

"Where was Simms supposed to be living?"

"At Randsberg."

"No one lives at Randsberg," Dalton countered. "Not if they can help it. What was his designated occupation? Truck driver?"

"Security."

"For whom?"

"For the Department of Transportation, specifically for the train."

"The sleep train" was his facetious remark. "This thing has bloomed way out of proportion."

"It has. I agree."

"Because of that I feel watching the hill will take two to be effective. Could you assign Margo Sam or George Maciel to me?"

"I can't spare the manpower until you have something definite. Just keep out of sight. You are ears and eyes only."

"Can you at least pull me off rotation?"

"For the next seventy-two hours," Marty said, sounding stretched beyond normal, "but then I need you front and center. One thing, Dal."

He waited.

"Du Bois must've maintained some kind of mileage log."

"I turned his place upside down. I found no evidence of one. The only log he kept were photographs of motels which Margo and I have identified."

"How about at his office?"

"Nothing aside from a handful of digital cameras."

"Odd, isn't it? I spoke to Lt. Taylor who told me he didn't come across a mileage registrar for several months."

Dalton raised his hands in a posture of inquiry.

"You think Ebenales has it?"

"He may. He was certainly in a position to know what Isaiah was up to. I interviewed him. He was extremely close-mouthed."

"If you can bring me anything to suggest he is storing his competitor's equipment in any of his warehouses I will send a man in as an employee."

"That won't be so easy. He says he's on the level."

"But he's the one with the reputation for beating a path to the door and exing out his competition."

"I know."

"I know you know. All I need is one piece of evidence that links him to these two murders. It can be as simple as a computer readout on that Ving card key. Or a hijacked item that turns up at a warehouse. Anything."

He'd do better with a fallback partner. He knew they were short staffed. He understood Lt. Walker had requested another position from the County Board of Supervisors and had been turned down.

He drove to his home and packed an overnight case. He made sure to bring the *PowerShot* camera and his *Sony* camcorder. This time when he sat on the mountain he wanted to be certain he captured the entire drama, whatever it was, on film.

THE CASINO AT ADELANTO WAS boarded up – someone's tax write-off. An orange grove competed with warehouses for water. Where it would get its water in a year was anyone's guess. The aqueducts were long dried now that Mono had cut off its flow, and the county was filling them in with sand. Except for the correctional facility which hired two hundred people, there was no lasting employment. The sarcastic wit of the old timer would tell the young passerby that you didn't want anyone to think there was anything out here to leap over the fence for, and the young passerby would sardonically respond that the state's three-strikes-you're-out-law was meant to spare the county from drying up jobs.

A truck blazed past him with enough force to push him off the road. *Oh God don't throw your truck on me,* and laughed. He laughed into Little Lake, the laughter poking holes in his tension. Signs of a desert economy had rusted into disuse: *Ecology Auto Wrecking, Auto Parts* being sold down the street, a *Granite Gas* tank stood waiting for something other than the hot sun to fill it or bring it back to usefulness; otherwise Joshua trees and sage stood ready to welcome descendents from the sky. Father had a U-Haul business and the kids at *Sunrise Raceway* raced their bikes amidst apart-ments going out of business – the desert and Time were elements to be reckoned with and the dwellers were stragglers who came from LA or Riverside or El Centro to start over in a place that wouldn't care what their pasts were made of. Places probably weren't expected to be here very long anyway; as long as the *Kingdom Hall* stayed and when it went, the entire village would go.

The road had all the flatness of an airstrip where a small plane could land unseen by anyone. The sign on Searles Station Road pointed the direction to the main gate at China Lake. Dalton rode toward the small stage that made up Randsberg. *Welcome to Randsburg* Jail stood at a crossroads, the Mojave in one direction and Atolia and San Bernardino in the other. Dalton passed the *Opera Cafe* and cute little Bodie-like houses. An old western town with a U.S. Mail look to it. Old wooden houses, an old steeple church newly painted in white and blue, hotels – and *Rands Mining Company* where gold was produced a century ago. All around were broken-down tin mine shafts, some buildings which were hard to know what they were. Piping lay on the side of a non-used aqueduct. Miles below lay a bluish green ocean of cacti. Emerging through this sea were gravel mounds exposing cement bunkers and doors – fallout shelters or dugouts or military posts inside which were rooms of computers tracking the flight of missiles and satellites not yet tested. Dalton ascended the road at eighty miles an hour passing a hollowed out tin shell of a gasoline station, several small airplanes awaiting repairs, a broken-down bus, all sitting at a crossroads truck stop. He thought about sophisticated surveillance equipment. About small airplanes and large ones. About computerized transmitters that could be sufficiently amplified to capture data being displayed on a target computer.

Dalton considered where the spurious economy left his hijacked truckers, as he prepared for a long night. Not in southern California, that was for damn sure. Nor on the telephone to a foreman or to a federal agent. If information leaked out slowly because it had to – the load wasn't worth your life nor having on-the-road harassment follow you from city to city. If the takers had a slick operation, if they were watched for years before any arrests were made, if access routes were cut off and interstate trade waylaid by state legislators suspicious of contraband making its way over the border into El Centro, if the hispanics came too far up the road into white- or Asian-controlled turf and threatened inland couriers on their way to the prisons, if the roadside monitors below Inyo county were black and the hijackers were white, you had to have a county ingredient besides local help. You had to be able to rely upon sheriffs who stayed off the road and attendants at gasoline stations who had ten seconds earlier gone to the bathroom and stayed there reading a good book for the half hour it took the thieves to corner the driver. If the hits were on *US Mail* trucks for a random collection - jewelry or stocks and bonds – sometimes car parts, high tech computer equipment or furs, cut lumber, munitions, any product that could fetch a solid dollar on the illegal trade market, you needed organized crime somewhere in the picture.

Just as in the San Fernando you had had water wars – long over with Mono Lake retaining its runoff from mountain springs – you had road wars. Vicious, antagonistic slimeballs who viewed prosperity as control of the road, plain and simple cargo kidnap, taking it anywhere they could get it. It was a hellish trip up 395 to the *Bishop* as the hamburger stand there was called. To an investigator a bishop hamburger was just that, a sardonic metaphor for a player on the board who didn't quite grasp that the bishop was the piece with the slash across its face. If most DEA investigated in pairs, how come Isaiah hadn't?

The more he thought about the hijacking the more he thought it was a continuing saga in a long war between a new underworld and labor. A long long war with thugs pitting the wage earner against yet another snake pit, a war in which the *duenos del noches* created every diversion the road had ever thought of. It was a long, long road and you wondered why in the midst of so much inner city violence and economic instability the government had to go out and invest in gold mines and violence in other countries in order to bring back the profits to continue the fight here. It just didn't make the grade at times. It's what Isaiah would've thought. Probably he did think it as he followed the hijackers and their connections from Ontario through San Bernardino's cities staging crude do-it-yourself checkpoints of unsuspecting motel managers. An African American CHP officer in the desert looking to spot trouble in a war where the booty was the claim of inner city black hoods had a blindspot. Isaiah was revered in San Bernardino's inner city; there he was loved and there he was feared – and out of that sea came men who cared nothing for black men who made it into the ATF, DEA, FBI or any other eschelon that had formerly excluded the black man or sought to make the black wage earner somehow less than he was by making him a token.

The dirtbag war, Dalton thought again, this time with animosity toward the man or woman who had taken Isaiah's soul and caused him to walk into the Colorado. In his mind he heard a familiar southern voice with its distinct twang:

A whole culturah heah of mo-bile homes with windahs punched out, like a weekend gathering of methamphetamine cookahs who bombed out their innards and took the money and ran. Yea sir, living in a tent is a mighty practical way of living. Why heck if you can't put your yurt up in the middle of th' road an' first lady that comes o'er the bend, you jus' flash your wares at her. But I'll tell ya I wasn't up fer that kinda living. No suh. Livin' out of a yurt; by time I'd get to work, I'd stink like hell.

The memory of the wanna-be senator whose righteousness for some reason stuck in his caw heralded back the IAD fiasco of a year ago: *That's what came of living three, four generations on the dole. When the state went to cut off AFDC after two years, if the family didn't take to the fact of working for a living, there was the road. Heck, if you was inventive enough, you could contract out the road for section work.*

THE MEMORIES FADED AND with them went the daylight hours. Night fell in shadows that stalked the landscape. Dalton fell asleep at least twice and awakened with the sense that sleep was unsafe. He found himself staring at the all too bright lights of two gasoline stations at Lone Pine. For a moment he thought he must be dreaming awake. In the far corners of his mind he saw two catsup red cabs carrying white sweetheart trucks bolt up the incline. Seconds before they became real as they rounded the bend and shot into the open past the Whitney Portal Summit, their engines pressured for a high speed run, he had reached for the *PowerShot* camera, focussed and snapped as many frames as he could. His hands were shaking. He leaned onto the dashboard to steady the camera. The two overbearing trucks killed their lights as an unsuspecting trucker barreled down past them. As the trucker passed them, they turned on their lights, turned on their music and charged onto the road at the trucker aiming for his left end. They rammed him and he toppled. His load crashed to the sandy shoulder. The two red trucks tapped at the tumbling rig causing it to catch the cab and drop it beneath the load as the load crashed over it and obliterated it.

Dalton removed the camcorder, snapped off the cap and fixed the focus on the falling rig. Then onto the red cabs. They had doused their lights again. They stood there directly across the road from him. If they sensed him or saw him he was dead. But he was certain he was far enough off the shoulder that he was unseen.

Somewhere in the hollows of the desert a wolf or coyote howled. Its wail sent a wave of panic through Dalton. He debated whether to run onto the landscape or to release the brake inside his jeep and roll backward. He didn't do either. There was no sound or movement by the truck drivers on the other side of the highway. The driver of the toppled truck was dead and there was nothing he could do about it. If there were any justice at all worth hoping for, it was that one of his cameras would record something useful for prosecution. He heard a door of what he imagined was one of the cabs shut with a bang and a man jump to the ground. Against his better judgement he crept out of his jeep on the passenger side to peer over the hood to where the sound had originated. The figure was sheathed in dark clothing; it moved quickly to the felled truck and cut open the back lock with a bolt cutter. The figure pulled open the doors. One door gaped as the other banged shut. Dalton watched the figure remove a bottle, light a cloth and toss it into the body of the truck. Almost immediately the motor of the companion cab started up, its lights still off. The figure returned to his truck, got inside and started up his motor. Dalton pulled back into the dark protection of his jeep, his heart coursing blood through his eardrums loudly enough to frighten him. Slowly the trucks pulled onto the road and headed toward Manzanar and Aberdeen.

He didn't dare follow. He sank to the ground, his knees to his chin and prayed the truck did not catch fire. He had a fire extinguisher somewhere in his trunk but he wouldn't look for it. It was too late for heroics. He heard the fire burst into a torch and whoosh into a roar. As he turned his face toward the road, he saw sparks of fire herald into the night. The container buckled as a fireball spit out of the rear. In a moment the truck was aflame burning out of control, a fierce yellow against a pitch black sky.

Dalton hurtled himself into his jeep, started up the engine and simultaneously released the brake. He stepped on the accelerator causing the vehicle to charge forward. Instinctively he cleared the dashboard. He rode with his lights off down the hill passing the two gas stations. Not until he had cleared the block of motels did he turn on his lights and slow his speed.

He knew he was in trouble. His entire body trembled uncontrollably. His body flushed into a cold sweat. He had difficulty swallowing nausea. It surfaced twice; finally he got out of the jeep and vomitted. He cried as he sponged his face with cold water from a thermos. He wished he were anywhere but on the road in the middle of the night, alone. He wouldn't return to the site for months. He knew if he had to go through another similar episode, he was washed up. He sucked on a wet cloth. Between shivering and teeth chattering, he managed to swallow a half cup of Gatorade and chew a piece of beef jerky. After a handful of minutes he returned to his jeep. He found a reasonably quiet road where he slept the rest of the night. Dreams abandoned him. Periodically heavy traffic sounds crashed into his subconscious. He came to while the sky was still dark; he took a piece of bread and a tin of water for nourishment and waited for the nausea to resurface. It never did. After twenty minutes he got back on the road and headed home.

HE DROVE WITH THE TREMOROUSNESS OF one who has come too close to death and barely escaped. He tried to think, but thought eluded him. He considered contacting Lt. Walker on his cellphone but did not. The desert divulged itself at the rows of tan tinted mirrors. At Kramer Junction he took 58 and headed toward 15.

He moved in bumper to bumper traffic. On one side the railroad cut through a gravel floor. Tumbleweed and sagebrush and yellow and pink wildflowers dictated the landscape. On the other side motel signs addressed the public from neon lights and an assortment of eateries. Daylight painted the windows in hues of crimson and orange. The aperture of his mind opened enough to allow him to understand the case was dangerous. Very dangerous. A CHP officer had been killed. A DEA responsible for bringing in truck loads of forfeiture was torched to death. Now this. He could not afford to guess wrong. He could not afford not to know what information Isaiah had turned over and he knew whatever it was Isaiah knew he, Dalton, had no clear knowledge of it.

He resolved in his mind to obtain a copy of the IAD report that had resulted in the disclosures of fraud and embezzlement. If nothing else, he had to start where Isaiah had when he relocated to Morongo Basin.

twelve

DALTON HIT *SAN BERNARDINO STEEL* with its three long hangars, three short ones. University Parkway leading to Cal-State San Bernardino jumped out at him and he took it. The university sat on Northpark, a tan tall building and a low grey one with many windows covered by green shades. Palm trees and Eucalyptus lined the streets. Above, the mountain in steel white girded pipes, poured water for 172,000 people. You could see the pipes at the north end of the valley. He passed Sweetwater Ranch Road to *Pine Creek* where at the top of the canyon adjacent to a white steel, peekaboo fence sat the victorian home of his wanna-be senator, a library peeking through the elaborate crystal glass.

Dalton parked his jeep and walked across the tiny postage stamp grass lawn and knocked on the red door. Bob Cobb's tall Chinese manservant opened the door with startled concern.

"Mr. Cobb is lying down," he said, with enough displeasure to indicate disdain.

"Just let him know I'm here. Please."

Dalton waited in the flagstone foyer among a hothouse bevvy of succulents. Thin panels of crystal glass looked onto a porch with rattan furniture and crysanthamums. It had been a year since he had seen Bob Cobb retired. Bob was the son of a horse's ass who could have been a halfway decent police chief if he had been content to work for a living. A solid lineup of police chiefs, his father had used his influence in city politics to sell off the Redlands and Yucaipa at a time when it seemed water would be forever flowing from Mono Lake.

"Why Dalton!" Bob Cobb strolled into the foyer. In his late sixties he was still dapper in spite of overweight and going bald. "Have you left your post at Yucca Valley?" He asked in his distinctly southern Baptist accent.

He escorted them both into the library and motioned for Dalton to sit. The manservant brought tea and departed.

"I'm still there," Dalton replied.

"Lt. Walker? Is he still your supervisor?"

"He is." Dalton left his tea untouched. "I wanted to know if it was possible to obtain a copy of the IAD investigation?"

"Whatever for, dear boy? It's very general, nothing a marshal deputy would evah need to see." He sipped his tea and without malice gave Dalton the once-over. "I understand Isaiah Du Bois died."

Dalton gave a nod. "Homicide."

"But how can you be certain? Officer Du Bois was a heavy drinker. Not only that, he was a homosexual who had one too many disappointments at love."

"He left behind an in-progress investigation."

"Well, I don't suppose death is evah timely. How did he die?"

"He drowned in the Colorado."

"I can certainly see why you doubt something so theatrical. He was not a theatrical man, although I suppose his lifestyle may be considered by some to be so." Bob Cobb held a defiant expression as though he expected to be challenged, or perhaps welcomed the challenge.

Dalton did not answer.

"You know what it said. The IAD roughly slapped us on the wrists for engaging in political indiscretions, among them using police officahs from Riverside and Imperial Counties to work after hours. I had planned to run for a position on the County Board of Supervisors. I might as well have thrown my entire futurah away for the damage it did me."

Dalton was sympathetic. If Chief Cobb willingly gave up his career for sake of a dangerous investigation, he stood fast as an upwardly mobile public damned him. "You gave fairly lengthy testimony about the routes those officers worked."

"I did, deah boy, but those weren't cocaine routes, if that's what you're after. Those routes didn't go into Arizona. They didn't penetrate El Centro. Those officers were a hundred percent legit."

"Then you won't mind if I borrow your copy?"

"It has to be *my* copy?" he asked without rancor.

"You have an unedited draft."

Bob Cobb stared at his heavily lined hands. "I have a son working in Kern County, Dalton. I'm not eager to see his prayers dashed to hell."

"If I find anything, I'll leave your name out."

He gazed at the leather-bound books that made up his library. "Your friend should nevah have considered a post east of Ontario." He seemed to be saying that when Isaiah agreed to the reassignment it was a matter of time before he became dog meat and for that Dalton was appreciative. But what other choices did Isaiah have?

Chief Cobb rose slowly, walked to his desk and pulled open the bottom drawer. "This is my only copy. If I had any sense I'd make you review it here."

"Thank you, Sir," he said humbly because humility seemed in order. He promised to return it in several days.

thirteen

T HE PAGE FLUTTERED FROM one of the notepads. Dalton bent to pick it up. It was written in Isaiah's cursive hand.

How does any man replace his life when it is gone? I am not that old but I feel as though I must be seventy, or eighty. I am emptied in mourning. If Eric's hardship was to struggle in the net that was his disease, then my hardship is simply to continue.

I long to cancel myself out, to stand in the dark and become darkness itself. This is a primordial calling like going home or finding oneself after years of being blinded and having been restored to sight is made whole. In darkness I might reshape myself. I long to see the imprint of the Anasazi who my grandfather was looking down upon shrinking crisscrossed fields of corn and squash and trees and creeks. I am afraid. Not of becoming crowded on too little space but of being made to pass through the poultice of grief. Of disappearing. Of watching all that I was become smaller and smaller and eventually being plowed under, myself gone, turned into roots, my lineage and history made invisible.

I am in agony. There shall be no sharp awakening for me. I am depleted. I am losing the life of my world as I was living, working, and as I was trying to hold to myself the knowledge of what it meant to lose one's value and lose one's self. In an instant I held Eric's sorrow, his waking and his rising, his abject terrors and the insideness of a shrinking world. This was not a gift he had given to me. This was the fear I carried for him — the fact that it is possible for one to be emptied of essence. That it is possible to lose all real sense of safety. Feel destroyed altogether. The refuge I grabbed onto once I escaped the inner city mind, of giving a voice to despair —

He should have written, I struck at you Hemal for hurting me. I lost and you won.

Dalton understood the inner city mind. It was not much different from the first world mind or the third world mind. When they couldn't hunt you down enough because you were still on some patch of land they thought they might someday want and they kept sending out soldiers to the city to find you, to bring you in or to surrender yourself to someone else's ways of living, then you lived with the knowledge of being perpetually hunted. Dalton understood this fundamentally. Isaiah had been expelled from the inner city because he had been effective. He had been shunted to a desert post with his reputation destroyed where no one should have been able to find him. The crime that cast him out lived on desert highways as it did on coastal and valley highways. Isaiah should have been seen, as Dalton felt he himself was seen, in the greater scheme of things. He felt he inhabited a section of landscape that few traversed, let alone built a house or relationship on. He was able, as once Isaiah had been able in the inner city, to escape the fact of being hunted. But when some part of you gets defeated, you become alone in a way you need to remain connected and you seem visible in ways that can hurt you.

If Isaiah was invisible in his investigations, Hemal found a way to throw him into the open. It seemed to Dalton that Hemal pushed Isaiah into becoming more and more self conscious until the awareness of self was painful. And all the while Hemal used Isaiah to deflect his own activities – used his jealousy, his need for acceptance and love, these qualities which make any of us human and humane, and thrust Isaiah onto an investigative landscape that caused Isaiah to become the target.

Dalton returned the note to the notepad it had come from. He wondered why Chief Cobb kept the notepads in addition to the report itself and then alternately wondered why the police chief surrendered it. Probably he had not known of the existence of the note.

fourteen

THE COLLECTIVE LAW ENFORCEMENT agencies for San Bernardino and Inyo counties convened in the Sheriff Department situated in Boron at the edge of the Edwards Air Force Base. The two lieutenants – Martin Walker of the Morongo Basin U.S. Marshal and Rydel White of Morongo Basin California Highway Patrol – headed the meeting. Present were twenty-two officers representing the Alcohol, Tobacco and Firearms; California Highway Patrol; Drug Enforcement Agency; Department of Justice, U.S. Marshal and members of Inyo and San Bernardino Sheriff Departments. Lt. Rydel White, Du Bois' CHP boss, had compiled a smattering of photographs which decorated the walls of the small room. He was a short slim man with a peppered crewcut and a harried expression that belied too much coffee and paperwork. To those who knew him, he had socked away thirty years of solid investigation before he put in for a desk job. It was understood he needed the increased pay to accomodate the rehabilitation expenses after his eldest granddaughter, a single parent of two whose marijuana problem took her on a nose dive off a freeway and crumpled the tin can she was driving, confessed to a twelve year substance abuse history. Lt. White's brain was a ticker tape that operated around the clock and interfered with the customary eight hours sleep a night so that despite his young fifty-eight years he seemed never quite caught up with the demands of the job.

Without rising, Lt. White began the briefing. "Eighteen months ago as a result of an independent commission appointed by the Justice Department to investigate the police corruption scandal in San Bernardino a handful of DEA were assigned to Morongo Basin. One was Sgt. Wally Simms, the other Sgt. Isaiah Du Bois. Both came on board in my department; both are dead, one of homicidal drowning, the other torched in a truck north on 127. We have another torch job but the remains have not yet been identified."

Lt. Walker stood. He distributed Zerox copies of excerpts from the IAD report and the findings by the Justice Department. "Chief Cobb ran the Police Department up to the time of the investigation. Released to the public were statements that his officers took bribes, released prisoners without authority, funneled DEA evidence into personal lockers and subsequently into payroll and equipment, misplaced bodies and on occasion they conducted their own star chamber going after or permitting others to go after witnesses to crimes.

"The facts are quite different. He arranged for police to drive trucks whose companies were under suspicion for bringing into the state cocaine bricks. He then arranged for officers to fan out all over the county to reside in neighborhoods where drug dealers lived, and finally he outnumbered drug dealers four to one on the street."

"Jesus, he took quite a fall," remarked a sheriff from Inyo County.

"He did," Lt. Walker said. "Even I was uncertain until I reviewed the entire report. It was probably the one way he could be certain of arresting longtime dealers. With the expansion of suburbs in the Inland Empire he also created a base of a thousand new homes in Del Rosa, Highland and in Morongo Basin. A new community hospital was built along with several satellite clinics. The police force in San Bernardino city expanded; so did fire departments and new fire trucks, public utility commissions, vehicle services, solid waste systems, regional parks, libraries, JTPA and GAIN welfare back-to-work programs, senior services, flood control, animal control and a host of other services. Cobb's division cleaned up with thirty new Lexus vehicles, laptops in every patrol vehicle, Livescan, and so on."

"He was a genius," someone said, speaking out of turn.

Lt. Walker smiled. "His idea was to overwhelm the drug dealers they had been tracking by expanding their markets and then posting undercover officers and agents who could get on film what they missed in prior years."

"Incredible," someone else stated.

"It was the first solid means we had," said Lt. White of Morongo Basin CHP, "for documenting means, methods and personnel hired by these operators."

"Very successful," a woman's voice from the back of the room.

A light breeze circulated from open windows through the large oblong room.

"Because of our abilities to share officers and agents up and down the highway and to produce a resulting decline in terrorism," Lt. White continued, "the state has funnelled another five million dollars into law enforcement for San B and Inyo over the next three years."

Everyone cheered and clapped.

Marty Walker held a hand, and the room quieted down. "One week ago the entire operation stalled when Sgt. Isaiah Du Bois was found drowned. Another undercover DEA was identified – Wally Simms."

A gasp in the room was audible.

"Two dead investigators —" An African-Canadian sheriff named Terence Jones underscored the gasp. "How on earth did this occur?"

"We don't know," Marty answered. "The investigation took on several adjuncts, one being surveillance equipment manufactured south of the border taken off the road somewhere around or above Inyokern —"

Lt. White interrupted, saying, "We're not sure if this is drug-related. It does seem tied to police forfeiture of high grade equipment we need to track them."

"Evidence was taken out of the evidence lockers?" A sheriff from Inyo County asked.

"These are police and sheriff items taken off the road." Lt. White read from his notes.

> Laser-disc-shooting simulator
> 12 9mm pistols
> Infrared nighttime aerial reconnaissance
> 5 Indoor-outdoor range
> $780,000 forfeiture from raids, stings and other activities including speeding violations
> 3 vans with packages of greenbacks wrapped in duct tape worth $1,100,053
> 25 "throw away" revolvers, 1300 kilos of cocaine and 280 pounds hashish
> 1 flatbed truck with sheets of drywall
> 1,000 pseudophedrine blister packs, 1 casement red devil lye, iodine crystals and flamables and oxydizers
> 1/2 ton methamphetamine packaged in pinatas

Lt. White resumed. "All of it had been seized and stored as *meat* in police-owned warehouses in and about San Bernardino and then was subsequently stolen. Some of it was stolen directly out of police warehouses, but most of it was hijacked while in transport from a crime scene to the warehouse or police lab."

"These thefts occurred a year ago?"

"Three years to a year ago."

"Why do you suppose the thieves stopped taking police forfeiture?" Marshal Maciel asked. "Did we clamp down and get better?"

"We became more efficient. Before he resigned, Chief Cobb asked that every law officer, deputy or agent have the same database system installed in laptops and that every patrol vehicle had a laptop. He also persuaded Department of Transportation to do the same. My guess is when we finally identify the hijackers we will find they traded police forfeiture in for commercial surveillance goods."

"So it's possible a ring of burglars went after police equipment in order to obtain access to certain carriers of surveillance equipment?" Maciel queried.

"Yes. Both Du Bois and Simms," Marty continued, patting a folded handkerchef to a line of perspiration across his forehead, "went after drug forfeiture and in the process discovered this ring of hijackers. Both agents were able to tie a few pieces of stolen police equipment to these hijackers.

"These slides," he said, as he switched on the projector and motioned with his pointed finger for someone at the back of the room to kill the lights, "were taken by U.S. Marshal Keys on two occasions." He showed a dozen slides of camera shots taken the previous night.

Lt. White put in, saying, "Both Simms and Du Bois carefully linked top players to cocaine and heroin shipments brought from Mexico into California by way of the southern cities situated on Highway 10. They had culled data as to who each man had working for him, where the shipments originated, approximate amounts, warehouse locations. DOJ could turn the cargo away from the various ports, quarantine cruise ships at the three-mile limit, shut down non-tower airports, and stop trains in the yards. It was a very effective operation."

Marty Walker resumed. "Chief Cobb and his henchmen went after anyone who they thought stood in the way of the prison action. Men who dropped out of sight will tell you that if he beat a personal path to your home he was for all purposes telling you he had his teeth in your dick. We called it the bristol brush; he left your hair standing stiff on your rolling pin.

"What you see here" and showed the figure of the red truck ignite the gasoline-soaked cloth tamped into a dark brown bottle, "is the first live indication of murder on 395. Once we get a positive ID on the driver —"

"What's the carrier?" asked a young DOJ agent.

"Unidentified," Lt. Walker answered. "Whoever's putting the killer or killers on the road, we think, is after people who can identify his operation."

"How many law enforcement are you planning to put on rotation?"

"Washington DC turned down our request for another thirty field operatives. Those of you in the room today comprise the work force that is going to tie the bows on these hijackers."

An ATF woman spoke. She was tall, compact with sharp facial features, a blonde who wore her shoulder length straight hair tied back in a pony tail. "You're saying Simms and Du Bois were murdered because most probably they could identify these hijackers."

"We believe at least Simms or Du Bois knew who the individual was in charge of the entire operation."

"Someone above Ebenales?"

"That's what we think."

She considered this. "Any possibility they witnessed murder attempts?"

"There was a case that this one dove-tailed onto. The Becker case."

"I remember. It was thought to be a serial killer who murdered a handful of men operating clandestine methamphetamine labs and deposited their bodies in train containers."

"That's the one," Marty Walker said. "There's some suspicion that this drug operator is cancelling anyone's ticket who tries to squeeze in onto his turf."

"Which is?" she asked.

"The entire San Bernardino desert."

"He'd have to have a sizeable number of dealers working for him."

"It is believed Ebenales farms out responsibility to a few men who handle the various routes that dealers are put in charge of."

"Ebenales was the operator that Du Bois was assigned to."

"That's right," Marty Walker replied. Behind him Rydel White nodded, and added, "Du Bois moved in with him."

"You are insane," she declared. "Why would anyone take that much of a risk?"

"Because he brings in the equivalent of a ton of cocaine yearly."

Lt. Walker placed a foot on his chair and leaned on his knee. "It was risky. For months Simms handled himself superbly. Then a week or so ago communications were cut off. He disappeared. We went after every known drug shipment east of 15 in efforts to learn what had occurred. Reports from DEA alleged he was carrying produce into Riverside to get more information on a driver. Inspection agents stopped every last trucker and came up with no sign of him."

"Do you have copies of any of his receipts?" Dalton asked. "It could be helpful to put together a chronology of his final hours."

"No, there's literally nothing. We went through his desk as well. When an operation is this dangerous, we disappear everyone who we can. If necessary we conduct fake funerals or report in the media that one of our agents died. After the first segment of the investigation including the Becker trial, IAD funeraled out two men who then came back as undercover agents with new names, new birthdates and new wives. IAD elected not to funeral Du Bois. In retrospect that probably would've been the safer thing to do, but then we could not have sent him in to observe Ebenales."

The need for secrecy told Dalton that White or some other lieutenant suspected there was a transportation problem at the management level and wouldn't take any chances.

"Was Officer Du Bois the only way you kept tabs on Ebenales?" The ATF agent inquired.

Lt. White replied. "We put Simms on the road as backup."

"But DEA also assigned him to a caviat of tasks."

"That's true. He was to keep an eye on rail activity. If he suspected drugs coming in by train with grain, beans or produce, he was to report to Admiral Jacobs of the U.S. Navy who would derail the shipment."

"Did he go after *Lucky* trucks?" A sheriff asked.

"No, those are meat trucks bound for Chinatowns up and down the coast off Highways 1 and 101 and if they carry contraband which some do, meat inspectors seize the drugs on the dock."

"Do we know what Simms uncovered?" Marshal George Maciel asked.

"He correctly identified those occasions when contraband and surveillance equipment were on board trains."

"For all occasions?"

"Every last one."

"He must have had a good eye," Maciel noted.

"He did. He also knew which load each of a handful of diversion drivers would receive and would signal ahead to sheriffs on the road which items various truckers were carrying."

Dalton asked Lt. White, "Any reason you didn't want to rotate Simms to the non-towered airports? Give him some down time?"

"Department of Transportation calls the shots. The lady who runs DOT for southern California highways gives us the timelines and the trucks she thinks may carry cocaine. Generally when she feels a mode of procedure is working well she tries to convince us it is worth our while to remain with the same team members in place. The problem," White conceded, "is we've been spread too thin for the problems we've encountered."

"Who did Transportation assign to monitor 395 most recently?" he asked.

"Nine out of ten guesses don't count," Maciel asserted sarcastically. "Probably last night's driver."

"Wasn't him," one of the three Department of Justice agents in the room answered. He was heavy set, dark complected and dark haired, with a casual air to him that frequently landed him as an airport or warehouse materials handler or crane operator. "This booby probably inadvertently talked to the wrong person. We don't stir up any action; we're eyes and ears only. When we see an illegal act we call into a central dispatch. From the operator, information is passed over to a DEA agent."

"Any link between what Du Bois came up with and what Simms may have learned? Did they flag the same shipment?" Dalton asked.

"Nothing we can prove," White responded. "Simms' cargo came from Needles. Du Bois could've been on water patrol at Needles. We have no way of knowing. We know what his out calls were because he wrote them onto his log."

Someone quickly inserted a question, asking, "Any possibility he went there to meet Simms who for some reason could not keep the rendezvous?"

"They were told never to meet in public. In addition, on that day Simms was believed to have been in the truck in which he was killed."

"Was Sgt. Simms supposed to verify for Du Bois that what left Crossroads actually turned up at Tecopa or Amargosa?" Maciel asked.

"Why didn't you yank him out of Ebenales' clutches at that point?" The ATF woman's tone was accusatory.

"Because we couldn't move *anyone*. We thought we might have a leak. We didn't know who or where," Lt. White replied defensively. "We're storing information in two different database systems to try to get a handle on what party is interested in law enforcement daily procedure. Both databases were deemed secure from external access."

The room was silent, stunned. It could've been anyone of them in the truck headed to Tecopa. It still could.

"What's next?" asked someone from the back of the room.

Lt. Walker answered. "We're going to send every last one of you into a known chain of warehouse locations operated by Ebenales. One officer wearing a wire to do the snooping, two teams of two outside to record the dialogues if there are any and to act as backup for the officer inside. You will each receive special duty pay because of the degree of risk. All of you will wear a lead vest and be provided night vision wear and upgrades. Questions?"

There were none now. Five or six hours later after people had spent a few hours with their families, the newer officers selected to go in on foot would be asking themselves the standard questions asked by every officer whose body could become a moving target. Will I make it out alive? Was the risk worth it? And, should I put in for a transfer to a desk job?

For every marshal who had signed onto this duty and been selected, they no longer asked the questions. Every desert shadow potentially hid a loaded pistol and every wall, a gunslinger who could shoot to kill at a range of a hundred yards with eyes closed. The nature of the work had long ago made them glory boys.

fifteen

D ALTON CREPT ALONG THE catwalk of the warehouse
at Red Mountain eyeing the surveillance cameras which overlooked aisles between rows of boxes piled high. Window panes
separated by thick lead typical of older warehouses had been painted
grey. Through the rafters he could make out two guards sitting in a
small office with a computer, phone and surveillance camera and
another man and dog situated at a desk in the middle of an aisle.
An interior dock held an eight wheeler truck and a black van, doors
of both open. He couldn't tell what was being loaded, if anything.
He froze the moment he saw Bahe in the dock with another older
man, modest height, thin with wiry salt and pepper hair dressed in
blue jeans and a flannel red and white checkered shirt rolled up to
the elbows.

"I can't make that schedule," Bahe snapped, obviously tired and
feeling compromised. "If you want me to play fetch for every mis-
take you make, you'll have to wait until I can pull a team together."

"I don't know what's the problem. You switch the players around too often as it is."

"I have to. I have sheriffs and Highway Patrol breathing down my neck everywhere I go, not to mention the assholes that are camped outside the warehouse at Needles."

"I'll tell you what. I'll give you four days but that's it. If we aren't on schedule by then, I'll find another carrier."

Vail Bahe stood without speaking for a moment, taking time to squelch rising anger. If his young years gave him an impetulance, knowledge of the road made for his maturity.

"We'll go in three days," he decided. "But you've got to bring in another rig. If I am continually spotted —"

"Vail, it's hot everywhere, not just in the San B. I-5's crawling with cops just itching for the take, 101's a microwave and Highway 68 into Salinas is covered with ants."

"I'll manage it, don't worry. Can you get me a rig? I have more than one load stashed in my barn."

"Not a problem."

"Equipped with a scanner?"

"It's done. You just be here. Thursday. If I have to, I'll line another carrier."

An African American guard had come into the aisle directly beneath Dalton. Dalton held his breath as the man stared in his direction, squinting to make out signs of movement. Not seeing any, he retreated behind a row. *The people looked the same.* The quote from Isaiah's journal came to mind; from a profile the guard did indeed resemble Officer Isaiah Du Bois. Worse, he walked and stood the way Isaiah had.

"What's the matter?" the older man inquired.

"One of the silent alarms was tripped."

The older man withdrew a pistol from a drawer and moved toward a wooden ladder that led to the rafters. Dalton turned and ran in the direction he had come. Shots rang out and a bullet zipped past him. He hurled himself faster flying through the air, his feet barely touching the wooden walk, no longer hanging onto the barely tenuous rope bannister, mindful only of the footsteps zeroing in on him.

"Hey you!" The man paused to fire another shot.

Dalton dove through the broken window he had crawled through and slid face down over a tin roof, somersaulting his body into a jackknife as he aimed for the ground near his jeep. The man behind him halted at the window and unloaded a round of gunshots into the air at him. He jumped to the ground and as he yanked open the jeep door, arms lifted him by the ribs and tossed him against the side of the building. The older man was stronger than he was, and heavier. As Dalton clasped both hands together and made efforts to pound the man's chest, the older man saddled him across the chest and pinned his arms to his sides.

"Care to explain yourself?" He asked.

Dalton winced at the pain in his left arm. After a brief moment he decided the bulldog mug on this man made him French Italian, or possibly some brand of Canadian Indian. "U.S. Deputy Marshal," Dalton said, wincing from pain. "I was following up on a complaint."

"I didn't notice you walk in through the front door."

"I didn't come in that way."

The older man reached into Dalton's pocket for his badge and flipped it open to the shield. Reluctantly he backed away giving Dalton room to stand.

He did so slowly, swaying slightly as his legs threatened to buckle. "May I have my badge?"

The other man handed it to him and watched as he pocketed it. Then came the unexpected blow, a quick thrust of fingers to the right side of the jaw forcing Dalton to turn like whipcord. He anchored himself on his feet, but the next chop to the waist took him more so by surprise. He jerked backward reaching instinctively behind himself to grab something to cushion his blow and toppled awkwardly onto his side. The man yanked him toward him and this time Dalton drew his legs together and clenching them into a rigid position aimed for the man's knees. The motion caught the older man off guard causing him to stumble. Dalton rolled onto his side and still moving squat danced onto his feet and thrust a punch at the man's abdomen. The man avoided contact and swung at Dalton who arched his back to minimize the impact of the blow. The man's fist grazed his chest. Dalton caught a movement from the corner of his eye and danced away. A guard carrying a rifle had come outside to join the hoopla. He fired a round of shots into the soil causing Dalton to stand stock still.

"You're on my property. Uninvited," the older man stated, with displeasure.

"You know anything about forfeiture police equipment?"

"No, nothing."

"How about windfall drugs?"

"Not here, fella."

Dalton didn't see the rope until it was already around him lasoo-style and cinched tightly, drawing his arms to his side. He tried to wrestle free but the African American guard kneed him and he fell, hard, fast, to the cement floor. As the floor rose to meet him he crashed into it, the block of warehouses whirling around him. As he felt himself go numb and black out he heard his backup pull up to the building and screech to a halt. What the hell took you so long? He thought as darkness burrowed him into oblivion.

*C*ONTINUOUS PRESSURE WAS WHAT *had undermined Isaiah,* Dalton thought ten hours later after he had gone to the Hi-Desert Hospital for Xrays and a patch-up for his bruises. In Nell's chalk colored adobe home tucked away in a ravine and partially hidden by low lying trees in Wonder Valley, Dalton accessed the county database for properties to learn the name of the owner for the warehouse at Red Mountain. The name *Hemal Ebenales, Manager* flashed onto the screen. Dalton pressed the cursor over the question for other properties. A list of ten locations appeared. He looked up the names for the owners of those warehouses also. Only Crossroads was owned by a man named Kyle Scott whose address was listed as a location on the river south of Needles. He pushed the *print* key and waited for the print hammer to complete its task of spitting out a list.

Next he worked with the *Identi-Kit* database to create pictures of the people he had seen at the at the warehouse at Red Mountain. He made adjustments as the faces took shape. He put in a call to Lt. Walker to tell him he would stop by his home in a few hours. Three hours later when he had a workable set of faces he FAXed them to the office for the clerk Evora to run them through DMV and the FBI. It would be at least twenty-four hours before he could expect to receive confirming names.

He worked another half hour completing the accident report form. Then he raised himself slowly and hobbled through the house. He said hello to Nell who was at her desk in the kitchen. Her agreement when they became lovers was he could call the second bedroom his own and when he came over she'd stay out. A calender with a midnight picture of Joshua Tree National Monument beneath a full moon hung on the wall above her self-made work station. Crumpled paper, styrofoam cups and uncapped pens littered the kitchen table where Nell had spread out a graphics art design she was working on for a new client, a small direct mail order company specializing in handcrafts. The blinds over the screen facing the desert were open. Joshua trees and sagebrush littered the landscape which otherwise was barren and wanting. Unlike the picture photograph of the moonlit sky, the scene before him was of diffused salmon light. Gradually the sky was changing color from the end of the day to violet and mauve.

"Are you alright?" She asked. She had gotten her hair permed so that it was wavy. It was pulled back from her forehead and held in place with a tortoise shell clip.

"Alive and breathing." He leaned to kiss her cheek. "It's a very dangerous assignment."

She nodded. "Ian called and told me."

Next to George Maciel, Ian Spender was one of his closet friends in the Marshal Office. Still he reacted negatively to hearing this, saying, "He had no right. Just because he wasn't assigned to this tour of duty —"

"I called him on another matter. My client knows him."

"Oh and you thought he could give you the inside dope on how to slant the ad."

"It was definitely worth the telephone call. Ian said my client takes all his ideas from natural surroundings."

He walked to her. "What'd you do?" and pulled her rough sketch drawings toward him. As usual they were as good as the sketch artists the Marshal Office hired to do crime scenes. She had sketched the sand as though it were a continuous wave and placed bleached driftwood and a cow skull in the forefront. She had given real thought to the shading and as a result the sketch looked complete.

"This is good, Nell. You've really captured something here."

"Thanks. You want me to start a bath for you?"

He shook his head. "I'm off to Marty's as soon as I eat dinner."

"Can I give you a lift?"

"No," he said, and kissed the top of her head. "It's a nice hairdo. Makes your face look softer."

He grabbed a soda and a slice of roast beef and went outside and sat on one of the rocking chairs. He needed time to think. He felt certain he was a few steps from whatever it was Isaiah had latched onto. He slowly moved his head from side to side to test for pain and stiffness. There was some residue.

He thought about the warehouse and about the man who resembled Isaiah. He wondered how often this man had been mistaken at a distance by other officers. The psychology that was being practiced against them disturbed him, not because a hired hit-man could ever sufficiently mimic a trained investigator in the field but because the visibility of such a man could weaken the natural defenses of civilians in a marshal's life. It made him wonder whether Nell or Lina's partner Max had ever seen this man and whether they had ever talked to him mistaking who he was.

"Sweetheart, I love you." He said on his way out.

"Love you too," she called out, as he closed the door to the two bedroom house.

Martin Walker's home looked down upon a dried creekbed that ended some fifty kilometers away in a concrete aqueduct. From his slate patio the rows of arched windowlike openings lit in pink and green soft hues by small lights positioned on the ground gave the suburb a feeling of being somewhere in Rome, Italy. The dried creekbed had been a creek before the county rediverted its drinking water. County services were slowly planting leafy trees and exotic flowers. In time the area would be turned into a small rain forest with hanging vines, bougainvillea, ginger and other typically hothouse flowering trees.

Marty poured two cups of coffee and set a bowl of coffee crumble cake on a small glass table. Dalton poured cream into his coffee and dropped two brown sugar cubes into it, then sipped it for taste.

Dalton removed his spiral notepad. He discussed the facts of the case. Isaiah had gone in undercover to live with Hemal Ebenales and to track his operations. He learned information Hemal kept on his computers and what items were stored at each warehouse. Dalton had no proof but he thought Isaiah had determined who continually stole police high-tech equipment. The police, ATF, DEA and FBI who had been reorganized after officers who helped bring in cocaine shipments were fired had been fanned out in all directions, some as train inspectors, others as highway cops and sheriff deputies. Dalton thought some officers involved in taking bribes had been repositioned into areas that saw little traffic. The clincher for these officers, he was fairly certain, was in doing business with men who resembled other officers they knew to be on this particular investigation. The confusion was intentional and must have led to miscommunications, errors in identification and contradicting reports.

Lt. Walker speculated aloud. Perhaps Hemal decided that in spite of an apparent physical attraction by Isaiah for Hemal that Isaiah was not the type of officer who would put love before loyalty. Hemal would have figured within a few weeks what Isaiah was up to. Knowing this he would have begun having Isaiah watched. He may have assigned a few people to him including men who resembled Isaiah's lover Eric Day. It was possible Hemal used this same strategy with Eric as well. Once Eric's disease returned, it was difficult to know whether Isaiah was outsmarted by the underhandedness of a quick old fox or whether in his state of despair and shock over his lover he had accepted too dangerous an assignment for his state of mind to cope with. Marty said he had to assume that Isaiah knew what he was getting into and took as many precautions as possible. He had to accept the belief that although Isaiah was mourning his lover's ill health he was still able to continue IAD's investigation. He had to assume that regardless of Hemal's honesty or dishonesty, Isaiah nevertheless had identified the players within his operation and within the police force, DEA and Sheriff Department, that he had correctly correlated with each warehouse the items stocked and regularly shipped, and knew when the shipments left the docks and when they were expected on the various highways. The only group of people Isaiah had not identified were the fences the hijackers turned to once they brought in the hijacked goods.

They agreed that Marty's summation fairly reflected the situation. Marty was also concerned about the number of lookalikes

Hemal was saturating the marketplace with. It meant successful convictions were probably not likely now or in the near future and that the Marshal and Sheriff jurisdictions would need some other corroborating evidence such as fingerprints, spilled blood, or objects the criminals had touched. If these warehouses contained the plunderings of law enforcement equipment, then Ebenales had the ivory coast sewn up. Despite the cooperative efforts of all the law enforcement agencies in the southern California desert and desert suburbs, his drug runners managed to move the goods into northern California, Oregon and Washington. He had to be considered a notable king pin by the underworld to have the airports, highways and military reserves continually watched and to keep products continually in motion.

Dalton poured himself a second cup of coffee. He savored the aroma before he returned his attention back to his supervisor. If Marty sometimes lost his patience in the office, in his home he was good as gold. They would sit all night if they had to beneath the veranda watching the star studded night sky and put the puzzle pieces together. Dalton recalled Margaret Bahe saying she hauled a load into Riverside County to Coachella a few times a month. She could have taken a tin of cocaine under her stepladder to someone in Palm Springs or Indio. Perhaps she did it because her son Vail made fast enemies in the towns where he spilled chemicals or dumped sewage and she felt he required additional protection from the heavyweights.

Isaiah had drowned on a Friday. The last receipt he had for a motel was a week prior at Needles. Two days before that at Inyokern. He had followed the route from Ontario up 395 probably half a dozen times if not more. He had satisfied himself as to each yard of the yardstick.

Dalton sat contemplative with his legs stretched, his feet crossed. There was no wind, nor sign of breeze. Just the night sky and invisible cacti. Marty told him what he thought – that Isaiah would not have given up until he knew the name of the fence and if the name correlated with a name of an officer Internal Affairs had turned over, so much the better. Marty doubted by this time Isaiah would have said much of anything to Hemal. If he didn't have anything on Ebenales he certainly had a litany on hijackers and dealers to nicely outfit a promotion up the career ladder.

Marty agreed with Dalton that at this arm of the investigation they required alot more information. Marty ordered Dalton to collect eight hours of sleep and then take Margo Sam to begin surveillance of Vail Bahe. If possible, Marty said, he wanted Dalton to learn what Bahe was storing inside his barn.

sixteen

"HOW LATE DO YOU WANT TO STAY?" Margo asked. Her two-day stint in Folsom was over and she was ready for some action.

"Until the house is asleep. Then I want to see if Bahe has a rig behind the barn."

She put on a baseball cap backwards. "You think Vail Bahe has cash on hand and a pistol under the horn cover?"

"If he's what I think he is, yes."

"Okey dokey." She sounded tired. She removed a flashlight and tested the batteries.

It was twelve-thirty when they snuck past the house into the barn. They shone their flashlights into a white rig with its hood popped open. They checked for typical masking smells: perfume, disinfectant spray, coffee grounds and gasoline soaked sheets that would be used as wrapping over cocaine bricks. In a closet where saddles would ordinarily be kept were vats of cleaning solvent that smelled like a cancer ward. They pulled open the latch and wooden door leading into a stall and found a freight pallet stacked with non-matching boxes. The two marshals worked quickly taking down a cardboard box and opened it to examine the contents. Inside was spoiled lettuce heads. Beneath these were oblong packages wrapped in plastic. Dalton slit open the plastic on one package. The smell of newspaper wrapping dumped in fumigator fogging solvent was overwhelming and caused Margo to pinch her nose. Right away Dalton realized the fumes could cause a skin or lung reaction. He threw a package to Margo who slipped it into her jacket. Then he redid the carton, packed it onto the freight pallet and adjusted the tight cinch until it held the mismatched boxes together without slipping.

He had hoped to look for other contraband or for the presence of guns but there was no time. The squeaking sound of a door opening caused them to break into a run. He followed her through the stable into the yard. Cloudcover hid a galleon moon. As their feet hit the dirt driveway they heard the clicking sound of a shotgun locking into place. Margo kept moving while Dalton turned around, jumped midair and kicked the assailant in the stomach. The young man dropped to his knees while trying to maintain his grip on the rifle. Dalton kicked the man in the arm forcing him to discharge the rifle. A light came on inside the house. Behind Dalton Margo started up the engine. He swung his leg catching the man in the chin. The jeep rolled forward at a mile an hour. Dalton ran to it skirting the rear to the passenger side. Grabbing the door he threw himself onto the seat as Margo stomped on the accelerator and floored it.

"You handled that very well," she said.

"Unless he recognizes us and brings us up on charges of trespass. If he discovers we have some of his product he'll come looking for us."

They agreed to leave his jeep at Nell's and take her husband's station wagon and return at once.

IN THE EARLY HOURS OF morning while it was still dark Margo and Dalton returned to the main road that fronted the cul-de-sac where the Bahe farm sat. They lowered the backs of their seats until they could lie without being seen. If they waited all day and into the next night, they'd come for nothing but instinct told him that the spoiled produce was meant to mask the presence of the gasoline-soaked wrapping inside which contained the cocaine. Bahe was ready to put the stuff on the road and the only delay Dalton could think of was perhaps a business partner who had yet to cross the Mexican border or who was joining up with him from another direction. Perhaps the partner would bring an eighteen wheeler rig with false walls which hid wrapped cocaine bricks. He thought Bahe's load was possibly meant to become road kill, diversion for another heist or road action occurring in another part of the county. Dalton figured that since Simms' and Du Bois' deaths, shipments into and out of San Bernardino were carefully charted by all law enforcement. Because Ebenales was a key southern California distributor, it stood to reason he had to secure other means of transportation and other people to gradually release the stash onto the road. The supply, wherever it was being stored, would be moved slowly along with other contraband or equipment.

Within several days Ebenales would redirect carriers depending upon the number of marshals and sheriffs on rotation who would be staffing the road. If Ebenales had to forfeit any of his trade in order to grease the wheel to get sheriffs into Tehachapi or Coalinga or a prison further north to protect a particular inmate, he would assign a driver who found it difficult to refuse a free offer of drugs and set him up for a take. On the other hand if he had no need to trade favors he would shotgun the cargo into as many drivers as he was able to line up and drive their vehicles in by night.

The rig that passed them was a tall cab. The container was standard sized freight. The label over the left side read *Azul Produce* in what looked to be apricot lettering over a green arrow. The rig pulled around the corner and parked in front of the Bahe farm. Dalton's watch read five fifteen. He nudged Margo who had fallen asleep and motioned for her to remain quiet and hidden. In the dark they could make out sounds of a forklift rolling what he imagined were freight pallets into the truck. There were more sounds of loading, and of a box tumbling free and of two men laughing. Dalton figured they had a good forty minutes to load the ham and salami he and Margo had seen inside the barn. As soon as the rig pulled in somewhere, he'd radio for backup and a K-9 dog who could do a sniff.

At length sometime after five-fifty in the still grey morning the back door was pulled down. The sound of the engine started up. Dalton hoped neither man saw him as the rig swung onto the street and moved past Margo's station wagon. He crouched up to eye the truck from the rear. It had a drop door similar to the metal doors seen at the entrances to smaller warehouses. A metal fender ran the width of the truck. They waited until it turned onto the main road that would access 95 before they put up their seats. Margo turned on the engine and pulled onto the road after them.

She passed through the intersection where the motel and market stood on one corner and opposite at the kitty corner, the modern olive structure and tinted windows that were the agricultural inspection station at Vidal. The truck bounded ahead traversing the chalky terrain spotted with clumps of wildflowers, sage and thirsty looking plants. In the foreground rose the Whipple Mountains. From Dalton's point of view they were bluish grey scallopped peaks with long downwind sides toward which an ocean of cacti drifted. The sun cropped over the horizon spilling warm light onto the mountains and road.

The road was a two-lane byway that without much variation. Dalton kept his eye on the produce truck while Margo began her morning ritual of taking a handful of vitamins with water as she drove. An occasional automobile sped past them. The air was chilly and windy causing the landscape, once the sun had made its path into the sky, to appear crisp as though every detail could be perfectly captured by the brain and observed. Chalk adobe houses and buildings, some with iron bars over the windows, popped out off the chalky desert surface. The suggestion of a river was everywhere in the vegetation even though the only water source, the Colorado River, lay some twenty miles over arid desert to the east. At one point the truck pulled over to the shoulder of the road and Margo drove past, pulling over where they could still see them but considered it difficult for them to see the station wagon. Bahe had a bag of sand which he poured onto the road for a hundred feet. *Lina's phantom*, Dalton told Margo as the young man retrieved a large jug of motor oil and washed the sand down with it. It was a nasty recourse for any competitor coming this way and a lesson to those who thought they would try to grab Bahe's cargo. Margo pulled back onto the road as the truck sped up and went slowly on purpose until the truck overcame them and the distance.

Margo and Dalton debated about Bahe's destination. Margo thought it was obvious the rig would be stopping at Needles because that's where Ebenales was. Dalton thought that afterwards the rig would put into Laughlin or Daggett. He decided they would travel west on 40 but only because of the manner with which Bahe soaked the road priming it for a major collision. Whereas there were numerous routes to Laughlin especially through Arizona, there was one to Daggett from the southern California state border. They smiled at each other when Bahe's driver put into Ebenales' warehouse in Needles. Margo passed a handful of road detail autobody shops some of whom Dalton recognized on spec as working for Ebenales. Margo drove to a coffee shop across the road and she and Dalton purchased a morning cup of coffee and a newspaper and waited for Bahe to emerge.

The newspaper reported a bust of a hundred pounds of MDMA, or Ecstacy. Almost as good as ice cream, he thought as he sipped his cup and watched trucks enter and depart the yard.

When he saw Bahe some twenty minutes later at the wheel of an unmarked meat truck, Dalton motioned with a head gesture to Margo that it was time to hit the road. She threw him the keys. They ran to the car and pulled back onto the road. He tried not to eye a handful of young men in their fancy cars on the side of the road as he accelerated past them.

In the rear view mirror the tree-lined waters of the Colorado River receded. The trees were quickly replaced by imposing salmon and beige mountains and by cement-cracked, ravine-riddled sand as far as the eye could see. The freeway was a smooth drive into the salt-and-pepper colored mountains that comprised the Sacramento and Piute Mountains. Bahe sped in and out of lanes obviously enjoying whatever responsibility for transportation was afforded him. He ventured off the road toward Essex on The Old National Highway that would wind through Amboy and eventually put in at Ludlow some two miles along the backside of the Marine Corp Training Center.

They speculated as to the transactions Bahe might be planning. Marine Corp officers were not outside the people who might expect drug shipments if indeed Bahe were moving the drugs that he had transferred from his barn onto the Azul carrier. Nor were officers immune to any other contraband such as illegal weapons or generators and hoses in order to put together mobile clandestine labs to manufacture methamphetamine, or dinosaur piss as marshals colloquially called it.

Rain splotches dropped in a sudden flurry onto the windshield and raced upward toward the top of the glass of the station wagon. The highway was one instant a crest and in the next a drop. Clouds overhead had turned dark grey. Long spindly cacti dominated the desert. A gusty wind slammed another few drops of rain against the windshield. Here and there bright yellow wildflowers clumped together like remote alien life huddled on the edge of an unforgiving strip of asphalt. This was a good place to collect rocks for rock art. Thoughts of his stepmother and the artistic collections she catalogued at the museum in Blythe crept into his mind and receded almost as quickly as they cropped up. Dried washes had turned to powdery dirt and turn-offs meant for fire trucks had become inhabited by low lying brush, proof that the desert resurrected itself quickly.

He focussed on Bahe. The truck had slowed as it exited at Chambless. Craggy basalt buttes rose above the soil, some like clinkerlike stone that blended with a sulphuric looking rock. At Amboy as soon as they cleared the post office and marshal and sheriff substation, Bahe stopped pulling under a shady tree beside a small trading post and market. Dalton pulled over too. He turned off the engine and yanked down his and Margo's visors to prevent Bahe from seeing them. All total there were about a dozen vehicles parked in front of the market. Bahe got out and walked a handful of kilometers up the road disappearing around a bend. Dalton removed some stick cheese and mixed nuts and made a lunch for himself and Margo. Depending on the length of time Bahe was gone, he'd check the load to see what Bahe was carrying.

D ALTON AND MARGO WATCHED the road for the more tedious part of an hour to make certain no one was coming for the load before they decided he would survey the inside of the truck and if needed she would take over at the wheel.

He jaunted with his cellphone attached to his belt across the road to the van. He pulled the ladder down to the ground, then attempted to raise the back of the truck. It was a drawbridge door, heavier than he expected and required two hands. As he climbed into the truck and discovered a lost Beringer sniffing machine originally purchased two years ago for the *San Bernardino Police Department*, he heard the sound of squealing tires. He eyed several pallets on a ridged T-floor and followed his gaze to spy out dead space between door and the roof. Then he lunged for the door pulling it shut, leaning against it to hear the sound of a vehicle skidding to a stop, of doors slamming, footsteps approaching. As someone slammed the ladder into place, he held his breath.

"Jesus, didn't you tell him? Lock the friggin door?" A man shouted angrily.

"Relax," came the irritated response from Bahe. "Pederson's never once stiffed me. He got a little careless, so what?" Speech slurred. "We got until seven."

"You got until seven, y'mean. No one's gonna be there to pay out if we get in after dark."

"Sure they will be. Hemal said they're expecting the shipment."

"Yeah, yeah. I promised my old lady we'd supper in is all."

"Why'd you do that? You knew the job with the return would take until about ten. Maybe later."

Ten o'clock meant Inyokern or Little Lake. It meant withered sagebrush, sandpaper lots and boarded up houses, unless they planned to double back to Indio or Coachella.

The first man grudgingly went to check out the key situation. He grunted something to Bahe who said he'd ride along in the cab as soon as he purchased a sandwich and a *Coke*.

"Yeah, yeah."

The truck engine started up and pulled onto the road in the direction of Ludlow. Dalton could hear Margo turn the station wagon around and follow the truck.

Dalton removed a pencil light and switched it on. The floor looked higher than normal and was irregular instead of level. He checked for a false compartment. He couldn't find one in the wall behind the cab. If there was one, he decided, it lay inside the side walls or beneath the crates. Next he tapped the walls for indication of an improvised wall. As he stepped around crates he came upon a laser speed-measuring device capable of computing distances. The police department in San Bernardino had to order a second and a third before one carrier made it to the station without getting hijacked. The presence of two expensive pieces of equipment suggested to Dalton that for some reason Bahe seemed to be pulling out all the stops. Perhaps with two dead agents the entire operation was feeling more confident.

He continued to tap the walls. Every so often the motion made by the driver sent him flying against a stacked pallet. He found fewer vertical ribs along the opposite wall. Number of ribs should match the number of corresponding riveted seams in the other wall, and didn't. A new or creased trim with fresh caulking and misaligned seams was evident where the roof met the sidewall. Utilizing a touch and tap technique he found a cache inside which an estimated forty grand in cash in a roll was stored with a continuous burrow of dark opaque plastic wrapped bricks. Very clever, he thought. He came across a torx-head screwdriver and a bag containing latex gloves. Not what he'd ordinarily expect. The torxhead was utilized to remove a window crank in order to pop off an inside door panel. The gloves were used to prevent skin from becoming contaminated by drugs in the event the driver was stopped by the police.

The truck swung to avoid someone or something on the road forcing Dalton to slide halfway across the floor. The small sniffing machine threatened to snap free of the binds that held it in place and the crates beneath it tugged at their harness. The motion of a passing vehicle caused the driver to swerve again. Dalton slid hard against the back wall. The crates pulled against the rope harness. Dalton could hear the rushing sound of trucks moving quickly in the opposite direction. He scrambled onto his knees only to be flung onto his back, sprawled out. They were climbing a low grade and moving swiftly. He was able to roll but when it came to rising to his knees, the force of gravity landed him on his back. The sound of the car motor hummed in his ear. The truck picked up velocity and sped toward its sought-after destination with its own wind.

He considered the operation. Obviously the work was done piecemeal. Bahe picked up his load in Needles just beyond the ten-mile stamp pad where he had smeared a few gallons of motor oil. Bahe then exchanged his truck. He drove the load into the high desert and deposited it on the outskirts of a military restricted zone where fifty minutes later a man from who-the-hell-knew-where hauled it up the road toward the Staircase. A stolen free-sniff machine that had already been paid for by the *San B. Police Department* and was used to slow down illegal cargo suspected of transporting drugs or explosives was in the hands of criminals. This was a machine that would have been used by police to assist in identifying cocaine; in addition, the laser speed-measuring device was originally meant to help law determine vehicle speed. In the hands of the crook it eliminated sophisticated technology that was otherwise expensive and hard to purchase.

Dalton suspected the route began somewhere around Bridgeport with an airport and came down to Bishop, made a beeline for Manzanar, put into Lone Pine, then into Little Lake or Homestead and an airport there or in the opposite direction into the middle of nowhere for some kind of switcheroo and then careened down the staircase past the PG&E circuit breakers, past Randsburg and the dried up inkwell that was once the gold rush, past Johannesburg with its thatch huts and row of apartheid wooden houses, past bunkers and toxic waste burials, past a railroad that normally carried motor oil to chemical plants or refineries, down a long descent to the crossroads where commerce moved single file, bumper to bumper, a still man-made lineup of elephants, maharjas, mahdis and sultans. All along the route the thieves worked – they dragged Mt. Cascade machines onto snowcovered wagon trails in the deep night and trained them onto unsuspecting cargo needed by another team further down the route. The laser machine could identify proximity of targeted rig; the Cascade machine could silence a radio and erase a laptop computer screen setting the stage to ambush a trucker leaving him stranded and vulnerable.

The truck driver hit the brakes and eased the load off the road. Panicked Dalton threw himself behind the stacked crates. He heard the sound of what he hoped was Margo's station wagon stopping and a door slammed shut. Footsteps strode over the gravel, crunching it, and climbed into the cab with the driver and Bahe.

Dalton wasted no time. He slid the drawbridge door up enough to squeeze beneath it. The lights of the truck stop blinded him for a moment. As he focussed on the afternoon hour he decided it was about two or three. The minute his boot touched the ladder, he drew the door down quietly and dropped soundlessly to the ground. Once he got his bearings, he decided he was at Kramer Junction. He slapped a tail beeper beneath the truck, then broke into a run into the market and found his way to the telephone booth to page Margo.

T HE SUN DROPPED OVER A congested landscape cluttered with water pipes and gas pipes and trucks moving in four directions. Pink color suffused the sky and turned gradually to rose and salmon and light purple. He spotted the meat truck. A black Porsche had pulled up behind them, their headlights trained on the worn asphalt ribbon in front of them. He couldn't see inside the car. The man talking to Bahe was a blond, youthful male, with a shrewd gaze fixed on the road, a cap turned backwards on his head. Eventually they'd put into port and he'd get a better look.

Night sprung from the desert. The soil seemed to extend itself to the sky and the sky, in its awesome vastness, seemed to drop to the road. A rabbit scampered across the road. The quiet gave him a solitude he hadn't felt in a while. It made him feel at peace with the desert and the animals and people living in it. His headlights took in the road and beyond it, sage and tumbleweed and saguro cacti. He went into the adjacent coffee shop, took a booth by the window to watch for Margo, and ordered a glass of milk.

He paid the tab, went outside as close to the truck as he could manage without calling attention to himself and lit a cigarette, and waited, straining to make out the two men's conversation, instead hearing only the whistling wind of trucks on the road. When the wind is the dominant sound it gives you the idea you are hundreds of miles away from civilization. You allow your guard down because as hours wear on, there's no need to tense for those confrontations you would naturally expect in the inner city. If the wind drives you, you are down, even if you are snug inside the patrol vehicle. The wind takes no hostages; either it reaches for you and takes hold or it echoes through you. If you're fortunate it carves in you a tolerance for anxious moments and long endurances.

The chill wrapped itself about him. He stubbed out his cigarette. He watched the road. The hour dragged on. He lit another cigarette, strained again to listen to the two men in the unlabeled meat truck and again heard only the wind. After another ten minutes it occurred to him they were taking a break or waiting for a connection to catch up to them.

In the distance tiny lights signaled their approach. Hope crested and then faded as he realized it was not Margo. The man in the driver's seat opened the door and jumped onto the road with barely a glance at Dalton and walked to his car and got inside it. Dalton's pulse sped as he saw Margo Sam's *Nissan* and ran onto the road to meet it. She pulled onto the shoulder several hundred feet ahead of the two drivers.

He got inside and rolled down his window. A frost had begun to settle on her windshield.

"God, are you alright?" She asked, and handed him a sandwich. "I'm sorry I wasn't right behind you. I ran into a checkpoint for produce at Barstow that took the better part of an hour."

"Thanks, I'm famished. That's them," he said, and unwrapped the pastrami on rye. "What a night. I thought I'd be stuck out here."

"Any idea what they're transporting?"

"Some of the equipment the San B. Police allegedly lost two years ago. A Beringer sniff machine and a laser speed-measuring device."

"About time those surfaced. Any idea where they're headed?"

"None. You have any ideas?"

"Not me either." She let out a sigh. She had changed from blue jeans, to a long sleeved pin-striped blue and black dress and a black jacket. "It's interesting, isn't it? I never expected to come across that stuff."

"Me neither. You ready?" He asked as the truck and Porsche and another smaller truck pulled onto the road. He tapped the window to indicate he wanted to go.

"I can do an all-nighter if need be." She waited a minute before she followed.

"Were you planning to stick a bumper beeper on them?" she asked.

"I did."

"Great going, Dal. I'm impressed." She said, and he beamed thinking it was true, he was a good criminal tracker. "What do you think we've got going here?"

"Cocaine trade. Bought and paid for. Druggies, maybe."

"Could be. You check out Lina's grease spot?"

"It's definitely Bahe. He poured sand and oil onto the road to prevent being followed."

"Do we know how the cocaine cargo will be distributed?"

"Not yet."

"A few days ago I got a list of all spills in the county in the past year. Seems you and Du Bois went out on a few of those calls."

"Those weren't oil. Those were chemical spills, toxic waste stuff. One was allegedly Anthrax although it looked more like grease and glass slivers."

"You think someone's loading chemical tanks for this one drug trade?"

He washed down the last of his sandwich with a shot of coffee from her thermos. He unwrapped a package of chewing gum. He offered her a stick. She declined. He took his time as he unwrapped a stick, rolled it up and stuck it in his mouth.

"The two calls I went on with Isaiah were off 62," he said, chewing slowly. "They had to do with the college storing chemicals on site."

"That's what you were told. But who in hell would endanger an entire campus? It isn't logical."

"I absolutely agree. You got a better idea?"

"Try this. There's a shutdown on expenditures for every department countywide. Anyone who was assigned to anything to do with that situation is transferred or reappointed. But the equipment is still on back order. Sooner or later it will hit the interstate. Word is out in the community that whatever was going on had to wait until the brouhaha —"

"But it did settle. The equipment was reported as lost and new equipment ordered and air shipped."

"And now you discover the lost equipment was sitting in Hemal's warehouse?"

"Right."

"So maybe Simms was actually meant to be Officer Du Bois' backup."

"It looks that way."

"Simms have family? A wife?"

"Your guess Is as good as mine. I assumed he was here on loan and because of it was a loner."

She handed Dalton a pack of *Cool* cigarettes and asked him to light her one, which he did. "Does it strike you as remarkable that the equipment that disappeared during the scandal were the things which if they weren't stolen would've placed the police head and shoulders above the crime elements in the county?"

"My guess is that is what Hemal does primarily."

She said, "What do we really know about Hemal? He has a warehouse in Ontario and a string of businesses across the county. Teak furniture, mahogany. He's the ivory trade from LA to the land of cloud makers."

"You know more about him than I do. He says he's not not hauling cocaine, but Bahe's truck came off his dock and is loaded to the brim with cocaine inside false compartments."

"What did he say when you interviewed him?"

"He was close mouthed. Said almost nothing about Isaiah. He was surprised to hear I thought Isaiah's case had anything to do with big rigs."

"Flying trucks. Flying elephants."

"Watch it," he said, as the direction finder that charted the direction of the bumper beeper beneath Bahe's truck showed the caravan ahead of them had turned onto Highway 27 and from 27 onto a dirt path.

She trailed behind by several car lengths at a slow five miles an hour.

"Get out the map," she instructed. "Where does this lead to?"

He rifled through the glove compartment before he found a map of Kern County. Leaving the compartment down for light, he spread the map over his knees and examined it. "It's a rugged road. It hooks up with 395 and on the other side with 14."

"What's the incline?"

"Forty-five hundred feet. We're straddling alongside the Rand Mountains."

"I hope this isn't an ambush."

"Kill your lights just in case they spotted us."

She did. They waited to adjust their eyes to the dark. There was too much cloudcover to see by moonlight. Dalton rolled down the window, grabbed a flashlight from her glove compartment and craned his neck outside. The flashlight shone onto the dirt path large enough for one vehicle. The truck would have difficulty negotiating the soft soil.

A dark fog was descending. The wet slapped the window. Margo turned on the wipers.

She said, "My guess is the purpose of the IAD investigation was to legitimately relocate people into the desert, to push them as far east as possible."

"That's what they did." He strained to see through the fog and the dark. "Go slow, will you? I don't want an accident if they've stopped." The flashlight reflected against the fog which by now was like a screen. "Why here? What's in the desert besides rats and squirrels?"

"It's chalk out here, nothing else. You think with the oil stuff it's just harassment to clear law off the road?"

"With Bahe? Competition, most likely. He's probably hired to break everyone's neck if they don't stay off 95."

She considered. "You read the IAD report?"

"Cover to cover," he pulled his head inside and rolled up the window. "The county was bouncing through hoops in every direction. Contracts were negotiated and four months into the fiscal year, they were defunded and renegotiated."

"And it told you what?"

"That money from several sources was earmarked for a bigger project than new roads outside Fort Irwin."

"If the IAD meant to farm agents into the desert, Isaiah tracked God knows who to this truck mess. He must have uncovered all their routes —"

"He did. He got the ones on the main drag as well as alternate routes. He and Simms were the lead men. It was their efforts that enabled DEA to pull in a sizeable load."

Her small *Nissan* knocked into a protruding clump of roots and soil. She moved slowly around the plant obstacle. The fog slowly dissipated. Through it, they saw the smaller truck ambling over the shoulder of the road after the unlabeled truck and car. A sliver of moon was enshrouded by a thin luminous circle.

Their direction changed and they headed east. The headlights of the truck shone on Joshua trees and sagebrush and ocotillo and saguro. A recent rain had washed away a rivulet of dirt. White wildflowers clung to the thin soil like irridescent stars. Overhead the night sky stretched infinitely, stars like distant fireflies or scattered pollen. It was impossible to tell where the horizon was but Dalton imagined the dark void that closed them off from a portion of the sky was the rising flank of Red Rock Canyon. The dashboard of Margo's car lit up an aqua neon dial that read ten minutes after nine. Dalton was afraid one of the travellers ahead of them would see the light from Margo's station wagon and stop.

Somewhere up ahead bright lights burned. The caravan slowed to a stop. Engines turned off and headlights were doused. Margo put the gear in reverse and slid silently down the dirt road until she reached the protruding soil where a tree's roots hung, exposed.

"Want to go see what they're up to?" Margo asked.

"I don't want to, but I know if we don't we'll kick ourselves for it tomorrow morning. You up for the look?"

"Absolutely."

They donned head masks and put on dark gloves. They put on dark plastic pants over their garb and slipped into dark jackets and dark shoes. They took digicameras and underwater wristwatches which they slipped inside pockts. They got out and quietly closed the doors, then sprang agilely up the ravine. Periodically Dalton clutched at the soil making his fingers clawlike to get a firm hold to steady himself. He was surprised at Margo's gait. She ambled up the slope, a thin limber figure capable of taking momentary loss of footing by shifting her weight. He imitated her, and together they climbed several hundred feet until they were almost upon the others.

Bahe and two men waded through a creek to unearth solidly wrapped bricks, either cocaine or heroin. They deposited these into cartons which when they were a third full were positioned into the back of the unlabeled truck. Margo removed a small hand-held camera and proceeded to take a handful of snapshots. Dalton cautioned her after five or so minutes and they moved past the trucks to a slightly higher vantage point. The dirt was uneven and unsteady and caused Dalton to fall to his butt a few times and slide down the slope. Margo took the erosion skillfully running lightly as any swift animal might, her ankles and feet providing support. He loped after her to a ledge on which she perched. They took a handful of photos between them of four men diligently retrieving bricks and loading them into cardboard boxes. They waited until the operation was completed. The ultrabrights were doused, doors were slammed shut, engines were started. The caravan proceeded east toward the small mining town of Garlock.

When Bahe and his men had departed Dalton and Margo walked to the small creek. The water was maybe all of four inches deep. The bank was indented below the water's surface with metal compartments big enough to slip cocaine bricks inside. They counted seventy-five slots.

Long after they reached the station wagon and got out of the dark clothing, she unloaded the camera rolls into small tubes as he removed a *Quick Pad* keyboard and began entering a narrative.

They slid inside and she laughed. "I learned ballet as a child. Believe it or not, it prepares your feet for unusual landings."

He nodded. "I believe you."

"You think this is what we came for?"

"Not in and of itself. I'm interested in their destination for the laser."

"My guess is that's for the top of the summit," she said.

"My guess. How do you suppose Ebenales knew when that piece of equipment was scheduled for delivery to the Baseline police department?"

"Someone notified him."

"From the warehouse?"

"Unknown. It could've been by the police."

"When I asked Captain Cobb for a copy of the report, he was concerned I not tell people what was in it. He didn't want his son to learn about it through the rumor mill."

She started up the motor. "He was asked to retire, wasn't he? Maybe he paid Ebenales to take the purchased police equipment off the road. It doesn't make sense, but perhaps he did it because he couldn't control the actions of some of his staff."

"The laser came from a Louisianna manufacturer."

"Perhaps the point of the purchase was to learn who crossed state lines into California for the market an illegal use of the machine might bear."

He agreed with her. Not much about the Internal Affairs findings made sense. He respected Captain Cobb as much as he had respected Du Bois and Simms. The investigation was beginning to have an alchemy of quicksand and the sandbars subject to torrential waterfall were not poorly anchored, plastic wrapped cocaine bricks but deputy badges of unsuspecting sheriffs like the two dead agents.

seventeen

IN WINTER GARLOCK WOULD BE knee deep in snow. For now it was still an Indian summer. Rectangular fields squared off by cut aspen fences lined the only street in town. At one end was an Exxon station and at the other elementary, middle and high schools, a library, a motel and a coffee shop and market. The primary source of livelihood beside the schools was a lumber yard which sat adjacent to the railroad like half a dozen or more small towns, among them Boron, New Cuyama, Lindsay, Badger, Chinese Camp and Truckee.

The caravan had pulled into a motel. Without much trouble, Margo learned the men had signed in as Vail Bahe, Jon Carmichael, Carlos Azul, Kyle Scott and Al Butler. Dalton suggested he and Margo hole up across the street at the market and wait until morning to get the men in plain view.

T HE *IDENTI-KIT* DATABASE produced five clear photo shots that the CLETS system operated by the U.S. Marshal and Sheriff Offices turned up names and addresses for. The two men in the Red Mountain warehouse were locals out of Barstow. The black man was Jason Carey and the hispanic Carlos Azul. They had grown up uneventfully, graduated high school, met one another in a church youth group and had gone off to the Army for two years. For a handful of years one lived by committing burglaries and by growing marijuana, while the other had worked as a mechanic in a legal foreign automobile chop shop.

If Ebenales didn't recruit them, it made sense they were independents, who could tag forfeiture flights in advance. Since they were both a central point for receiving windfall from downed aircraft and were a drop-off point for hijackers, in order for them to remain in the desert close to China Lake meant they had entrepreneurial support. Dalton assumed that because Kyle Scott drove the Porsche he was the businessman. It was even possible he gave instructions to Hemal Ebenales.

It seemed Bahe organized the transporting personnel. Dalton surmised Bahe relied on twelve to twenty people from high desert towns. Frequent rotation kept the likelihood of identification and arrests low. It suggested contraband transporters, and possibly hijackers, lived off a handful of jobs a year or had some other type of regular income. Dalton believed many would prove to have criminal records for illegal possession of a firearm, armed robbery, burglary, theft or possession of a stolen vehicle. At an average age of thirty-five they were unemployable by virtue of their criminal histories and the fact most probably never made it through high school. If a few had families, the others were part of a criminal class who otherwise rotated through the jails and prisons serving sentences up to a year and then back onto the streets to try their hand at automobile detailing or car repair or welding until Bahe or Ebenales could offer them a job.

The assignments had to be relatively straight forward for the warehouse men. They watched for a small aircraft that had been tagged and when it came onto the screen they took a van or jeep and went to meet it after the pilot brought the aircraft onto their runway. The aircraft was subsequently reported as lost. It didn't make sense that this outfit would take high tech equipment and forfeiture off a plane, strip down the craft, repaint it, outfit it with a new flight recorder box and put it back in the air to fly to a private party, well within satellite view of China Lake.

Dalton considered. If this operation had been in place for about a few months, it seemed logical if law enforcement did not know of its existence, then neither did Simms or Du Bois. Last night's action led by Bahe took Carmichael, Azul, Butler and Scott to Garlock. Photos taken at daybreak matched those taken at night at the creek. Carlos Azul's family shipped produce throughout the southern California desert; Jon Carmichael was Bahe's ride up the mountain, and Butler was presumably Nick Castille's − owner of Blue Water Casino − charge who couldn't straighten out no matter what help he was given.

The noose was tightening around the investigation. If he could discover who the trucker was who had been torched on 395 he'd be another step closer. He placed a telephone call to the Department of Transportation and learned the burned man was a longtime trucker by the name of Charles Nestor. Nestor had flown planes after serving in the Army in the Korean War. He had allegedly been handling equipment similar to police forfeiture to lure Ebenales out of the woodwork to determine how his operations worked. He could have determined that Bahe was sidebar action, of no consequence to IAD or to the Marshal Office; or Bahe could be a beacon for the roadrunners.

The man at the DOT told Dalton they were closing in on potential witnesses. A man had been seen northeast of Lone Pine hauling material waste to a dumpsite near Mt. Cerro Gordo when

Nestor and his load were torched.

DALTON DROVE OUT TOWARD VIDAL and the Bahe home. Night fell with the italicized style mark of a minor notation. He felt sorry for any law enforcement officer who had to take on county departments in order to demand an accountable criminal justice system. What did it mean for rookies to learn after two years on beat patrol that some of their their salary benefits might be paid for by drug forfeiture? What did it mean for lieutenants and captains to question the work of top-notch detectives who took in a few thousand pounds of cocaine every year and with it, a quarter of a million in bills and were forced by death threats or a chain of harassment to look the other way? Had any of the San B. boys taken twenty percent off the top before turning the remainder over to the boys in DC?

He pulled alongside the Bahe farm and shut off his engine. The elder Bahe was pumping water at the well. Half a dozen chicken and geese fluttered about in the dim light. Through the open barn door Dalton could make out stacked bales of hay. He returned his gaze to Barry Bahe. Disappointment must have weathered him because he looked resigned, as though the separation from his wife and the responsibility for raising a son had all but taken every source of energy. He fed the animals, then trucked the water inside the house. The lights came on one at a time.

Dalton tore open a protein bar and chewed it thoughtfully. He'd wait a while to see if the kid showed up. If he didn't, he'd talk to Bahe alone. Colors of the sky changed from blue to mauve to dark purple.

Dalton lit a rare cigarette. He was in a dirty business with an abundance of dirty secrets. Desert children were growing up to be desert hoodlums. It used to be they grew up to be farmers or mechanics or railroad buffs or Top Gun pilots or firemen enthusiasts.

Dalton got out of the jeep. He trudged up the grass to the house and knocked on the door.

The man who opened it was broad shouldered, heavy in the face, hunkered down with beers or a sedentry life. "You a cop?"

"U.S. Deputy Marshal Keys." He produced his badge and Bahe squinted at it. "Any idea where your son Vail is?"

"Gone to see his mother, I reckon. Spends half his time there. At least that's what he tells me."

"Mind if I come in?"

"Sure. House is a bit messy. It hasn't seen a woman's touch in years."

Dalton followed the older man inside the ranch home. The living room although cluttered had been built with the southwestern adobe in mind. Log pole beams ran across the ceiling. Lace curtains hung between heavy drapes. A worn leather sofa faced two dark green upholstered chairs with the bottoms falling through. A stone fireplace faced a wall on the other side of which was the kitchen.

They sat at a thick round oak table in the center of the kitchen. A refrigerator and icebox stood on one side of the grey tiled counter and sink. On the other side were three open, floor to ceiling shelves packed with every imaginable type of jar and box. Two bedrooms with a bathroom between them let from the kitchen.

"Nice place you got here," Dalton remarked, thinking the house looked bigger from the street.

"It's alright. There's another living room and bedroom with a separate entrance on the other side of the house but it hasn't been used since Margaret moved out."

"I was wondering about that. Your place looks fairly large."

"Yeah, everyone remarks. Originally I bought this place for us and my dad, but then my dad passed on. Margaret and I were fighting all the time in those days —"

"How long ago was that?" Dalton interrupted, and removed his small spiralbound notepad from his breast pocket.

"1994."

"And your wife moved out when?"

"Well, I was saying we were fighting constantly. She moved out and stayed there and that was okay until she came at me with a gun. I told her to get out and get out she did. She took off and Vail went with her until he came back because he couldn't stand all her bickering."

"The place has been empty since?"

"I can show it to you if you like."

"Sure."

Bahe took Dalton through the bedroom on the right and with a key hanging on a chain opened a double door. The inside door opened onto a musty room inside which the table and bed were covered with sheets. Dalton looked inside the living room and small kitchenette. The furniture – a sofa, round lamptable, kitchen table with four chairs – also were covered with sheets. The air was damp and cool.

"No pictures," Dalton said, as they returned to the inhabited side of the house.

"I boxed them up. I couldn't stand to have anything that would remind me of her."

"How come you don't rent it out?"

"Don't want the headache, I s'pose."

"Do you mind me asking why your exwife pulled a gun on you?"

"I don't mind." He stared at his large hands. "She wanted to work. I didn't want her to."

"She's a truck driver."

He conceded with a nod. "She used to carry crates to Coachella a few times a month."

"And you didn't want her to augment your pay? How much were you earning?"

"It wasn't the pay. I made enough for both of us. I wanted her to stay home to look after Vail. I was worried about him."

"What concerned you?"

"He fell into a bad crowd when he was around fourteen. He —" His voice trailed off.

"Did you notice it at the time?"

He shook his head. All the inevitable sadness of having failed his family surfaced. "I lived for them, you know. He was a wanted child. But Margaret wasn't cut out for the child rearing. She wanted to be out on the road, talking to other truckers, playing country music all day long."

"She couldn't take being cooped up."

"No. Getting Vail to six years old was about all she could do." He looked at Dalton. "I had to earn a living and trucking was all I knew. The money was good. My employer let me pull a double whenever I wanted. The farm is paid for, believe it or not.

"You want to know what happened to Vail? I'm from a large family myself. My father had a farm and my grandfather had one too. All five generations from somewhere along the Colorado. We raised squash, corn, fruit and sold it at a roadside stand until the motels opened up. Then we were the first ones they came to. Could we triple the crop? They asked me. Grow it on rotation? Mind you, this is before agribusiness. This is back in the Fifties when the country was looking at how to get back to being farms after the war.

"When I was Vail's age I wanted to get as far away from my family as possible. The farm life was hard. I could see that straightaway. It's just you attend a farm schoolhouse and you meet other children who live differently. I guess I wanted to be on my own at an early age."

"Where'd you go?"

"Nowhere. My grandfather wouldn't allow it. But I always remembered if I ever had a child and he wanted to cut out to be on his own, then I would let him go to it."

"At fourteen?"

Bahe considered, his tongue against his cheek. "It's young, I won't argue you. It wouldn't have been a problem if Margaret stayed home. Vail couldn't have gotten so far away. In his mind is what I mean."

"How did he get away?"

"It's anyone's guess. Sergeant MacIntyre would call me to come get him. Cops had found him riding the freight trains."

Sergeant MacIntyre who had been sent into retirement by IAD. Maybe there had been a bad cop in the bunch. "How often did the sergeant come out?"

"Whenever Vail was in trouble. One thing added up after the next. He hotwired a car, then he broke into some man's house and broke into his safe, then he was picked up during a drug raid in the country. After Margaret took off, I cut my hours down but it wasn't enough for me to stay at home."

"You must've married late in life."

"I did. I was forty-one. Margaret was thirty."

"Were you forty-one when you took over your father's farm?"

"I was. Someone had to stay to help out."

"Was this it?"

"No, we were out near 178. We had a good operation until agribusiness bought us out."

"Then you bought the farm here?"

"Not straightaway. I travelled for two and when I returned the place wasn't the same anymore. I took a test and went to work as a truck driver. That's how I met Margaret."

"You know who your son works for?"

"He's his own person. Nothing I can do about that," Bahe answered defensively. "I'm happy he comes home at all."

"Is it Hemal Ebenales?"

"Sometimes. The man calls him up to bring in a few loads. He's been working for him since he was about fifteen."

"Do you know the name Scott?"

"Never heard of him."

"What about Azul?"

"Yeah, five brothers. All went into shipping lettuce clear up to Mammoth."

"And Carmichael or Butler?"

"Yeah, Carmichael. I drove Vail once to his place. It's down at Vidal toward the river. Crazy idiot, if you ask me."

"How so?"

"He has cock fights down there twice a year. My opinion that sort of thing makes you mean."

They sat silently, both ill at ease with whatever each thought was suggested by that information. For Dalton, the fact that it was Sergeant MacIntyre who introduced Vail Bahe as a teen to Ebenales suggested the San Bernardino Police Department was not above trafficking in the corruption of teens.

"Can I offer you coffee?" Bahe asked, after a moment.

"No, thanks. Has Mr. Ebenales ever been here?"

Bahe scoffed. "I told Vail in no uncertain terms he is not to bring that man to this house."

"Has Vail ever been to Mr. Ebenales' home?"

"I wouldn't know."

"Do you want to know what your son has done?"

"In the way of crimes? No."

"I may have to arrest him in the next few weeks. For hijacking electronic equipment."

"I often wondered where he got all that stuff from."

"What stuff?"

"Looks like transistors, little black boxes, monitors." Bahe got up, kicked open the door to his son's bedroom and showed Dalton to a closet inside which was stacked Radio Shack surveillance equipment.

"This the only time he's stored this stuff here?"

"Naw. He has a handful of men who come by for it. Does this all year round."

The older man left the room and Dalton followed. In the

kitchen he took a business card out of a drawer beneath the counter and presented it to Dalton.

"Kyle Scott," Dalton read. "Who is he?"

Bahe shrugged. His mood was less disgust than it was sadness. "He wants to buy my property. He says it's to put a road through here to the river. He's offered me a handsome price."

"What've you told him?"

"I wouldn't sell no matter what the price."

"Did he threaten you?"

"He said he would ask until I said yes."

"Who's he with?"

"I don't know."

"You think Vail knows him?"

"I would never forgive him if he does."

"Why?"

"I think this is land they want to put under water."

"Is that what Mr. Scott told you?"

"No, he said the county wants to put in a road."

A road to the river, Dalton reflected as he drove home. After years of resisting development, it seemed the county was finally giving in. It meant there wasn't enough water to meet the needs of tract homes stacked back to back from Vidal to Crossroads.

In his mind's eye he could see Isaiah tracking truck loads of stolen goods from Independence to Needles and Vidal. He was bothered by MacIntyre's presence in this young man's life. It was possible Vail had been sent to Ebenales by the powerful then-police Chief Cobb to handle certain indiscretions the police could not afford to enter into its ledgers. Disappearing cocaine evidence and equipment could be reported as embarassing losses and cash proceeds as campaign or church contributions. Certainly Isaiah must have wondered what decisions led the county to park him in a remote spot in the desert where heaven met hell for a few brief hours a month as automobiles slugged their way through sand and heat to make drug deliveries from Coachella to Ontario. As the wheeler dealers pumped cocaine over county lines, the county extended its legal arm ever further East. A low cost housing development answered a lot of problems if the basics could be easily hammered out. Narcotics could be brought in on time schedules, first to the penal facilities and then to the suburbs to industrial warehouses for night shift distribution and easy heists could put flailing companies in the red on the books until the fences recycled the goods back to the companies for the price of a finder fee. It was one pessimistic attitude to have and Dalton did not want to believe it. He wanted to hang onto Cobb's goodness and onto the hope that only one cop was dirty and he had been fired and an entire restructuring had been orchestrated after he left.

eighteen

DALTON SAT AT HIS DESK WITH a legal sized notepad and reviewed what he had written. He had placed beside each bullet a summation of rulings made by the county Board of Supervisors. Over a ten year period the supervisors voted to rescind previous rulings and to put into place committees to study demographics and small businesses. Of the small businesses in the Inland Empire fifteen were transportation. Trucks hauled fiber optics to assembly plants for telecommunications panels; they sped to Adelanto to FedEx computer parts to installation plants; they winded down the narrow to bring digital cameras to direct mail marketing shops, and delivered a host of other equipment to stores up and down Baseline and to outlying areas. These businesses were funded in part by Small Business Association loans in alliance with a handful of banks whose stocks on Wall Street rose or plummetted depending upon insider trading and the international value of the dollar or lira. On the Internets and America On Lines of the roadways these industries were succumbing to road seizures by armed bandits. Twice a month, they climbed onto the stepladders of rigs, yanked open the doors and grabbed the trucker by the collar and flung him onto the asphalt. Sometimes they flushed him out with hoses from chemical tanks, other times they wrapped the coil around his arm and cut off the blood supply to his hand. Without two hands he was permanently off the road. After several months drivers grew to expect the violence at the sight of a scarlet tall cab appearing in the left hand rear mirror and they pulled over and took an hour-long coffee break behind a tree on a half inch bedroll pad of foam.

The loans were funded by special state and county monies to contract commercial carriers in San Bernardino, through Victorville and Oro Grande, dropping a delivery in Inyokern and up the Staircase through Lone Pine and Big Pine and to a host of small towns, among them Lee Vining, Conway, Walker and Picketts. Each carrier fleet was given a vehicle repairman who rode in an automobile or pickup and stopped to crank up the hood and perform minor repairs. In addition drivers could pull into a handful of motels to bed down for the night at no cost to the driver nor to the employer. Each rig was outfitted with a radio and laptop that hooked the driver into a central dispatch to announce, much the same as any taxi, towns he or she was passing through as well as times of departure or arrival of small aircraft the driver had to connect with.

Except for the elder Bahe's statement that Sergeant MacIntyre had baled the younger Bahe out on numerous occasions, there was no overt link to the county plan and to the highway henchmen who were thought to bilk thousands of dollars from unsuspecting carriers. When at last the county was forced as a result of the Internal Affairs investigation into the Police Department and Highway Patrol to pull out from offering backup and marshals and state bureau investigators were brought in, it became apparent that the network that created twenty-five hundred jobs had also given the illegal black market a boost unequal to contraband markets elsewhere in southern California counties.

Dalton appreciated the intentions of the County Board of Supervisors to draw a thousand new residents into the newer neighborhoods of Highland and Del Rosa. For the first eight years the expansion plan seemed perfect. Then with a crash the Becker case took every newspaper across the forehead. On the heels of a gradually souring trial corruption within the police force made for the fatal scalp job. With no correlation to raised taxes the police purchased fifty acres of land worth a million dollars and built a new department, jail and morgue. They rotated men like Simms in for four months on a per diem basis, then sent them home to Chicago, New York and Miami.

It seemed young men like Vail Bahe, Carlos Azul, Jon Carmichael, Al Butler and Jason Carey had found a permanent field of interest. Hijacking rigs, fencing stolen equipment or selling it back to the employer or in some instances returning it unannounced to the shipper after several months was routine. Bahe was tied in person to pulling over the rigs. Who was at the back emptying out the contents or unhitching the load was anyone's guess. But Dalton had partial IDs of four people he thought were Jon Carmichael, Al Butler, Dani Gardino and Liam aka Kelly MacDougal. If sentencing judges required hard photographic evidence, the evidence was slow in coming if it came at all. It appeared that Isaiah was a lone dog trying to film these episodes. Because he was unable to capture them adequately he brought in more sophisticated equipment and as he did, the incidents seemed to dry up. In reality Ebenales or some other individual, or both together, redirected the death rides until these men were cleared off the road.

Dalton eyed the evidence he had accumulated. It consisted of closeups of a team of four men and one woman hijacking a truck at night under less than desirable circumstances. He had their names, he also had addresses, criminal history sheets and whatever else on the CLETS database was available. He had a warehouse of items including infrared aerial equipment that could stall an airplane engine of an airplane flying in the vicinity. Also he had a clear link with photographs of drug transporting by Bahe in one carrier normally used for produce transportation. He could place Isaiah at the scene with an unidentified female and place Simms on what he suspected was the same route for bringing in new untagged small trucks destined for Red Mountain to be used in transporting either stolen equipment or drugs. None of this was enough to put behind bars an entire gang for life. The problem was that after a year or two these men recycled back into the communities where they lived and committed the illegal acts. He knew Lt. Walker would want more. On the murders they needed a direct tie with hard evidence – the suspect's fingerprints on the stolen equipment, a dead-on face shot during the commission of a crime, hair and fiber belonging to the suspect at a crime scene. Anything.

And finally Walker would want solid investigative narratives for every hijacker or suspected associate. Dalton clasped his hands behind his head and surrendered himself to the exhilaration of knowing he was about to learn something no single hijacker knew about the others on the team or about the man paying out the payroll.

H E SAT IN FRONT OF KYLE Scott's riverfront Cross roads home. It rested in lavish greenery at the water's edge behind a brick wall and was made of wood with wall-length glass window panels, sky lights and a cement walkway bordered on two sides by hedges. A copper door and copper roof, both turned blue with age, were the only acoutrements that said the man had money to burn. Dalton asked himself how he would link the last county administration with the names he had turned up. Isaiah had kept no obvious information on his computer nor in notepads in his home. If there was a connection today it was well hidden. He sipped coffee from a styrofoam cup and considered Scott's connection. Dalton guessed he was the man who paid off the fence for the hijacks.

When the man emerged from his garage driving an El Dorado, Dalton recognized him instantly. Although older, tufts of white at the corners of his forehead, he was a man who some twenty-odd years ago had approached his father to sell his land. By now, if he had served time, he probably had a rap sheet of aliases. Even without that orange and yellow necktie with the road running from the knot to the nap, Dalton remembered him well. Dark hair cut scalp short, a narrow forehead, aquiline nose, small mouth, darkish complexion, probably Italian, threads made of polished tweed, black alligator shoes, white gold cufflinks sparkling at his thin wrists. Dalton remembered a shiny black Datsun, the man's confident step, his speech about being neither with a bank nor with a title company. He represented the road. It was probably something he told unsuspecting new home owners whose properties along the Colorado he was seeking to get his hands on.

Scott turned onto the road. Unobserving of Dalton he swept past Dalton's vehicle. Dalton pulled onto the road after him. The ride to the boathouse was a short one, led through Needles to 95, then out onto a white sand landing that rested upon the water. Scott parked in a small lot. The asphalt had newly painted white lines on it. From a distance they were a string of dashes, punctuation marks on shiny black asphalt meant to be a visible landmark for an incoming airplane. Dalton gave the man five minutes before he turned off his engine and followed him to the small wooden pier. Scott was gassing up; his boat was a sleek motorboat made of light wood with twin jets and aptly named, *Chase*. Dalton paid the market fifty dollars for use of a steel outboard. He ran down the pier, stepped rather clumsily into one of two outboards, donned a lifejacket and cap and pulled the cord to start the engine.

The water was salty green with six inch waves. He tracked

Scott downstream making sure to keep a good distance. The air was breezy, a humid seventy-five degrees. Scott rounded an inlet and disappeared from sight. After five minutes Dalton took his boat to shore, turned off the engine and wading over rocks camped it securely in the beach. The water was cool but not cold. He walked across the sand to an inlet from which he observed Scott shed his clothes to reveal a wetsuit. The man lowered a mask and snorkle over his face and put on flippers, then jumped off his boat into the water backwards. Dalton crouched uncomfortably waiting to see what Scott would do next. He waited in the hot sun at least twenty minutes. He smoked a cigarette and considered why this particular team of criminals utilized creekbeds and riverbeds. Obviously it was to stash waterproofed cocaine and heroin bricks. It was a chancey thing to do though. If they were seen, competition could move in and swiftly steal the stash.

At length Scott surfaced. He wrapped heavy cord to the hooks at the side of the boat. The cord was in turn tied to some kind of haul beneath the water's surface. Scott climbed up a small ladder, removed his flippers and mask and started up the motor and backed the boat slowly out of the inlet. Dalton scrambled down the hill to return to his boat. He dropped a fishing line over the side and sat, cigarette in mouth, cap worn backward. He eyed Scott who raised a hand in salute and then returned to his task. When the *Chase* had disappeared from sight, Dalton marked the area with a small yellow buoy. From the river a hundred or so meters away the color would be invisible. Later, in the evening or after nightfall, he would return to scout the underwater area to determine what provisions Scott had made. He reeled in his line. He negotiated the rocks with one of the oars until the boat slipped into deep water. Then he started up the engine and followed the other man upstream.

The wind had died down. He passed a houseboat with sunbathers on the roof. He steered around a log floating downwind. The air temperature was pushing a sweltering eighty or eighty-five. Sweat bathed his face and neck in perspration. He chewed a piece of beef jerky and sipped coolade to replenish the salt in his body.

As he entered the water closeby his home, Scott killed his motor. His boat drifted, rocking in the wake of another passing motor-boat. Dalton rode across the river to the bank and holed up on the sand with a pair of binoculars. Through them he watched Scott don his water gear again, slip again into the water, untie the cords and pull them and the load they pushed up against a brick wall that faced the rear of his home. When he reached the wall he pulled on some kind of lever. A shelf much like a repository of a book deposit safe for a library lowered. He parked himself on a stair or stone platform and gathered an opague plastic bag toward himself. One by one he inserted brown plastic wrapped bricks onto the shelf. When he had about twenty bricks on the shelf he raised the lever. The shelf appeared to release the bricks into a cache on the other side of the wall. He then pulled the lever toward himself again until the shelf lowered and placed another twenty plastic wrapped bricks on the shelf. Dalton observed Scott perform the task a third time. He counted sixty bricks when Scott completed the task.

Scott moored his boat to a hook on the wall at three feet above the water. He then climbed out of the water passing through a gate. Dalton waited another ten minutes to see whether he would return to his boat once he took the bricks into the house. He de-bated the worthiness and risk of calling for backup now to make an arrest. He still didn't have all the information he felt he should obtain. He didn't know who Scott's buyers were. He didn't know the size of the underwater cache nor how many such repositories there were along the Colorado. That could mean months of sur-veillance. But he was itchy to do something to dent the man's trade.

He got inside the boat, started the motor and rode to where Scott had moored his boat. He eyed the wood and glass home wondering whether it was likely Scott could see him there at all. Dalton thought Scott would keep the bricks in his basement if he had one until he was ready to make a sale. He stepped from his boat onto the *Chase*. He loosened the rope from the hook. Next he pulled the throttle to allow water to flood the valves. Within twenty minutes this would cause the boat to flood and sink. He stepped into the outboard clumsily, almost falling as another motorboat passed at high speed and sent a churning wake in his direction.

When he departed the scene and cruised downstream to the pier and market, he reconsidered the scope of the operation. In all probability it was since Isaiah's death that Scott relocated his operation from Needles to his home. Once the heat was off Dalton thought Scott would return to *Blue Water* or to some other resort closer to the southern U.S. or the Mexico connection.

D ALTON TOOK REFUGE IN a cafe at Earp overlooking the bluish green river. Nursing a glass of iced coffee, he contemplated the actions he thought Ebenales would have taken once he realized his card key was missing. A chain of alarms would have been triggered. Ebenales would have contacted Bahe telling him there was a problem with the road. Who he would've conveyed the problem to was most likely Scott. Next Ebenales would have told Bahe to shadow Isaiah as Isaiah charted his way from Ontario through San Bernardino cities following the team of hijackers. The fact that he was in possession of the plastic card key may have been enough to convince Hemal Ebenales he was left with a very serious threat to his enterprise. But the real clincher would have been a look-see at the warehouse at Red Mountain; that would have told Hemal the FBI knew he stored forfeited equipment belonging to law enforcement. It would also have told him the federal boys knew he was putting lookalikes to their agents on the road to confuse truckers and local police. This knowledge would've told Hemal his fishing days were over. And Hemal would have flexed his muscle to permanently remove Isaiah from the road.

What made the infrared aerial system that Dalton had seen at the warehouse important was that the system was used to spot waterproof encased packages of cocaine placed along the shoreline. The infrared aerial could spot images in the water and provide depth perception. Since anyone and anything crossing the border was heavily searched by border patrol in and out of the water, it was possible divers brought the contraband up the river. If Isaiah had scouted the river and seen the divers at night or if he told Simms and together they closed in on the routes the team used to bring drugs in from Mexico —

Pretty big ifs, Dalton told himself as he paid the tab and leisurely walked to the parking lot to his jeep. But it was the only real answer he could see as to how Isaiah came to have a fair amount of confidence wading into the Colorado.

He started up the engine and pulled onto the road. A wind blew a crumpled carton into sagebrush. The road cut a weathered line through two mantels of sloping desert. He could feel a breeze move off the water and at points could see the placid waters crinkle like tin shining in the sun. He moved slowly. As he passed the sign that said he was crossing over the invisible line between Arizona and California, he considered the problem again. The divers probably made a beeline with cocaine packages for the California beaches. Arizona contained the Colorado River Indian Reservation as well as the Chemehuevi Valley and Fort Mojave. Because of jurisdiction the FBI patrolled the Arizona side. The California side was shared by marshals, sheriffs and highway patrol. Also Highway 95 on the Arizona side was a straight shot to Laughlin and Las Vegas. Although less than five towns rested on the California side they were desert shanty towns with no culture, no family environments nor sidewalk pavements to recommend them, merely a string of warehouses and plenty of storage.

Nothing from nothing makes nothing, you gotta have something if you want to be with me, the song bleated from the radio. Dalton tapped his hands on the steering wheel as he shot down the highway into the beige wilderness. Isaiah had successfully defined the entire scheme from A to Z. Once the divers brought the packages onto dry land, they bolted the stuff inside vans and cars and drove to the various motel sites for distribution. Perhaps Isaiah or Simms had intended to search the river banks along the San Bernardino for the containers of cocaine and heroin and someone who knew them well enough to identify them clobbered Simms and then intercepted Isaiah and sent him unprepared into the cold Colorado River.

nineteen

BY MOONLIGHT DALTON SET UP the underwater cam-
recorder. Video cassette inserted, he wedged the recorder into
the sand until its viewer was level with the water packing the sand
around it to ensure it couldn't be seen. The truth struck him as
ridiculously obvious. Isaiah invited a person he knew and trusted
onto his boat and the person knocked him into the river where
unknown to Isaiah one or more divers was preparing to transport
or to hide contraband. The diver would have pinned Isaiah to a log
or worse, lasooed him and held him captive until he died.

Dalton planned to return nightly after dark, remove the cassette and insert a new one. Eventually he hoped to catch one or
more of the team of divers on tape.

Moonlight caught the desert in a spellbound trance. Sagebrush
sprung up in one dimensional blocks. Even the road seemed without proportion – a mere strip of asphalt in his headlights unfurling
in a wake of absolute darkness. The double yellow line matched

the speed of his jeep. Out here anything could happen, and did. Fortunes were spent and lost. Men came to tamp out what remained of their uncertain lives and women followed them or abandoned them or betrayed them. Flash floods carved ravines into the plateaus and but for four inches a year that was absorbed into the ground, rain evaporated mid air in humid striations. If squash or beans or corn survived, the take was meagre, nearly withered by the time harvest arrived. So it went season after unyielding season. The distant mountains cast an uninterested eye to the road and the road coughed up little more than subsistence living for most of the families who would venture this far.

You could live and love or love and live, however you measured the songs you sang. One minute you were stumbling to a confession, the next minute confessions galore seized you in a pathetic clutch at what might be the only tangible, visible act you would recognize yourself making. Dalton imagined what Isaiah's last minutes held for him as he struggled to free himself of an actual or invisible net as surely as though he were Simms staggering from a gunshot toward dying under the merciless draw of a cowboy's gun. *I got you mother-fuckers, I got you – you goddamn crap of a whore's behind* singing into the night as the river pummeled angrily to the shore. *Ah want you to know the fucking misery you caused me, the trouble ah went to, hiding and dancing in the fucking wind, my piss scared frozen because of you!* And Isaiah thinking the moment before he invited the man or woman on board that he had the odds beat. As any deputy knew about a hard man toughened by years of criminality anger makes a man dance. This man would do his dancing in a boat or in the water or beside a rig he'd taken, laughing into the night.

The moon disappeared behind cloudcover. As he pulled into his carport and turned off the engine, the moon reappeared again causing mottled shadows to pass instanteously over the landscape. How much stress did Isaiah have stacked against him before he became incapable of comprehending the seriousness of any act?

The question stared at Dalton as though from some abysmal wind high up above the soil. Isaiah was seriously depressed long before he chased a man in a boat named *Chase*. Long before he rented the boat or swam out to meet the man whose boat he boarded. The algae found in his lung was the same algae that grew in the river. To go down for the last time swallowing water and algae and diatoms and grains of sand and whatever other minute particles made up the watershed only told Dalton that the river beat him. This all-powerful snake of a river that gave life took life and the man or woman who pushed him into it and the one who held him down had to have something that branded them for what they were. Isaiah had made some serious errors. Stealing the card key, tracking the motel route, bringing Bahe's mother on part of an investigation, failing to arrange backup - Hemal's role was to wear Isaiah down to the point it was obvious he was making mistakes.

DALTON PARKED IN FRONT OF Chief Cobb's beautiful Victorian two story home. Further up the mountain water slammed through large girded steel pipes to feed an entire county. He took the stairs two at a time.

The front door stood ajar. Dalton pushed it open and paused on the threshhold listening for voices. After a few minutes he entered tentatively. The home was quiet as if the help had been dismissed for the weekend. He wandered down maple hardwood floors and paused in front of the library, then took himself to the next door which housed a computer room, and past it at the end a room encased in windows with plants of all types and lengths situated on wooden bookshelves and crates and antique furniture. He knew as he walked the entire length to the foyer that Chief Cobb was not inside his home. He was away for the week or in a pub somewhere drinking up his retirement or out on the town with a woman.

Dalton's first instinct was to call 911 but he disregarded his impulse and instead climbed the carpeted stairs to the second story. There were two bedrooms, one for a guest which the chief had presumably cluttered recently with picture albums and left them splayed over the floor and quilted bed. He had half a mind to open a window to let the musty smell. He paused inside the room beneath a series of framed black and white photographs of Cobb and his wife, his son, his men on Vice squad, several generations of Homicide, one which had been separated out for some reason of Isaiah photographed with Sergeant MacIntyre and a side view of Kyle Scott – before he understood the meaning of the sight. Isaiah had been chosen by MacIntyre and pointed out to Scott. He backed into the hall making mental snapshots of the scene. A box of cigars sat on a lamptable beside an empty coffee mug. Bifocals showed beneath a folded police journal on the opposite lamptable. A silver money clip with twenty dollar bills rested against a white opaque lamp.

He stopped for a look-see in the guest bedroom at the photographs, most of them posed shots of Cobb's family and son and half a dozen more homicide detectives.

Cobb was a cop's cop. He was the man who hired on the first African American cop in the Department. If he was pictured with MacIntyre and Scott, if he knew what they were up to, he knew these things because men had had their lives threatened on the Becker case and he did what he had to to hide them from the evil that was wending its way toward them. He lied for his men and they lied for him. Isaiah took a tumble with evidence lost in the evidence locker. He did it for his boss, the only authority he respected or trusted, and he must have done it without knowing who in the Department was dirty, taking the eventual tumble with the rest of them.

"You are trespassin', my friend," a voice said from behind in a southern accent.

Dalton wheeled around, terror in his chest.

Eustace Dimes was a slightly overweight white man with a balding hairline and an ever lower hanging gut. Those who knew him didn't perceive of the menace his voice manifested for those who didn't know him well. His gaze dropped to the bound copy of the IAD report.

"You come lookin' to argue testimonials, Dal?"

"The front door was open."

"I left it open when I went for a stroll in the garden, deah boy."

"Do you know anything about Officer Du Bois' death?"

"Not a thing, Dal. What causes you to ask? Am I mentioned in that manuscript therah?"

"No, you aren't." He handed him the report. "Will Chief Cobb be home soon?"

Eustace jammed the report under his arm. He shook his head, saying, "We nevah tell after we bury our ghosts. You should know that."

"Who was the ghost?"

Eustace Dimes tucked in his double chin and peered at him through watery blue eyes. "Why that was our Sergeant Bowman. He pulled that arrow as far back as the bow had stretch in it and shot for the man's balls and got him."

"Who did he get?"

In the hallway below the door whined as it opened. "Dimes?" came Chief Cobb's query. He stepped into the gallery, looked up and seeing them, gave a nod and said, "Dimes is my daughter-in-law's father."

They went down to meet him. Chief Cobb wore a black shawl across his shoulders over a sweater. Cotton trousers made him seem more dapper than he had looked in his career.

"Thank you, Sir," Dalton said. "It was an interesting report."

"Care to come in for a sherry?"

"I think I should be running along."

"You do, do you?" Bob Cobb looked at him and then at his

long time friend and relation. "Whah'd you tell the marshall, Eustace?"

The other man chuckled. "I told him who shot Bobby Kennedy."

Their laughter followed Dalton into the night. Maybe in addition to sharing a few grandchildren, they also played golf or attended a bridge game once a month at the Lion's Club or Rotary Club. Dalton hadn't liked either of them but he respected them for holding down the fort.

twenty

H E HAD BEGUN TO add up the pieces. The beach crime scene of a week and a half ago still felt a little too fresh. Snapshots fired off like synapses gone wild in the head of a man with stroke. The imaginery sound of patrol cars whining off the road across the asphalt onto the sand, their red lights flashing, one snapshot. Officers rushing up the stairs, squeezing through the narrow frame of the mobile command unit, another shot. Lined up one after the next the images were like an endless tablet of mirrors each capturing a redundancy – the table of maps, boats crowding onto the water, the navy divers, the syringes in his neck, chest, arm, leg - all to stimulate a pulse – and the eventual rush of crime scene photographers.

"How many teeth do you suppose Dimes had in Ebenales's dick?" The question resounded down that long corridor of redundant images.

"The Man'll nickel and dime you until the cows come home,"

Isaiah had told Dalton after the military laid down its own corridor of Anthrax after someone had burned a truck on the road just outside Twenty-nine Palms.

"Well he should," was Dalton's retort.

"You forget who you're talking about. This is Indio making its way a few markers up the highway."

"It's not the mob, trust me."

"Oh I trust you, Dal. Indeed I do."

Dalton had looked bewildered at him. He remembered thinking, did Chief Cobb know who was setting trucks on fire near the non-towered airports? Did Sergeant Hague know?

"Give up? It's us," and Isaiah howled with laughter, hands holding his sides. When he quieted down, he said soberly, "It's a black man. Or a white man. Two riding ducey do, shotguns tucked under their arms. They decided come the twenty-first century, they too will double in the night as Buck Rodgers."

MAYBE ISAIAH THOUGHT ONE African American man was laying a trap for another African American man. Maybe he thought it was ironic that a team of drug dealers was playing *I gotch you* with a handful of law enforcement agencies. Or maybe Isaiah recognized a man from one of the gay bars. If the man came on board when evidence from the train case involving a dead teenager and a child suffocated in a refrigerator hit the headlines, then it seemed there had to be a connection. Perhaps what really happened was the feds gave the train victims and their families a funeral and put them into a witness protection program. If the child had accidentally opened the refrigerator and climbed inside it, perhaps someone had placed the refrigerator onto the train hoping it would be identified in another town. If Chief Cobb knew what had occurred, if Ebenales told him the story or an officer who discovered the child's body and suspected who the killer was and suspected the situation could become dangerous, perhaps they engineered the disappearance of the refrigerator as well as of the fingerprints and saliva smears. Or perhaps there had been no child but there was no other way for the police to impress upon an addicted community of adults not to allow their small children to wander outside their homes.

Dalton closed his eyes and breathed in the desert fragrances. He had planted gardenias this spring. It wafted sweet and sickly, too pungeant, on a sudden stir of wind. The need to be sheltered had driven him to Nell. That need kept him with her. You were on the road all day, waiting for whatever it was that was going to occur. Some days had that characteristic to them. Hot blowy days got the chemical spills. Cool nothing days saw the caravan of drug ivory. Hazy, no-visibility days got you busted rigs. You sat on the road, scrunched down like a desert hare or tortoise and you prepared yourself for hours of nothing. Some days you were antsy, irritated and you didn't want to be there. Shadows of clouds stepped up the irritation; you thought you'd bite your nails to the raw or eat yourself into insanity. Other days you thought you could sit on the road your entire life and if you saw no other vehicle it didn't matter. There were ups and downs, gullies and ridges. You took your place on the low side and waited, sometimes all day for the rig's windowshield to flash in the sun like a rhinehart bauble. You were head up for the task of sitting the moment you filled up your thermos and made your sandwich and the appreciation of being one of the chosen ones stayed with you until nightfall. Night in the desert reminded you that you'd been waiting all day. The reminder blew you like dust across the cement-riddled soil into your house and into sheltering arms. Sometimes it drove you. Sometimes you thought you could evade it.

This was the same desert Isaiah worked. High noon was the same for Isaiah as for Dalton. Red dawn, all those stupid cliches you heard during shift change as either you headed home or you prepared to work a double shift. Isaiah was human – he would've clutched desperately to Eric if the road sent him home in that condition.

With Eric's death Isaiah had all the time in the world. Perhaps he asked for a Staircase assignment. Perhaps Cobb thought he was the best man for the job. Perhaps he went after Hemal to vindicate Eric's death. He must have known how money changed hands. If someone other than Vail Bahe arranged meetings, Isaiah would have learned that as well. It was not possible to live with a man who was married to his cellphone and not overhear conversations and determine who the players were and what their plans were.

Dalton looked at the expanse of sky. The night had become darker and the flush of stars more visible. He made out Orien's belt and the Seven Sisters, star formations his father had taught him when he was a child. He thought about his father and about calling him. When he completed Isaiah's investigation, he would return home for a short stay.

If it was important for Bahe to have as few connections to the team who regularly hit the trucks, he had to assure someone like Isaiah or Simms could not identify them nor they him. Bahe must have hoped that by using motels he could eliminate the problems he had with identification by officers. With the rental of a handful of motel rooms the times for transactions could be changed. Motels could be changed. Motels could be sold and new owners could remodel the premises. Drop-off points could be changed throughout the week. Parks, zoos, river banks, dams, highways, restaurants, truck stops, hilltops - anywhere a car could pull over a drug deal was being made.

Isaiah lived with Ebenales and tracked Bahe. He must have been playing a percentage game going after the runs that would pull in the largest action. Hemal had to have known what Isaiah was after and been plenty conflicted over it.

Dalton walked inside his house. There was a message on his voice mail. Probably Nell. He'd listen to it in the morning. He showered and dried himself and as he got into bed and set his alarm clock, he wondered if what tipped off the man who murdered the agents was the fact that the refrigerator could be traced back to him. Most certainly Hemal had tipped the man to the fact that Isaiah was a problem by hiring a man at the Red Mountain warehouse who was Isaiah's double.

Sleep overcame him and he drifted toward a recollection of the day's images. He forced himself awake an idea pressing into his thoughts. When Isaiah took the card key, he eliminated Hemal's ability to tell Bahe's drivers on which train the rest of the contraband was coming in on.

Isaiah had aced Hemal. Cobb, Dimes, half a dozen top ranking police had to have known this. So what the hell happened? Why did Isaiah get murdered?

twenty-one

THE FIGURE IN THE WETSUIT CAPTURED on video cassette was a bony angler who walked confidently onto uneven stones in a fast moving current without falling. Probably someone who had been wading or swimming upstream since he was a child. Dalton had decided on basis of height, weight and body structure alone that he was Jason Carey. His place was in a warehouse inside what was, for all he knew, a replica of a hangar, the aisles masking marker numbers of an inside airstrip in an area where hijackers were bringing in cocaine.

Dalton grabbed his empty soda can and went inside his house. In his study he flicked on the light and punched in the code for the sheriff database. Once it showed on his screen he placed his photograph of Jason Carey on his FAX machine and relayed it into the database. He waited as the computer screen began processing the new request through its vaults of terminals. Carey's face showed on a personal file. Dalton left the computer on to process the volumes of agents and statewide profilers to produce a hit on any agent resembling Carey who may also have resembled Officer Du Bois.

He fried hash browns with celery and red peppers and added a dash of pimento and basil. He broke an egg over the potatoes and placed a pan cover over the egg. After a minute he scooped the meal onto a plate and ate slowly, unable to use much nourishment. He recognized his reaction as a typical sign that he was nearing the end of a case. He chased down the meal with a non-habit forming relaxant given him by a physician over a year ago with the last of his coffee. When he returned to the computer, the information on the screen gave him chills. The man was listed as DEA for Chicago, Illinois. His name was Alex Rudy.

Dalton dialed the number for Drug Enforcement Administration in San B. and asked to speak to Alex Rudy.

"Rudy here," the man spoke with a clipped accent that was vaguely reminiscent of a Mexican or Panamanian.

"Deputy Keys. I have a security clearance for you as a doer on a hijack case."

He laughed. "Your suspect work in a warehouse at Red Hill?"

"At Red Mountain." Dalton corrected him and nodded into the phone. "You came from Chicago with a man named Simms?"

"I personally escorted a truck worth of high tech forensics designed to pick up serologies, microscopies and trace and drug chemistry from the College of Pharmacology at the university."

"And you've been here since?" wondering why he hadn't run into him.

"I have a desk job. I compile leads all day off half a dozen databases for homicides committed in various cities. We're looking for links into transportation."

"Jesus."

"Yeah, the implications are far reaching."

Dalton calculated quickly – DEA was trying to hook up a handful or criminals possibly grownup gangs to long distance routes.

He told Rudy the names on his list asking if he had come across any in the southwest states.

"How 'bout I drop your names in the mainframe? It'll take a few hours."

Dalton gave him his telephone number and hung up.

It occurred to him he had missed the level of sophistication used by Ebenales and Bahe's team of target poachers. Just as an outsider was unable to pinpoint where a plane might be once it landed and taxied into a hangar, Ebenales had at his fingertips equipment and instrumentation designed to mask an entire operation. The same technology used for under water recovery was also being utilized inside an aircraft or a vehicle to sweep the beaches for boats that might be targetted by the Coast Guard or the Air Force or FAA. If Ebenales were bringing in the cocaine by any route – automobile, boat, barge, aircraft or diver – then the real reason law enforcement required a bevvy of cops with different abilities in many specialties was because the ivory trade had become an entanglement of obstacles. The ivory trade too used emergency locator transmitters to help see aircraft in fog and haze, infrared aerials to help detect objects underwater, sonar submersibles to chart radar screens by which someone like Jason Carey could locate underwater or buried drug stashes, and beacons to select last point of contact in weather conditions of poor visibility. Part of the problem was there was not much depth perception over the Colorado River near the Davis Dam to begin with, nor real horizon to chart pings, or other visible landmarks other than houses that blended into the landscape, fish and rocks. If you saw the shoreline, chances were you saw nothing else.

Isaiah was a can opener in a world of tilted tins, steamers and fishing crews. The lid he popped was not to a bait or worms or a shaving cream aerosol of diamonds but to powder venture, with names and false identities and false passports and diversions. Dalton doubted the Carey/Rudy match was unique. Probably for every agent there was at least one dealer who looked identical and assumed that particular agent's eccentricities.

TWO HOURS LATER DEA agent Alex Rudy had transmitted by FAX a name of a man seen bringing in stolen, high powered technological equipment designed for and purchased by law enforcement. His name was Adam Beutler.

twenty-two

D ALTON COMPLETED THE paperwork necessary to obtain a search warrant of the truck and premises of Adam Beutler aka Alan Butler. He and Marshal Lina Crandall rode from the Joshua Tree substation in Morongo Valley to the southernmost tip of the county. They said little on the way. The flat beige wilderness spread out before ravine-riddled mounains of the inspiring peaks of the San Jacinto Mountains. Heat immersion rose off the hardened sand as though the illusion of water promised a future that the unforgiving rock was incapable of rendering. On a square of crumbling shale sat a vast network of PG&E poles. Wind turbines rushed into the narrow at the juncture of Highway 62 and Highway 95. The trail to Gomorra lay on a low road through boron bleached hills and wind-devastated adobes that perched barely visible through sage and cacti. Men wound up in this windswept postage stamp married or unmarried but sworn to the servitude of creating dollar wisdom in poolrooms and dog fights and balywicks that allowed them the sought-after privileges enured to wild youth of readily available pocket change, cheap thrills and a desert coffee shop full of ex-cons and wannabe terminal inmates.

Adam Beutler was one of those men who had chosen to make do with the simplicities of living in favor of some eternal fountain of free time and noncommitments. Although he had married twice and divorced twice and went through relationships as one would cellular telephones, he had turned down companionship in favor of a hot tub and porch of hayburners situated on a hill with a dried creekbed and a train of old refrigerators, a few which were useless to the methamphetamine industry because they had no doors.

A scarlet truck cab sat in a cement driveway behind a soapdish convertible red Chevy with fins and a nondescript baby blue VW bug. Dalton and Lina peeked inside a garage and saw radiators and tubing and stainless steel sinks and a half dozen unplugged refrigerators inside which methamphetamine manufacturers froze a solution of chemicals including sulfer, acetone, and No-Dose tablets purchased in batches of thirty thousand dollar quantities at Home Depot or Longs Drugs. All too often the meth lab operator blew off a few refrigerator doors and then a roof. A dilapidated barn stood at the edge of the property, its rafters visible. Situated across the rafters were ultraviolet grow lights for the hundred or so potted marijuana plants that filled the floor. What you saw was what there was.

Dalton recognized Beutler instantly, although the thin hipped, muscular man with almost no neck showed no sign of remembering him from Ebenales' warehouse at Needles. Dalton handed Beutler a warrant that ordered a search for cocaine and heroin bricks wrapped in plastic or opague masking tape; for bags of marijuana seeds or leaves; and for listening posts, Radio Shack transmitters and surveillance equipment, and Beutler sardonically invited Dalton and Lina inside a white marble tiled structure with one permanently open, ten foot by fifteen foot window aperture to the stone desert. Dalton explained how the search would proceed and invited

Beutler to stay closeby. However after showing the deputies the lay of the land, Beutler retired to a patio and swing chair beneath an awning of golden yellow nylon, see-through fabric.

The home was small, two bedrooms with a kitchen and living room divided by a floor to ceiling bookcase and planter. Dalton began running his hands beneath shelves, while Lina checked behind mounted paintings and beneath couches for secret compartments. Dalton inspected the fireplace for hidden ledges, in closets and inside shoes, shoeboxes, beneath clothing on hangers. Lina ran her hands beneath clothing tucked in drawers, beneath desks and tables and sinks. Dalton stood on a chair and pushed open the crawl space to the attic. There he found an alarm system. He inched into the crawl space and made his way slowly between insulation panels tapping the pink material for any container he thought might have drugs. He checked for panels in the floor of the crawl space. With a slab floor home, if there were no drywall evident behind a stairwell or in a garage, sometimes the crawl space hid drywall concealing drugs or guns. At the end of the crawl space he found a trapdoor. He pulled it toward him and found a wooden space the size of a tub with a wetsuit folded neatly on top of a scuba mask with an infrared shield. Nice stuff. He hung almost upside down to retrieve the waterproof flashlights, handful of water proof wrist watches, a private stash of forty wrapped bricks which could either be cocaine or heroin and a black bag inside which appeared to be a hundred thousand dollars. He bagged these items and inched his way back to civilization.

As he climbed from the attic, he heard Lina give a whoop. An engine was starting up followed by the whir of blades. He ran from the house in the direction of the sound tossing the booty of wetsuit and mask, wrist watches and drugs and money to Lina, who pointed toward the barn, and gathered momentum as he shot past her and burst around the barn in time to see a crop duster take off. Dalton calibrated a course for the plane running toward it with every last energy he was capable of. He grabbed onto the tail as Beutler lifted the plane for higher airspace. Dalton reached for a steel girder shifting his weight toward the center of the wing. He swung his feet and legs onto the rear seat and braced himself against an upside down manuever. The plane's shadow bounced over the chalky rolling hills, then careened sharply as Beutler veered suddenly into the bright blue sky. With the agile confidence of one who has trained in high school and college sports, Dalton crouched over the seat and moved toward the pilot's compartment. For a moment the sky whirled and the ground seemed to whirl also. Beutler couldn't keep up the theatrics. He challenged the buffetted air once before the plane shuddered. As he drew the throttle toward his chest, Dalton limbered to him and holding onto another steel girder he wrapped his feet tightly around the other man's neck. Searing sunlight caught the plane in its grasp. For a second as Beutler let go of the controls the plane lost altitude. It spiraled toward the ground. Dalton had half a mind to tighten the pressure on Beutler's neck but as he glimpsed the ribbon of road coming dangerously quickly toward them, he thrust himself backwards through space, falling free form for a moment before he hit the ground.

The plane came down hard, wing to the road, the force of the crash on the asphalt severing the right side of the two wings, splintering the body of the craft as it split apart in a gust of smoke and flying debris. Dalton rose, his body unsteady, blood coursing through his veins and charged after the plane and after Beutler. Part of the plane had skidded uphill and rested precariously at the crest of the ribboned road. The stench of burning rubber and plastic left little doubt in Dalton's mind that if Beutler survived the crash he did so with broken bones, fractures and severe head trauma. Yet when he came upon the portion of cockpit, he found no pilot nor flying cap nor evidence of the man. Scattered about the second seat were a few boxes labeled *Radio Shack*. Later when he had time he would find they contained a handful of surveillance equipment used typically in sighting the writing and colors of rigs, in capturing pictures off their laptop computers, intersecting radio calls, and interferring with spedometers.

He jaunted up the road. Burning plastic and wood lay in remnants over the downslope of the crevice-cracked beige landscape. Whatever diamonds this man had yearned for, the shocking bright sun had found a way to cancel his dreams. Specks of ore and granite glinted in the flood of daylight causing the horizon to shift as if with unstability or fluctuating bands. He stood mindful of the rising vapors. The land was an illusion itself, one moment like an expanding and contracting lake, in the next instant dry as chipped clay void of the mercy of any rainfall, even those wisps which vanish a hundred feet above the ground. This was the way a sane man learned to live with uncertainty, by staring at the sand or chalk shifting landscape until it offered up a consistent, liveable surface.

The heat burned down on him causing him at once to be thirsty and nauseous. At the periphery of his vision he saw or thought he saw the movement of a man's leg. He focussed on the spot wishing he had in his possession binoculars, knowing also in some anterior part of his brain that he was too shaken to use any instrument to advantage. The motion appeared again – the briefest shadow causing the gravel hill to fold over on itself. He ran to it, gravel causing him to slip. He picked himself up and ran as men practising an amphibian drill ran, feet equal distance apart, shifting weight from foot to foot, his body semi squat. The sun seemed at once to suck the air. He gasped and panting now, sweat bathing his arms and back in a film, he launched himself at the crawling man.

Beutler let out a mean wail. "You fuckin asshole cop motherfucker." His voice was reminiscent of the night at Lone Pine. *I got you motherfucker in my sights, I got your mean ass coming in a sling, I got you, I got you* – the words and that drawl echoing through that chilly night into the envelope of the moment. Beutler turned onto his side and cast Dalton a look of vile contempt. *I dare you*, the look declared. Somewhere in someone's computer data bank flying fingers would register a matching thumbprint, a matching profile photostat, a Department of Justice federal identification number along with his social security, driver's license and date of birth. Dalton reached for the man's collar and lifted his neck and back several inches off the ground.

"Was Simms crawling toward you or away from you, you dumb fuck?" Dalton yelled.

Beutler grimaced as if to say, you never went down before DEA, CHP or US Marshal without at least one eyefuck.

"You gave the bricks to Scott who secured them in the river, didn't you?"

Beutler howled with maniacal laughter. "I pissed in my pants," he said, and tried to raise himself off the ground but was unable to do so. He began crying, slobbering.

"And what about Officer Du Bois? Did you push him into the river or were you the one who held him under?" He wanted to thrash the man, kick him, break his face, open his gut, but he did not.

"He came after me, chasin' me through the water like some bat flying outa hell. Ah didn't invite that mahn on my boat. He done climb outa the water and topple hisself inta my boat!"

"Who the fuck held him down in the goddamn water?" Dalton yelled down at him. He wanted to annihilate him but out of the corner of his eye he glimpsed Lina running toward him. "Jesus, what the fuck did he do to you? Did you think if you got rid of one, you'd show the system? There's whole squadrons of us! You'll never outnumber us." He yelled into Beutler's face, "I mean, what the fuck did you kill him for?"

Realization gave him a sickly pallor. "That black asswipe broke our code," he replied with entitlement.

"You mean, he swiped a goddamn code key."

"I mean, he fucked the computers! He left friggin' magic wands in every direction. We couldn't land our planes! Couldn't get the shit out of the air!"

Dalton broke into a grin. "Imagine all that hardware fucked to hell because he screwed you with your own screws."

Beutler was yelling, "Hemal said he wanted Du Bois any way anyone could snuff him."

Beutler opened his mouth to protest Dalton wrestling him to stand. Somewhere between starting to yell and telling Dalton to go to hell, he figured it out. "Therah was two a them. Two DEA." He pronounced the letters, Dee E A'ah.

Dalton yanked the man to his feet. "Did you know MacIntyre or Dimes?" His anger was subsiding.

"MacIntyre belonged to Hemal. Same as Bowman."

"You're wrong about Bowman."

"I got rights, don't I? You're fuckin' with my fourth amendment, boy!"

"Just say the word."

"I gotta right to an attorney. You shoulda read me my rights. You done fucked with my rights."

"Save it for the arraignment, Beutler. My guess is you're never coming out. The Man'll have to make one shoebox just for you."

Lina arrived, out of breath. "You read him his rights?"

"Why don't you?"

She did.

They'd bagged a big one. There'd be no more hijacks for a while. They'd get a handful of nobodys in addition to Bahe, Azul, Gardino, Carmichael and if they were lucky, Ebenales and Scott. With Scott they'd take care of the stuff coming in from over the borders.

L T. WALKER HANDED OUT the beers. Dalton uncapped his and took a chug.

"What'd we find out?" Margo asked. She stood over the firepit, an apron tied around her waist, monitoring hamburgers and hot dogs.

"Beutler went after Isaiah. Personal vendetta, after Isaiah apparently took their bar codes and reprogrammed their entire operation. Their entire run had been decoded."

"Why MacIntyre?"

"Easy way to keep rolling in the profits. He knew the players. I mean, let's be practical. He helped the county engineer the economy. I guess the temptation to sell off the stuff in the locker room was a big one for him."

"We have any real evidence on Bahe?" Lina interjected.

"Enough."

"How about Ebenales?"

"Keep your fingers crossed."

"And who the hell was Cater?"

"An alias for Scott. He's the head honcho."

Marty Walker was in rare form in shorts, a Geiko shirt, and black tennis shoes. "The forfeiture runs were monitored to the teeth after IAD fired the first batch of officers. The whole point of sending Isaiah into the desert was to learn the relationships of takers on the route for people Ebenales and Bahe moved."

"How many hijackers?" Lina's friend Max asked.

"Seven. Beutler, a John Martin – he's the mechanic for a dozen carriers – Dani Gardino, MacDougal, Carey, Azul and Bahe."

"Jesus, a woman!" Max said.

"Yup," Dalton replied. "Sort of hard to imagine, isn't it? And she's got two young children to raise."

George Maciel with his blond athletic good looks who was sunbathing on a float in the pool yelled, "Ebenales is going to face a lot of questions on the death of Isaiah's lover. I mean, who knows what he did? Could've given the man HIV and watched over him to make sure he had it."

"Now, now," Lina said. "He'll probably get off."

"Not with his man Carey in a warehouse where Beutler worked

a few nights a month when he wasn't delivering haul there," Dalton said.

Marty said, "Lina's right. Too circumstantial. It's not illegal to hire a man."

"The code key belonged to him. Beutler said he called the hit," Dalton persisted.

"You watch. His lawyers will eat holes in every line of argument."

Maciel yelled, "Good work, Dal. Time you bumped up the ladder."

Lt. Walker looked soberly at Dalton. "There's a post available on Baseline."

"Not interested," Dalton answered. "Too much politics."

Lina stalked across Marty's backyard to the cooler and helped herself to another beer. "I've got a better idea. Why not give Dal a go with a special task force?"

"He could join the DEA," Ian Spender quipped, from a lawn chair as he kept an eye on his two year old on a blanket. "Or INS and do border patrol," he added.

The entire group laughed.

"Good job," Margo Sam told Dalton. "You got any plans for time off?"

"I thought I'd go home, see my folks."

"You taking Nell?" Evora who worked dispatch asked.

"Not this time. I'm feeling possessive of my time."

"I know the feeling," said Ian. "When you return though, why not put in for after hours? We'll do it duo."

"If it's anything but drugs."

Everyone laughed.

Lt. Walker disappeared inside his house and returned a minute later. He had handed Dalton an orange bow tied box with light orange wrapping. The gift turned out to be a Compaq Pesario laptop computer. "For you, on those lonesome days."

Dalton placed the computer on the picnic table along with a remaining portion of humus and garbanzo dip. "One thing I have to say. I keep only one female at my bedside."

More laughter. Lt. Walker glanced admirably at the members of his unit. "The laptop's not for the bedside. It's for the road. It's to replace the relic you're using."

"This is incredibly generous. It must've cost a fortune."

"It did, and you deserve it."

Everyone clapped.

Dalton stood and raised his beer in salute. He said, "I'd like to say Isaiah pulled off a brilliant investigation."

"Here, here," said George Maciel. "Wish you were here, old fella."

Lt. Walker gave a nod. A breeze stirred up the paper plates stacked on the picnic table. Lina walked to the grill to request a well done hamburger on a toasted sesame bun. Ian put his son on his lap and bounced him, and Marty came over to Dalton.

"I'm driving down to Salton Sea this weekend. You and Nell want to come?"

"Thanks, no. I'm driving to Needles to spend some time with my father."

"Just thought I'd ask."

They watched the others mill about. As usual Ian was the life of the party. Maciel had settled to the task of wood whittling. The wooden door to the garden opened and Isaiah's supervisor Lt. White entered.

"Someone invite him?" Lina asked.

"I did." Marty Walker replied. He walked over to him and pointed out his coworkers and their families.

THE END